TRANSCENDENTAL MUTILATION

RYAN HARDING

PRAISE FOR TRANSCENDENTAL MUTILATION

"[HARDING] IS AN ABSOLUTE artisan of extreme horror...A definite must-read for hardcore, strong-stomached fans of the extreme...and quite probably next year's Splatterpunk winner for Best Collection..."
—Christine Morgan
Splatterpunk award winning author of *Lakehouse Infernal* and *Trench Mouth*

"*Transcendental Mutilation* is the pus covered, bloody, vomit-inducing, and savage heir to Harding's masterpiece, *Genital Grinder*. This collection is perfect for fans who have no boundaries and love well-crafted stories. While every story is amazing, "Angelbait" will test the resolve of any hardcore fan."
—Daniel J. Volpe
Splatterpunk award nominated author of *Left to You* and *Talia*

"From Splatterpunk master Ryan Harding, prepare for ten obscene tales containing: necrophiliacs, nudes, zombies, dendrophilia, and more. *Transcendental Mutilation* is brilliant, revolting, and the only collection you need to read in 2023."
—Christina Pfeiffer
Uncomfortably Dark

"There is a level of depravity within this one that will either spark the dark side of your mind or send it screaming the other direction. Or perhaps both.
—Lisa Lee Tone
Bibliophilia Templum

"Ryan Harding conjures the inner spirit of David Cronenberg as he exposes flesh enhancement and anatomical horrors."
—Mike Rankin
Horror Bookworm Reviews

For *The Night Stockers* (co-written with Kristopher Triana):

"A literary Niagara Falls of irredeemably explicit violence.... This is top-of-the-line hardcore horror!"
—Edward Lee

For *Reincarnage* (co-written with Jason Taverner):

"A total fucking blast and a must-read for fans of all the great 1980's slasher icons."
—Bryan Smith, author of *The Killing Kind* and *Depraved*

For *Genital Grinder:*

"Think you're hardcore? Think again. If you've handled everything Edward Lee, Wrath James White, and Bryan Smith have thrown at you, then put on your rubber parka, spread some plastic across the floor, and get ready for Ryan Harding, the unsung master of hardcore horror. Abandon all hope, ye who enter here. Harding's work is like an acid bath, and pain has never been so sweet."
—Brian Keene

Published by Death's Head Press,
an imprint of Dead Sky Publishing, LLC
Miami Beach, Florida
www.deadskypublishing.com

Cover by: Don Noble

Edited by Shawn Macomber

CONTENTS

Prelude to Repulsion

My first collection, the delicately named *Genital Grinder*, came out in April 2012. I wrote all those stories between 1998 and 2003, with a little revision and expansion in the months preceding publication. Taking inspiration from Bret Easton Ellis' *The Informers*, I linked the stories with recurring characters or allusions to characters/events. I've continued this with *Transcendental Mutilation*, which also occasionally recalls *Genital Grinder* as well as a certain phenomenon in the towns of Morgan and Sandalwood from *Reincarnage* and *Reincursion*, my slasher homages with Jason Taverner. *TM* is still very much standalone, though.

I'll see you in the postscript with some notes about all of these stories.

Speaking of being there at the end, though, Chase is waiting in a couple of pages.

Ryan Harding
July 2021

THE CORPSEFUCKER BLUES

Off the grid no longer exists. Not in this world where we are seen, recorded, and mutated by everything. Even if it did, I am sure it would still come with that deep, unnamable loss and corresponding lack of fulfillment assured by our lives on the grid—because we are all connected, if only by the profoundest sense of disconnection. And what is a grid, if not a web?

—*Transitory Bodies*, Dr. Braedon Obrist

I.

CHASE RAN HIS FINGERS through the first woman's hair, dry and tangled like tumbleweed. He clawed through the knots, yanking out a small tuft in the process.

She offered no encouragement or complaint.

He held the clump of hair away from their nude bodies and let it float to the ground. It didn't have far to go with him draped upon her prone form on the hard earth. Despite the bed of grass, the ground rubbed his knees and elbows raw. It's why he'd never consider camping out in the woods.

But for *this*?

Chase was only too happy to make an exception.

The harsh and uncomfortable environment scarcely mattered with her body so soft and inviting beneath him, slicker and wetter than their last time together; always wetter each time, as if augmented by his own rising desire. By herself she would have satisfied him completely, but, of course, one didn't have to suffice tonight.

When he raised his head, he found the other woman's toes right in front of his face, poised in midair. They belonged to a thicker woman with wider feet than most of the ones he saw around the office at work. He thought they were magnificent. He smiled up at her, though the shadows of the tree obscured her features. The toes drifted slightly back and forth, teasing him. He could see them in a hint of moonlight. He thought she had painted them an electric orange, though the paucity of available light did not permit him to confirm this. He reached up and stroked her calf, round and smooth. His fingers slid down until he found her heel and coaxed her foot forward. He fit four of her toes in his mouth and moaned appreciatively. They tasted sharp.

Years ago, he might have thrown up, but he'd come to appreciate the intensity of the flavor.

Something tickled his scalp. *Several* somethings. Exhibits 587-594 why he hated the outdoors. Nothing to do for it, though. He never could have brought these lovely ladies without an audience.

The discomfort of the woods hardly equated the drawback of the lack of privacy most anywhere in the city.

Chase found himself doing it, too: peeking through the spyhole when he heard voices outside his door—especially from an occasional argument—and cataloging the comings and goings of neighbors. Just part of the urban assimilation process. He'd notice if someone on his floor had company; ergo, he needed to stay the hell away from home to enjoy the delights of his special ladies. He brushed the crawling things from his hair, never missing a stroke in licking beneath and between the toes stuffed in his mouth.

He rubbed himself against the woman beneath him. *Maria*, he thought. Or maybe the electric orange toes were Maria's. Regardless, one was *Maria*, the other *Esther*. He'd known the difference at some point, but not now. He only remembered his incredulity that such a sexy woman would have a name like Esther. That had to be a family name, donated by a family who obviously didn't care if a lot of guys laughed at the thought of calling someone Esther while they pounded her quim like a railroad spike. He felt his mouth curling into a smile around Esther's toes and let them slide out of his mouth.

Maria (?) felt almost twig-like now, as unyielding as the earth. He should have brought Esther to the ground instead. Her larger body would feel much better. Not too late to amend the error, of course, but he'd save that for a little later. No need to have the best stuff right out the gate.

It was a marathon, not a race.

More things landed on his scalp, one of them alarmingly heavy. Bastard things. Chase swiped it away. This wouldn't do for much longer. It was becoming too much of a distraction.

He peered down at Maria, the moonlight enough to see her face. A tangle of worms formed a squirming mass in her eye socket. Even now he felt some of that atavistic repulsion he thought he'd left behind. He thought he could hear it above the persistent ambient noise of the woods, the network of slippery bodies sliding across one another. Too many to be contained within the skull now, bursting through the eyeless hole in her face. The decay had reached a stage that moistened her skin all over, fish belly white and glistening. A cavern at the left side of her face revealed her teeth with an overflow of flailing grubs oozing through the egress.

He wasn't prepared to give up just yet. Chase was the kind of man who would eat the gristle off his steak, after all. A few places with a flimsy texture wouldn't put him off. He flattened his palm and spread his fingers against her belly, rubbing against the smooth expanse. It wasn't just slick now; the juices were thick enough to spatter the tops of his fingers. He caressed the mound of her breast. It felt like wet leaves. Cringing like someone trying to creep up a set of stairs but setting off every loud pop, he squeezed the spongy tissue. The flesh sloughed right off, the whole clump like the sodden skin of a fruit stuck to his palm. He flung his hand away and the layer of her skin mercilessly sailed off somewhere beyond the moonlight.

Still loath to completely abandon his post, he clamped hold of her thighs and attempted to pry them open.

Chase might as well have been trying to shatter concrete with his bare hands. He strained anyway, hoping for more give at knee level and, when he heard the dry snap, an instant of terror at the thought that it might be one of his arms. But, no, it had just been Maria's leg cracking, now sickeningly close to the shape of a capital *L* with a near right angle formed at the knee by the shattered bone.

Hmm. Definitely won't be a "girlfriend" experience with you tonight, Maria.

Judging by the steady drip of crawling bodies on his head, Esther must not be faring much better. He boosted himself up. Esther's feet swayed ever so slightly above the ground. He had a better look at her sturdy knees and plentiful thighs now, and the silhouette of her head.

He'd tied her flowing hair around a massive branch—which had *not* been easy. The process required him to tie it at a lower hanging point of the branch then climb up and move her in increments until she lifted off the ground. He'd expected the branch to collapse under the weight of them both—or maybe for her scalp to simply detach like some dangling jellyfish—but it held.

That whole Rapunzel story was evidently no joke.

Something landed on his face. More damn grubs, pouring out like the sand through an hourglass.

This would have to be the last time with Maria and Esther, unfortunately.

For now, there was the bitter disappointment at the inevitable conclusion of the cycle. Though he came night after night as long as he could, it was never enough. The familiar self-loathing—knowing he could probably count on one hand how many people in the entire world were facing this same moment of disappointment and despair; i.e., the *corpsefucker blues*—would truly hit later, like a hangover.

Chase wiped his face and sighed.

"What do you say, Esther? One for the road?"

The patch of hair on her belly swayed at eye level now, which had been the whole point of the hair-hanging endeavor. He spread her thighs and stepped between them. Her head eclipsed the moonlight, but it showed him things moving somewhere in her hair, and lower still, a death factory cranking out a new maggot model every couple of seconds. Somewhere in his mind, it astonished him that the remarkable thing about his inexorable descent to her vagina wasn't him going down on a dead woman dangling from a tree branch—branch notwithstanding; *that* was old hat—but that her name might be Esther.

The process involved plenty of turning away and spitting at first, though that wasn't so unlike the removal of an errant hair on the tongue with lovers who shared the complete absence of an obituary. He brushed away as much of the sarcophagus activity as he could, pushing his fingers between her lips and swiping away what he could. Her nether lips offered dryer putrefaction, unfortunately, and he'd have to put in the work if he wanted something he could slide into without an entry arid enough to peel all the skin off his member. There were lubricants, of course, but he couldn't bring himself to use them. He wanted to do it himself. Otherwise, he may as well buy a sex doll or one of those weirdo devices from InterphaZ.

And that was just pathetic.

He maneuvered Esther's legs back over his shoulders after the clearing initiative to bring her right up against his face. He buried his mouth in her hole. He'd missed a few of the maggots—or could be the ol' assembly line had cranked out some more—but it would do for now. It even *sounded* like the real thing for a moment: the slick, squishing sounds of oral congress. He didn't know why he should cherish the token reflections of normalcy in something that was designed to be complete-ly aberrant, but he did, undeniably. He supposed he must be something of a romantic.

He had to give up the fantasy rather abruptly when the rest of her weight fell upon him and knocked him down to the ground in something that resembled a poorly executed profes-sional wrestling move. The wet white bone of Esther's skull lay completely uncovered.

He groaned and exhaled, looked up at the sky. The moonlight had shifted enough to reveal the lower branches of the tree where a wig-like remnant of blond hair still dangled from the branch, the red and glistening underside of a scalp at its roots. He laid there as it dripped on him, thinking that a complete hand wasn't required to count the people in the world currently experiencing a moment like this.

No, just one finger...probably the middle one.

II.

Diary of a Corpsefucker, August 20th.
Dear Diary,
I can't keep doing this. God, I shouldn't even be writing about it because what if I get hit by a bus or die in some kind of freak ac-cident? Someone'll find this and then what seemed like an awful tragedy might start to seem like karma. Well, handy thing about screwing a dead body...you won't find anybody talking about "an eye for an eye."

It's sick. I know it is. I swear it's always the last time, and then I turn around and what do you know, I'm back in the old cadaver saddle again. Yee-haw.

I hate myself for doing it. I stare in the mirror and think that this couldn't be the face of someone who'd do such a thing, but the kind that does must be right behind it somewhere.

Everybody has a secret face.

Would it be different if I didn't have to kill them?

It would be so much easier if I didn't.

But...it's too dangerous. I'll probably get caught someday as it is even without working at a morgue or a funeral home, but it'd be that much easier to get busted if I did. They've probably got security cameras just to discourage that sort of thing. They don't think anybody would really do something so deviant, but might as well throw some alligators in the moat.

I just hope if it ever happens...if I do get caught...that I have time to kill myself. I don't even want to imagine the headlines if I have to face my crimes. We haven't had a good murderer/necrophile in the news in a long time as it is, and this would blow everybody's mind.

Writing about it helps a little, if not nearly enough. All the stuff I've written in here about The Urge, it doesn't really communicate the power of it. It feels like I'm out of control, completely out of my mind. I feel like I have as much choice as a werewolf on the night of a full moon. So...I have to go to the meetings. I've said that a hundred times in here before, but I'm really going to do it. I've said that too, but next time I write in here, Mr. Diary, I'll be telling you what happened, and probably what a waste of time it was, but I'll have at least gone. I don't know what I'll say, but the best lie stays close to the truth, right? So what? I find coma patients irresistible?

I have to try.

I have very little hope it will cure me, but it's something.

III.

Chase rubbed his hands on his pants. He couldn't get them dry. It felt less like a room of his peers than a jury of them. He'd seen classified ads for the sex addiction group for the past couple of years and, while it seemed about as appropriate a place for him as a daycare, he figured it was his best bet. He still couldn't believe he'd actually gone through with it and come. They held the meetings at a community center downtown. His nightmare was that there'd only be two people, including himself, but there were six others. Not enough to fade into the woodwork altogether, but enough to hopefully spare him from getting his arm twisted.

What brings you here tonight?

Can you talk about that?

You'll feel better if you do.

We're here to listen.

No judgments.

Don't be shy now...we've heard just about everything you can think of...

Ha ha ha.

Yeah. Right.

There were two women and four other men, with one of the latter playing the role of moderator. His name was Neil. He'd thrown away his first marriage because of a pornography addiction.

That's it? Chase thought during Neil's introduction. Whacking off too much to porno was no great shakes. You may as well have a chronic jaywalker trying to tell hardened rapists and child killers that they too can turn their lives around.

And that's when the sweaty palms really began; with the realization that some part of him actually believed he would feel better about himself by listening to other people's struggles.

Unless some guy walked in late and announced he had a predilection for sodomizing roadkill, Chase doubted he would be granted any absolution.

They sat in chairs arranged in a horseshoe shape. The whole atmosphere couldn't have been more awkward. Chase cursed his failure to sit closer to the door. He'd done it so he wouldn't try to bail out in the middle of the meeting if nerves got the best of him. He was trapped on the side of the room. Everybody seemed acutely aware of one another while simultaneously trying to pretend they weren't all thinking about what degenerates they were deep inside.

Neil cleaned his glasses as he continued his story, the "icebreaker."

"I couldn't stop. I was spending most of my paycheck on hardcore pornography, week after week. We were falling behind on our bills, but I didn't care. The only thing that mattered to me was buying the new *Gaping Anus* movie, even if I had to pay sixty bucks for it sight unseen."

The man beside Chase, a rather hirsute individual with a military style coat and dog tags, spoke up. "Why didn't you rent them? They had a bunch of those *Gaping Anus* flicks at Movie Heaven."

Neil put on his glasses again and shrugged. "Most of them were four hours long. I had to see every ass-pounding minute." He exhaled and laughed a little. "Can't go down that road again, though."

One of the women asked, "Is Movie Heaven even still around? I thought after that nutcase went on a rampage..."

After someone pointed out pretty much all video stores had gone the way of the woolly mammoth with or without bad publicity, Neil resumed his narrative. It played out like Chase expected. His wife's happiness plummeted while stock at Jergens and Kleenex soared. He hit rock bottom when she found some nudie mags stashed in the child's nursery for the nights when it was Neil's turn to pacify the brat's sob sessions. She hit the road before the sun came up and left Neil as the king of his empty castle—a castle with a foundation of jumbo box *Gaping Anus* videos and XXX-themed magazines, the mortar supplied by the jizz of an 8-jacks-a-day habit.

"But I haven't bought any movies in seven hundred and thirty-seven days," Neil reported. "And I get Kinslee on the weekends." There was polite applause, as if he'd done something truly noble by trading his videotape habit for Internet ass-bang clips. It was probably easier to find a payphone these days than hardcore pornography on video cassette. Chase almost asked how long it had been since Neil bought any magazines, since he'd surreptitiously left out that detail but decided that the guy living in a glass house of dead body orgies didn't need to throw any stones.

G.I. Joe went next. He admitted to a profound foot fetish. He'd shadow women in shopping malls for hours if their feet caught his fancy. He usually masturbated in the public bathrooms when the lust got to be too overwhelming. He was afraid he was going to cross the line soon and find a way to do it where he could look at the target's feet while he stroked.

That's what he called them—*targets*—and Chase wondered if his military background extended to clock referents.

Got a couple of froth-worthy soles at nine o'clock, I'm ready to fire at will.

G.I. Joe had this idea, see, where he could buy something at the food court where they'd give him his order in a tall paper bag. Then he'd hurry far enough ahead of the target and cut out a hole at the bottom of the sack through which he could cram his dick then feverishly work his inches upon the target's approach while doing a primo acting job of relishing a hamburger.

He even had a name for it: *Operation Hot Lunch*.

The woman who'd asked about Movie Heaven hooked one ankle over the other and shifted her feet as far beneath her chair and out of sight as she could. The man who pointed out the collapse of the video industry then offered a grim forecast for the life expectancy of the local shopping malls. The zealous light that radiated from Joe's eyes while explaining his prospective masturbatory caper dropped from a hundred fifty watts to thirty.

Chase would have laughed were it not for his despair. GI Joe's tale—he'd given his real name, but Chase hadn't paid attention—was sad and pathetic, but compared to his own, a virtual triumph of the human spirit. Joe *hadn't* crossed the line in his paraphilia yet, whereas Chase had blown past it like he was speeding on the fucking Autobahn, never sparing so much as a glance back.

Everyone offered token assurances to Joe that he wasn't going to sink to this feared level of (even more) public self-gratification.

Chase nodded as if he agreed, but he knew better: Joe was a dead man wanking.

He'd been a regular at the meetings for a while, but it was obvious it would only take that One Special Target for him to double-time to the food court for a combo meal and extra napkins.

Joe's moment of therapy expired at last, and Neil looked around. His gaze fell on Chase and for a heart-stopping moment, Chase knew he was going to be called on, just like the old high school days in French class when he had no idea what the hell anyone was saying.

Mercifully, somebody else volunteered.

"I'm Cynthia." She gave a little wave to everyone. Chase had almost forgotten about her since she was more in the corner of his eye. The other woman had asked about Movie Heaven and seemed like she might be more forthcoming, but she hadn't drawn any attention to herself since trying to make sure her feet didn't launch Operation Indecent Exposure.

Cynthia had black hair and certainly an attractive face, but her voice especially took Chase in. That was kind of funny because it was the sort of thing that really didn't matter for his needs; his lovers didn't tend to be big conversationalists, after all. But he liked the sound of Cynthia's. The women at his office had a uniformly chirpy bombast that dogs would probably flee from, but her voice had a smooth and alluring frequency. He thought of Adrienne Barbeau in *The Fog*. Then he thought of her tits. Then he thought of her rotting in a shallow grave somewhere. He adjusted the front of his jeans under the guise of fixing his belt buckle as he listened to Cynthia.

"I guess I'm here because I can't control myself sometimes." She laughed with fake mirth. "Okay, *most* times. I know what I want. And I know how to get it. So I take it. People don't like it much if women do that."

"Unless the women are doing it to them," one of the other men said.

There was a round of laughs at this. Chase wished everyone would shut up so they could get back to Cynthia. He was mild-

ly curious what brought the Movie Heaven woman here, but
didn't care to hear the sorry tales of panty-sniffing and frottage
with which the other guys would probably "regale" them.

"You get so many chances, it's kind of hard not to do it,"
Cynthia said. "I kind of feel like I *have* to."

There were sober nods at this. The room would be empty if
they weren't all locked in that cell, Chase especially.

"None of us are here long and there's only so much we can
do with it, isn't there? So, I do it. I'm not always glad about it.
My boyfriends *definitely* aren't."

Chase heard his laugh over everyone else's.

Cynthia shrugged. "I wish I could stop. I'm not sure I can."

Neil took this opportunity to weigh in. Chase tuned him out,
watching Cynthia like she was still the one talking. It should be
too early to tell, but she excited him. Not because she'd make a
great cadaver—though God, yes, she would at that—but some
combination of *that voice,* her smile, and the apparent "wide-
spread' availability that would ultimately alienate the men who
fancied her...he wanted more of it. They were *something* alike if
they were both here, he thought, selectively forgetting his rote
condemnations of the entire group for being nothing like him.

Cynthia caught him looking and smiled, absently brushing a
hand through her hair and using the moment to turn away from
him.

He wanted her to keep looking. He wanted *her.*

———————

They actually had a refreshments table. Come air your dirty
laundry and then have a cup of punch and a cookie, horn-
dogs. *Nice touch.* No big surprise that Cynthia and Linda, who

never opened up about her reasons for being there, kept their open-toe sandaled distance from Joe. They all tried to talk about normal things with one another as they stood there eating stale cookies: Their careers. Safe anecdotes about family members. An upcoming lecture from Braedon Obrist that Chase couldn't wait to avoid. The hobos who wandered around this block and how intimidating they looked.

Speaking of, did everyone hear about that woman who disappeared from the soup kitchen? She'd volunteered out of the goodness of her heart, and some stewbum creep probably hacked her to pieces for the police to find in a shopping cart somewhere. Bet that same scumbag snuffed Geisha Hammond and ate the evidence. Just awful. Chase's collar felt tight but that Isabella woman wasn't his handiwork. He only *wished* Geisha Hammond was one of his.

Those dead puffy lips on his cock?

Lord have mercy.

When he glommed back on to the flow of conversation, it had moved on to a new sandwich shop. Their meatball sub was, apparently, no joke.

Banal exchanges, the safe white noise between the obsessions.

Chase had been compelled to introduce himself to the group, or at least to Cynthia and the default bystanders. He floundered, supplying a vague description of irresistible urges which said nothing at all; truth without reveal.

Linda left first, which made what happened much easier. Normally the women would have paired up to exit for safety, particularly downtown—those hobos might want more than their pocket change. Maybe it started that way for the missing soup kitchen volunteer. Instead, Cynthia begged off on the elevator out of claustrophobia and Chase asked if she wanted him to tag along on the stairs, just in case.

She stopped on the second floor, leaned against the wall, gave him that smile, and said, "Do you like me?"

He didn't speak; just closed the distance and kissed her. She nodded in the direction of a security camera and grabbed him by the waist band of his jeans.

"Come on. I know a place where there isn't one of those things."

IV.

Diary of a Rehabilitated Corpsefucker!, September 22nd
A month!

Are you my cure? You don't know how badly I want that. Wouldn't it be hilarious? I went to that stupid meeting and came off like a total retard, but I'm better than I've been in a long time. It had nothing to do with the meeting, of course.

God, what a bunch of losers, the whole non-corpsefucking lot of them!

I'm trying not to get my hopes up, but you're working like a charm. And it's the best live *sex I've ever had.*

I know things at the beginning of a relationship are always the best. In some ways it's like the Other thing, when you think about it, Mr. Diary. You feel like you can do anything at all, you don't see anything you don't like, you're excited about it and it meets your expectations night after night after night.

But then it starts to rot. Pretty soon you can only see where it's going bad, and then you're only doing it because you've already come this far, so you might as well. And then it's making you sick to be around it all the time. Then you cut your losses and swear it off for good, until you find yourself doing it all over again, and it's new and exciting. At least the dead have a tangible sell date.

But maybe I'm not talking about you here. Can it last?

Please, please, please *last.*

This time might be different.

Must *be different.*

Don't make me do it again.

V.

Two months.

Chase's smile felt chiseled on his face; unfaltering, though his eyes couldn't always match it. Cynthia didn't seem to notice. She talked a mile a minute across the table from him, couldn't be happier.

"I was getting these weird vibes from him, too, you know? Like Dennis from group... the one you call G.I. Joe." Cynthia laughed. "What if he worked in a shoe store? He's had to have thought of it. Wouldn't that be just...*creepy*? Like a sex offender doing children's parties as a clown. Gross."

Rehearsing: *It's not you, it's me... You're exciting, and vibrant, and alive. Well, okay, I admit, it's at least a little you, and the fact that I'd be a lot happier with you if you were dead.*

Chase doubted he would get any points for originality. He kept his mouth shut and the smile in place. He fought the symptoms, the backsliding.

Okay, it wasn't perfect, but you'd have to be an idiot to think there was such a thing when it came to a relationship.

Cynthia still turned him on, which helped enormously. He liked to hear her talk—the way and the sound.

Things in the bedroom—and backseats and doorways and
stairwells and bathrooms and park benches and movie theaters
and...everywhere else they'd managed to perform at least a partial sexual act—were good. There was the one time he'd "teased"
her about lying deathly still with him on top of her and she'd
obliged as a joke for about ten seconds, but she hadn't seemed to
notice how much more passionate he'd been that night or that
he'd quickly blown his load like someone had stood by the bed
with a stopwatch and a million-dollar cash prize.

"He looked so heartbroken the last time we were there, and
I didn't wear sandals. What was Linda thinking? She doesn't
want him to look, but she keeps wearing shoes that will set him
off. Maybe that's her kink. Addicted to teasing and looking for
targets. I always thought half the guys who went to the meetings
had to be perverts out for total nymphos."

I'm okay, Chase assured himself. *Doing just fine.*

He looked around the restaurant. Mostly couples, all staring at each other like they knew a secret. No screaming brats,
thankfully, just murmured speech and incessant clicking and
clinking. A warm feeling, warmer still with a nudge from Cynthia's foot in his crotch below the table. He peeked down to see
she'd taken off a shoe. The foot play was new. She seemed to
have an inexhaustible supply of such pleasantries. He stiffened
immediately, thinking of Esther's orange toes even as he told
himself he wasn't thinking about that at all, trying to reshape
the thoughts from something past to something forthcoming.
Namely himself with Cynthia grinding against him, the way
women who are alive tend to do.

"Maybe that's why *you* went," Cynthia teased. She prodded
with her toes on the *you* and *went*. "On the prowl to use someone's lust against them."

He knew he'd have to think of Esther to get off later. The cold and shriveled lips of her sex as his tongue moistened them, the once soft flesh all but petrified and her vagina as cold as the sleeping earth beneath them as he fought his way inside, the only lubrication his pre-coital drip and a hastily applied slathering of pus/adipocere/assorted putrefaction around his organ; the fear of some horrifying form of genital disease so extremely short-lived with the blissful immersion into that rotted sheath, buoyed by the liquefying death doll, this complete stranger he had strangled because the thought occurred to him that hey, this beauty would be heavenly to come inside after she'd prettied up with a little rigor mortis.

"You had the look of a man with special tastes. I wondered what you had going on inside."

Her toes in little waves, a teasing stroke that would have had G.I. Joe exploding in his camos like a Claymore.

Yes, special tastes. The strong chin and measured head tilt of a man who finds more masturbation fodder in a forensic textbook than one of Neil's ass-bang stroke books. That's me.

"I'm going to the ladies' room." She continued to knead him expertly, massaging, squeezing. "Maybe you should check on me in a minute to see if I need any assistance."

Comp*romise*, not de*mise*, he thought. *This is going very well. Six weeks. Everything is fine.*

"Hurry back," he said, a bit loudly over the mutterings of the other couples in the restaurant, as though to intrude on their secrets.

She paused as she slid her chair back against the table. "Oh, and some food for thought while we wait for the dessert menu: My parents have a cabin up in the mountains that they won't be using again for months. How's your weekend looking?"

His smile, unfaltering.

VI.

Diary of a Rehabilitated Corpsefucker (?), October 17th
The big test. How's your weekend looking?
Partly cloudy with a 50% chance of a dead fuck.

I have to try to do this. If I can resist, it means I'm safe. Not
cured—*I'll never be cured any more than an alcoholic, but an*
alcoholic can walk away from drinking. Anything could happen
with you after the weekend, but just knowing I resisted the Ulti-
mate Temptation, it would help.

Fact is, though, you opened your mouth at the restaurant
tonight and for a moment I saw a clump of worms spilling out.

Okay...65% chance.

But I have to try.

VII.

"You nervous?" Cynthia asked.

Chase drummed his fingers on his thighs. He gave her a lopsided grin. "Kind of steep."

She laughed. "Well, yeah. This isn't like those other mountains...you know, the ones that *aren't* steep?"

"Ha ha," he said.

She patted his knee. "This isn't four-wheel drive, but I've
come up here plenty of times. We'll make it."

He nodded. He had no worry about that because he'd made
it in his own car several times, and that thing looked like it might
blow away with a strong enough wind. Even though they'd gone
way past his turn-off point, it had still freaked him out, like she

was taking him directly to the site of his sins. A necrophiliac intervention.

Please give up the corpse sex, Chase. I care about you.

It brought back nauseating memories of some little girl named Sarah Putnam who went missing awhile back. Search parties with bloodhounds swept through the forests like ticks, and he'd waited on pins and needles for The Discovery, vowing to give it up forever if they didn't stumble over his ——wet work.

The universe bestowed its favor upon him: They didn't find any of the corpses or the little brat, after which Chase's solemn vow lasted about three months before he found himself blasting his payload in another rotting twat. A wide enough niche in the trees allowed him to pull his car off the road, out of sight. It wasn't heavily traveled anyway, especially at night. He worried more about crossing paths with a bobcat than a potential witness. Once off the road, it was a simple matter of hauling the body out of the trunk, tied up in a sleeping bag for the laborious process of dragging it for hours deeper into the woods. He doubted a marathon could compare to the exhaustion of this process through the uneven terrain and obstacles of roots and branches, not to mention two or three—usually three—hefty protein deposits along the way in frenzied pit stops which left him spent and light-headed. No telling how he would have survived this before the advent of Red Bull. Hours in body-drag time proved far less in hands-free travel the subsequent nights, but apparently enough to ensure the secrecy of *Bang*ri-Lah. At least so far. Best of all, no cries of *serial killer!*

The disappearances had not been connected.

People disappear all the time.

You can walk down the street and right off the edge of the world.

It was funny because he never thought of himself as a serial killer. He derived no pleasure from the act, only the selection and the aftermath. The strangling was purely functional, like pushing a button on the microwave for a frozen meal. He'd only known one of the women, and he hadn't been involved in her life to a degree that anybody would have associated him with her vanishing. Someone he'd known years ago from college who had all but forgotten about him. He'd thought about *her* a lot, though, and the fantasy converged with opportunity a few years ago when he followed her home from Swag, a business since demolished as if in solidarity.

RIP Donna.

RIP Swag.

He never thought he'd really go through with the impulse, even as he'd put together the whole protocol in his mind in the preceding years. It had seemed harmless, like the one fantasy where he got in a fight with some douche at a bar and whipped his punk ass right in front of his gape-mouthed bitch.

"Am I going too fast?" Cynthia asked. "Your hand is balled up pretty tight."

"Oh." He looked at his hand like he didn't control it, and let his fingers spread out again.

He smiled disarmingly. "No, I'm fine. So, you come up here a lot?"

"Not for a little while. It's a nice place to escape, though."

Or vanish.

The city seemed worlds away this deep into the woods. They'd seen one car coming down the mountain, but nothing in the twenty minutes since.

"My parents don't use it much. I didn't even tell them we were going."

Chase had not met her parents, nor had there been talk of such an introduction. That wasn't a step he had been looking forward to, and one she didn't seem in any hurry to make either.

They don't know what I look like or how to reach me—maybe not even my name. And they don't know we're going there.

He started drumming his fingers on his pants again. All the sex they'd had in the past couple months combined would not be as fulfilling as rutting with her dead body once. All the way out here, it would be a hell of a lot more than once, too.

A whole weekend. With an actual bed. Anything I want to do.

Cynthia turned off on an unpaved road that almost seemed camouflaged. It was not a straight path. Within moments they could not see the main road behind them.

Anything I want to do at all.

They'd gone to a few of the meetings since they met to keep up appearances, but nobody knew they were together. He could drop in a couple more times and feign surprise at her absence. He suspected he'd be in a repentant mood again anyway.

He knew it was a risk to do this with someone he knew, someone he'd been seen with, and that he should really think this through, but the prevailing thought wasn't to let better sense prevail...it was that the longer she was alive, the less time he'd have to explore her the way he truly wanted to—no, *needed to*—before Monday.

I can call in sick! he realized. Considering what Chase would be doing while he was supposed to be selling ad space for the marketing division, it wasn't exactly a lie.

Three-day weekend!

Cynthia looked at him. A bit intensely, he thought. "You look awfully happy."

He took her hand. "Why wouldn't I be?"

He'd miss her voice, but nothing she could say would be as good as this weekend.

Nothing.

If he wanted to hear her that bad, he probably still had her saved on a voicemail.

Hmm. Come to think of it, better destroy her SIM card.

After another mile and a half, the road opened onto the actual cabin. "What do you think?" she asked, pulling the car to a stop.

Looks like a cozy place to spend the weekend with my dick inside every hole your cadaver can offer.

"Very nice. They keep the *Book of the Dead* in there?"

She looked puzzled. "What?"

He shook his head. "Not important. Want to give me the grand tour?"

She took him by the hand and led him to the front. She'd worn jeans. He wished there had been a skirt with stockings, as he'd purposely not taken anything for strangling to help psychologically dissuade himself from going down that road.

Didn't even make it to the cabin before I fell off the wagon.

No matter. There'd be something inside: Rope. A lamp cord. A tie.

The cabin stood two stories, rustic but well-maintained. He bet anything there would be an animal head mounted to the wall. He planned to joke about how fast it must have been running when it hit the house. That's what a normal guy would do.

"There's a Jacuzzi upstairs," she said. "Feel like a bath?"

Good idea. I can just pull you up by the ankles until you drown.
Even less trauma to your body than strangling.

"Sure. Want me to carry you over the threshold?"

She slapped him lightly as she fumbled the right key on her ring into the lock. He felt precisely zero surprise at the buck head over the fireplace as the door swung open. The bear skin rug, though, he hadn't counted on that. He couldn't think of a more perfectly tacky touch.

Evidently, he wasn't the only one fascinated with dead things.

Before he could make his joke about the buck head, Cynthia said, "It's cold in here," and seized him by the crotch. "Come on, let's get you upstairs."

"You don't want to bring in our stuff?"

She laughed. "We already have more than we need."

Cynthia led him upstairs and through the master bedroom at the end of the hall. A king-size bed, he noticed. He'd have all the room in the world. By this time tomorrow, she'd be virtually perfect. He felt giddy with the excitement. His first time might last about four seconds if he was lucky. He wasn't worried, though; he had a way of recharging really fast. Maybe Cynthia's dad kept some Viagra in the medicine cabinet. She'd be leaking his ball sauce from her nose and ears by Monday.

They entered the bathroom. The overcast sky outside issued pure gloom, but it seemed bright enough even without turning on the overhead lights. Cynthia bent over and twisted the knobs on the faucet. He admired the view. He'd experienced it many times, but it seemed new now, uncharted territory. If there was anyone he could have felt uninhibited with, it was her. It still didn't matter: He didn't want to share her life with her, only her death.

"Okay, you strip down and I'll be right back," she said.

"Where are you going?"

She thumbed open a couple of buttons on her shirt, revealing the white skin beneath and a black bra. "Fireplace. I'll heat things up downstairs and you can take care of the upstairs."

She turned. He saw her shirt drop out on both sides as she freed the last button on her way out.

Showtime.

Chase stripped his clothes off in seconds as if it would give him more time to prepare, but there was really nothing to do but wait for the tub to fill. He tried to strategize, though it would really depend on what Cynthia did when she got in. Most scenarios he envisioned would lead easily enough to his goal.

He shuddered a little; it *was* cold in the cabin, especially standing there naked. She hadn't returned when he shut off the water, but he wasn't going to wait on her. Mercifully, she'd set the temperature to almost unbearably hot. He eased into the water, sighing. He might want to wait for the water to cool a little before he dragged her under. He'd rather she be strangled than scalded.

Cynthia appeared in the doorway seconds later, undressed. She carried towels and bathrobes folded over her arm. "How is it? It looks divine."

He gestured. "Come see for yourself."

She knelt and set everything down by the tub, leaning over to kiss him. He thought about hauling her in right then, but he wanted to avoid any kind of struggle where she could claw him. Besides, when her hand slid down between his legs and stroked him, he didn't see how another thirty seconds of life was such a bad thing. He leaned his head back, relaxed.

The pain exploded in his throat a second later.

His eyes shot open to see he had grown a new brass extension somewhere below his jaw, a union Cynthia initiated. Blood exploded in a wave of hot sleet, splashing into Cynthia's face and on her breasts like the blowback of rainwater across a windshield, momentarily blinding. She blinked her eyes, expressionless as a reptile. He felt the artery pulsing in his throat, the crimson pumping through his sieve. Cynthia twisted the instrument in his throat clockwise and back, then wrenched it free.

Where are you going?

Fireplace.

A poker.

Chase was too stunned to move, or maybe the bloodletting was too immediate. Red spooled through the water in the tub, spattering within and along the sides. And all the while, her other hand continued to stroke him, wordlessly watching as jets of blood gushed from the slashed artery. It was the weirdest sensation, as though her manipulation of his genitals had created an orgasm in another part of his body, one of pain rather than pleasure. He marveled at his hardness, fully erect even as his eyelids gradually drew shut forever.

VIII.

Diary of a Relapsed Corpsefucker, October 18th

What was it I said, Mr. Diary? "You get so many chances, it's kind of hard not to do it. I kind of feel like I have to. None of us are here long and there's only so much we can do with it, isn't there? So, I do it. I'm not always glad about it. And my boyfriends definitely aren't. I wish I could. I'm not sure I can."

Well, I gave it a good try. I really did want to stop, but evidently not hard enough.

And speaking of hard...you still are. They don't always finish that way. I'll be depressed about all this later, I'm sure, but right now I'm a kid on Christmas morning. The tears and the vows to stop doing this will probably start again on Monday, but I'm going to make the most of it. A hard man is good to find, as they say, and a hard dead man even better, as I say (now).

In fact, why go in Monday at all?

Screw it. I'll just call in sick.

Three-day weekend!

THE SEACRETOR

Is it reassuring that there are still worlds unknown to us? Our reality is mapped and enforced by algorithms we do not see, whose influence we accept. Everything runs in accordance with them. Yet there are places beyond the maps of reality, of consciousness. Fractures in the thinnest places that we don't even know to look for. I wonder less about how our influence will one day change these strange oases than the ways in which they may change us.

—*Transitory Bodies*, Dr. Braedon Obrist

I.

GRANT FUCKED THE TREE on the sixth day.

I watched him do it from down below, near the massive letters we dug into the sand which spelled *HELP*. We did this on both sides of the island, which was thirsty work even in the shade.

We didn't ration our water so effectively, which was why he and Tanya drank the tree jizz on day five.

I guess I'm getting ahead of myself, though.

Let me back up.

II.

The *Seacretor* was Grant's boat.

The whole invitation felt like an opportunity for Grant to play his demo reel for Tanya. You know, *All of this could be yours, if you just tell Ben thanks but no thanks and take a hit of my dick instead.* I don't think he wanted her initially, but she met both of us at the same party and started dating me. It must have wounded his ego. How could she choose the guy who couldn't have attended such a prestigious college without a lacrosse scholarship, had to work in the library on top of that, and owned a secondhand car? What sorcery made me the better option than the trust fund prince with the hot-shit dad whose load hit the floor first during the Illuminati circle jerk? He was *Grant!*

We were barely friends and only because I tutored him last semester. He could count how many houses his family owned (three) and on how many continents (two), but otherwise his math skills left much to be desired. An owl could solve a Rubik's cube before Grant passed his courses on his own, so I came to the rescue. Grant escaped with a C-average and I earned a summer invite to his family estate on an island, which, he said "you've probably never heard of."

And admittedly I hadn't.

Tanya and I privately called it the Island of Dr. Maroon at first, but she stopped doing it when we got there. I wasn't sure if Tanya and I would last, but neither of us planned to go back home for the whole summer, so an exotic month-long vacation was hard to pass up. I needed to get away from my roommate, too, and his random stories about accidental incest and mutilated hitchhikers.

The mansion was impressive, I'll admit, with a view to the beach from most every window, but also an indoor pool if you didn't feel like walking a whole three blocks. Tanya fell for it immediately. I was more reserved, anticipating a thirty-minute head start to run for our lives before disaffected rich guys with pith helmets and elephant guns hunted us down.

After a week, Grant grew tired of the scenery, or at least he felt like he'd impressed Tanya as much as he could with his home, the beach, the scenic hikes, and the exclusive island club. He insisted we take out the *Seacretor*—he was *way* too proud of that name—for a few nights, get a taste of other islands and their posh restaurants, hotels, and cuisines, and make passive-aggressive reminders about me working in the library.

I proved to be as adept with the sea as Grant with equations. Lots of puking over the side into the Pacific. Bonus time for Grant and Tanya. I wondered if he purposely kept us out in the ocean longer when he saw what it did to me, and that may have been why we came across the island instead of docking a couple hours earlier when we had the chance. He claimed a leper colony set up shop there.

"Is it even okay to call someone a leper?" Tanya asked. They debated while I spewed over the side again.

I thought Grant played it up when he said this island wasn't charted on his deluxe mapping system. He moved in for a closer

look, with Tanya giddy at the prospect of an adventure. A couple hundred yards out should have been enough to conclude
nobody bothered mapping the place because it sucked, but the
Seacretor drifted closer as Grant and Tanya hyped this mystery
island and I held my head in my hands and tried not to puke.

"I bet there's buried treasure," Tanya joked.

I was about to opine that Grant needed greater riches like R.
Kelly needed a diuretic, and that's when a spire of rock smashed
through our hull. A few minutes later we stood drenched on
the shore of the island after a hundred-yard swim, each of us in
sodden shirts and swimming trunks or bikini bottoms, all signs
of our vessel erased like paint smeared over a landscape to hide
a mistake.

III.

"I don't know where the hell that rock came from," Captain
Fuckface swore as we took stock of our inventory—a hastily
grabbed first-aid kit, flare gun case, a torpedo-sized bottle of
water barely halfway full—my doing after heaving my guts over
the side—and a smartphone reluctant to power on after its dip
in the ocean.

MacGyver could build a submarine from that, but we'd be
lucky if it meant a three-day-lease on life.

Tanya patted Grant on the arm as he stared at the site of the
shipwreck, or the approximate spot since it was hard to be sure
now. It's no wonder vessels and planes can disappear out here,
swept under the globe's largest rug. We'd seen no other boats
the past two hours since we drew away from the last island.

We were all alone.

If there was a silver lining to our predicament, it was that no expense would be spared on behalf of Grant's rescue. They'd send the armada for the golden boy and tell them to grab his friends, too, if there was room in a shipping crate.

We set down our supplies far from the surf and took stock of our environment. Yes, it seemed strange it did not appear on a mapping system—this was far more than some little outcropping of rock barely big enough for a seagull orgy—but it wasn't much to look at from our current side. We saw a dwindling shoreline alongside a tall column made of pure rock. This hill rose overhead roughly a hundred feet and stretched half a mile, kind of bony in appearance and unblemished by any trees or bushes on our side save for a lone tree at the top. I hoped that meant we'd find more signs of life on the other side of the rock.

Grant took point toward the nearest end of the island, far enough ahead to allow me a moment to talk privately with Tanya.

"I don't believe this," I said.

"Calm down. We'll be okay." Despite the assurance I thought she sounded annoyed with me, even though I wasn't the one who just crashed our ship and instantly cast the three of us in a remake of *Robinson Crusoe,* currently filming in the style of un-found footage.

"You don't think he should have paid more attention to the *sonar* than his *bo-nar?*"

Ten days ago Tanya would have laughed until she snorted that one.

Now she rolled her eyes and walked faster until I was left alone with my shadow.

IV.

I caught up to them at the end of the shoreline. The rock extended past the sand and we couldn't see all the way around to the other side. Waves exploded off its surface in bursts of white spume. Too easy to imagine a swimmer slammed into the wall repeatedly until sharks did him a favor and ate him.

"I bet it's the same on the other side," Grant said.

Well, he was certainly the authority today on obstacles we couldn't successfully negotiate, so I didn't argue.

We walked back the way we came until we found a decent spot to ascend. It was more of a punishing hike since we never truly climbed at any point. Ten minutes or so later we all stood by the tree, sucking wind.

The trunk had burst through the surface of stone, but for all its aspirations, it was a rather sorry excuse for a tree in the end. No leaves, no fronds, minimal shade. It looked like the withered three-fingered hand of a giant stickman.

"Yuck, what's that?" Tanya pointed to a limb on the far right. Something oozed from it, dark and syrup-like. She drew her hand away like she wouldn't be able to stop herself from touching it.

Grant smiled. "Bring any pancakes?"

Tanya tee-heed while I seethed; *bo-nar* was way funnier.

"Forget about the tree jizz." I gestured to notches in the trunk without sticking my fingers in them. "What's up with all these glory holes?"

Tanya's smile evaporated and her eyes went cloudward again. Grant shook his head like the joke was beneath him and brought us all down as human beings.

I examined the holes as if I actually cared. Turns out, Grant and Tanya were missing out on a sensational discovery. Each one opened to a disc of apparently rotting bark and a true hole in the middle. I didn't pry since they glistened, probably from more of that fluid.

The top of the bluff stayed level twenty yards past the tree. We walked to the other side for essentially a mirror image of where we'd landed, except it had shade. After being in the direct sun for half an hour, we were ready for some of that. Otherwise, it had nothing else we wanted or needed.

"This place sucks," Grant said.

"Yeah."

I wanted to remind them how excited they were about the island before. Their indifference now was too little, too late.

"There's nothing to eat." Tanya squinted as if we were over-looking a bucket of fried chicken somewhere. "Hey, is that a cave?"

She pointed. Turned out her eyes were good for more than just rolling at supremely funny jokes. Down and to the right in the shadier section of the rock jutted a protrusion that partially obstructed a deeper black. You could almost write it off as a shadow in the crag, but it was an opening for sure.

The path down required more care than the other side. Everyone made it fine, but soon wished we hadn't bothered.

We all picked up stones before we entered the mouth, I guess in case we had to mount a coordinated effort to bludgeon a deadly cave parrot to death, but there were no birds. In fact, we hadn't heard so much as a gull since arriving. The cooler air felt heavenly, if tempered by the confirmation of no water source. I'd been hoping to hear it trickling from somewhere in the recesses, but there didn't seem to *be* recesses. We dared to venture slightly beyond the reach of the sun and the passageway narrowed and lowered considerably until we were practically walking on our knees.

We turned back. The cave would make a good shelter from a storm but we didn't care to linger. It smelled musty and its tight confines suggested jaws struggling to clamp down on us.

We agreed to sleep on the beach instead.

"Someone will come," Grant said as we looked out at the ocean. "Someone has to."

But we could see for miles.

And no one was coming.

V.

We slept the first night on the side we washed up, close to where we dropped our supplies. I should say we tried to sleep, but I never felt like I made it. The coolness of the night quickly lost its initial pleasantness, but Tanya showed no interest in huddling close for warmth.

Digging *HELP* in the sand was my idea and warmed us up in the dawn before the sun started bearing down. Tanya suggested we use rocks to spell it on top of the hill too. A passing plane might see it, but I was more hopeful someone would aim a satellite our way and do something about it if they saw our signs. If they zeroed in closer still, they might mistake Tanya's eye rolling for grand mal seizures. The long night hadn't softened her any and the feeling was mutual.

We waded out to catch fish but they apparently had better things to do than hang out near the mystery island because opportunities were few and far between. When we saw a stingray, we hauled ass to the beach. Grant threw a rock in its direction like a shotput which splashed only about twenty feet from the target.

"This close," I said, holding up thumb and index finger.

Grant flipped me off peeled banana style, which made me hungrier.

You can guess how Tanya reacted.

Day two felt like six days, minimum. The smartphone wouldn't power back on after teasing us with the partial burst of Grant's ringtone, a loop of that Corpsefrother song. I can never remember the full name—it takes longer to say the name than to listen to the whole track—but I'm sure you know the one. (Supposedly Grant wanted to christen his boat the *Beef Broth* in homage, until he saw on the news someone already beat him to it.) Anyway, if boredom were edible, we'd have been okay. Instead, we sniped at each other for being thirsty and hungry. Or, rather, I sniped at Tanya and Grant and they took turns sniping back as a tag team. We tried to distract ourselves, often making it worse. Grant asked what our desert island CDs would be, and they ganged up on me for saying, "I don't know, let me see what I grabbed off the boat before it sank."

"This is such bullshit," Grant said at another point. "We've got all this water out there—we never stop hearing it, for Christ's sake—and we can't drink any of it."

"We could," I said, "we'd just dehydrate faster from the salt."

"Dehydrating from drinking water." He laughed humorlessly. "Man, that's just not even fair."

"We'll probably have to drink our own urine after we run out of water."

Tanya had the face of a child hearing the urban legend where the babysitter discovers the calls are coming from inside the house.

"Don't listen to him," Grant said. "It won't come to that. Even if we don't get rescued right away, it won't matter. It'll rain."

We looked to the horizon and the pure azure sky, not a single cloud in it, fluffy white or otherwise.

If the ocean didn't ripple, you could almost confuse one for the other.

"It'll rain," Grant repeated. "It has to."

VI.

It didn't rain, not the next day when we used up the last of our water or the day after that. Plenty of clouds floated past but always wispy or as clean as snowfall. We named the shapes, but no one bothered forecasting rain from anything we saw. The skies darkened only for the arrival of night. I'd never seen the stars clearer in my life.

Like I could have shattered them with a stone from the ground.

"What about the tree?" Grant said on the second day with no water.

We were hiding out in the cave. I'd been playing sentry beneath said tree with the flare gun for unknown hours before this, having stretched my shirt and one borrowed from Grant out across two limbs to create some shade to sit there and watch for passing ships. There wasn't enough to comfortably shield two people so Tanya had a ready excuse to stay behind with Grant. We decided to stay on the side with the cave since it offered shelter from the sun, and we had a look-out to the other side with a little hike from the cave.

"I've been thinking about it too," Tanya said. She often seemed to have been thinking about the latest thing Grant said, funnily enough. I suspected she'd make the same claim if he'd said, *What about animal husbandry?* I also suspected they were fooling around, even though it would have been stupid of them with no fluids to spare. I could creep to the edge of the bluff and see what they were up to, but who knew what happened when they holed up in the cave. That's when I usually made it a point to clamber down for someone to take my place. We were deciding who should take next watch when Grant made his proposal.

"It's something, right?" He sounded excited, and he and Tanya both stood up.

"Yeah, we'll die if we don't try something. I've never been so thirsty in my life."

"Wait a minute." I followed them out because they weren't stopping for a dissenting voice.

The sun nearly melted my contrarian attitude by the time we attained the summit. It would have been easy to roll the dice and sip. If I didn't automatically hate everything Grant and Tanya agreed on, I might have caved.

"You don't know what's in that stuff," I said.

"We know we can drink it," Grant countered. "That's a better offer than the rest of the island is giving us. That's good enough for me."

"Me too," Tanya said. "Have some of your piss if you're too scared, Ben."

"At least my piss definitely isn't poisonous."

"Poisonous?' Grant laughed. "Dude, it's a tree, not a mushroom."

"There's poisonous sap."

"Ben, it's not poisonous, okay?" Tanya said.

"I guess we're about to know for sure."

They stood near the coated branch, the only one of the limbs with that glazed appearance.

Tanya winced from the sickly odor of the ooze, something that kept me from giving its consumption serious consideration during the hours I watched the sky, parched with thirst and stomach gurgling. It reminded me of disease for some reason, subdued my hunger with nausea.

"Here goes nothing." Little syrup stalactites stretched from the limb and Grant knelt beneath them with his tongue out. A couple pooled on his tongue like motor oil until he drew it in and swallowed. "It's not good," he reported. "But beats dying of thirst any day."

Tanya guided her face below the branch for her first share. She clearly wanted to spit it back out but finally swallowed it down. When she licked the residue from her lips, I thought of rubber cement.

I shook my head when they asked if I wanted in and they gave me disgusted looks, although less so than from the act of drinking the tree jizz a couple more times. It satisfied me enough to know it was there as a last resort, like a cyanide capsule in a false tooth. I did drink my urine that morning before they got up—it almost looked orange—but it hadn't helped and I'd nearly thrown it back up because of the wretched aftertaste. The thirst started consuming me again, would have been all I could think about if not for Grant and Tanya, but I wouldn't trust my fate to mystery ooze while I had the chance to see its effect on them overnight.

I could hold out that long.

I hoped.

"See?" Tanya gestured. "We're both fine."

"Yeah, man," Grant said. "You're depriving yourself for nothing. FYI, we're eating you if you drop dead."

I doubted they would cry themselves to sleep tonight over that so I didn't say anything, just walked back to the cave with them.

I wondered how many more times I could do that without being so dizzy that I pitched over the side.

Or how many more times I'd have the strength to make the climb in the first place.

VII.

The sun had nearly emerged from the horizon as if borne of the water when I woke up and made sure Tanya and Grant were fortunately (I guess) still alive. They also hadn't spent the night doubled over puking or shitting their guts. I suppose I looked quite the fool for my protest, but I'd gotten comfortable with that role in the past couple weeks.

I examined them as they slept. Sunburns notwithstanding, Tanya was undeniably pretty, almost painfully so in such a time of need. I didn't mind seeing so much of her ass and legs each day. I had a fantasy of her pulling her bikini bottom to the side, telling me to fuck her. That ship had sailed, though, or at least smashed itself to pieces and dropped to the ocean floor.

Grant, on the other hand...

"What the hell..."

A disgusting insect poked through one leg of his swimming trunks, something like a giant grub/millipede hybrid. The bulge ran all the way to where his package should have been. I didn't understand how he could sleep through that, and expected him to bolt upright amidst much falsetto shrieking. I seized a nearby stone with hopefully enough heft to smash the little bastard dead. (The insect thing, not Grant.) I tapped the rock on the ground, hoping the thing would withdraw to investigate, but it didn't move.

My rock cast a shadow over the pillar of disgust. It had little rubbery fronds along the visible duration of its length, which looked greased up with something like pus, and had the thickness of a garden hose. It made me sick to look at it.

I tried once more to coax it away from Grant, tapping it through the fabric and nudging it in my direction.

"Ben, dude, the fuck?" Grant said.

So barely brushing the fabric of his trunks disturbed his sleep in the way some dick-sucking insect couldn't.

He sat up straight and scooted away, maybe thinking I was about to smash his junk. Instead of evicting the thing, it went with Grant even when he stood up. The tendril just hung there like a curtain cord.

"What?" Tanya rubbed her eyes, groaning as she strained upright.

I pointed. "Grant! In your shorts!"

He looked down and his eyes popped. He slapped at the thing like a lick of flame. I stood ready with the rock, ready to crush it as soon as it dropped off, but it didn't release.

Grant ceased his slapping almost as soon as he started. "Oh shit...oh Jesus." He collapsed on his ass in the sand, holding his head in his hands, chest hitching like he was working up to a scream.

"Is it...latched on?" I advanced with the rock. He held up a hand. "Stay back! Don't touch it!" Tanya stood beside me, wide awake now.

Rather than trying to yank the thing out, Grant pulled his trunks down below his waist so it would cover it up.

"You want the rock?" I prepared to pitch it to him, though he had plenty of alternates in reach.

"It's not latched on," he said, returning his hands to his head and shaking it miserably. "It's...*me*."

He kept repeating this as if it could help him integrate the madness with reality.

"Let me see!" Tanya took a step toward him. He drew up against the hill, burying his face in his arms, ordering us away.

Ostrich syndrome with a side of millipede dick.

I shook off a twinge of jealousy. She didn't want to see it because it was his thing. Which she'd probably already seen, sucked, and fucked. It was more like the morbid curiosity over a two-headed calf, but she wouldn't desire such a thing, even if that two-headed calf owned an island estate.

"Come on," I said, "let's give him some space."

As we walked away from him and the awkward sound of his crying—the real reason I wanted some distance—I couldn't help thinking, *The winner...by default...Ben!*

But there was no real joy involved. The ramifications were as hideous as they were impossible: The tree did that to Grant. And Tanya drank from it too.

I kept a hand on her back. "How do you feel?"

"I'm fine, really," she said, but pulled her bikini bottoms out to check. I wasn't sure of the etiquette there so I looked to the ocean and tensed for her scream. It was hard to reconcile the beauty of the sun-dappled waters and the renewal of another day with Grant's mutation. The natural and the sickeningly unnatural.

"All clear," she said.

I turned back as she brushed away tears.

"Maybe it only has that effect with guys," I said.

"Maybe." The tears continued and I put my arm around her. I didn't believe for a minute she was out of the clear, and she didn't either. I was ready to pull away from her at the first sign of a change. I wondered if Grant still wanted us to be found.

Tanya stopped walking. "Not too far. We have to make sure he doesn't start digging into the first-aid kit."

"Why's that?"

"It has scissors."

VIII.

Grant volunteered to be the lookout, like nothing had happened. I wondered if he planned to throw himself off the top. I wasn't sure what to say. They didn't make a greeting card for genital transformation.

I went up with him to watch him per Tanya's request as well as to clean up the *HELP* sign with that side still shaded. The tide had eroded the crescent of our *P*. I was less concerned with some satellite-savvy grammar Nazi ignoring our plea to teach us a lesson than just getting away from Grant so he could do what he thought he had to do.

Shade or not, the heat crashed down on me in waves of its own and I thought I was hallucinating when I looked up to see Grant doing what he thought he had to do with his trunks around his ankles, thrusting with abandon into the tree as he hugged the trunk. The thrusts were disturbingly long with the added girth as the mutation hadn't been all bad—he'd packed on those extra inches that allowed the visibility of his new appendage past the hem of his trunks. He was the Johnny Wadd of biological abomination, for what that was worth.

He shuddered visibly and slumped against the tree for several seconds. Then, like a child determined to learn to ride that bike without the training wheels, he started pumping away. He chose a different hole.

The *P* was neat as you could please now and the furrows of the letters nice and symmetrical, but I wouldn't go back up until he'd returned to his post.

It took a lot of hip thrusting and spasms before he withdrew and planted himself back on the ground, shoulders hitching. If a destroyer cruised by, he would have missed it. I began the hike back up the hill, convinced it was the last time. I wouldn't have the strength to do it again. The sun could do its magical dance along the ripples of the ocean again two mornings from now and I might be rotting to a dry husk in the sand.

I was going to pretend to have missed the sex show to avoid the awkwardness and keep the status quo.

"I can't stop fucking the tree," Grant said measuredly the second my shadow fell across him. "I'm about to get up and fuck it again. I can't stop, Ben. It won't let me."

I thought I'd maxed out at wanting to be anywhere else in the world before then, but it turned out there was still another level after all.

Grant continued. "Wants me to fill it up. I must. Soon. You were right. Never should of done it, Ben. Never should of drank the tree jizz."

Thankfully I at least had something to say now. "Pretty sure it's you shouldn't *have drunk* the tree jizz, man. Just sit tight and holler if a ship comes, okay?"

I noted that the ooze now hung from the underside of the limb for nearly three feet, stretching to within inches of the ground. Longer, thicker than before. I walked away fast as I dared. He'd resumed the tree vigil and begun grunting behind me at roughly the same time I heard Tanya's screams.

IX.

I found her in the cave, a writhing shape beyond the reach of the sun. I couldn't see her, only heard cries of horror and pain on my way down which sounded disturbingly less identifiable as human by the time I reached her. The heat and lightheadedness played spatial tricks where the darkness looked like a black train racing away from me endlessly, and a swarm of blue spots filled my eyes from the reduction in light. When she slumped into the path of the sun, I trusted my sight even less.

She had stripped off her shirt and her skin rippled all over, as if taking a liquid form. I thought of the golden specks of sunlight this morning from a marginally saner time. She had swollen all over like a puffer fish, half again her size.

Tanya held her hand out to me as protrusions undulated through her arm, some moving toward her hands, others to her shoulders, while a couple more spiraled around the limb. I thought she tried to say *help,* but she'd been reduced to choking sounds.

I might have been screaming that whole time too, as it seems like I'd already begun before the burrowers started to emerge from Tanya's mouth. They looked similar to the thing Grant had been sticking into the tree, but this was a colony of them, pouring from her gaping mouth like raw meat through a grinder in a mass exodus, and the crank kept churning them out in an unbroken stream. Hundreds of them, maybe thousands. And not just her mouth either: others sought a more immediate exit than the long line for the oral aperture. They pushed through her eyes, nudging them aside to spill from the sockets. They left a snail trail in their wake upon flesh and stone, the same pus-like discharge as Grant's mutation. Her bikini bottom bulged as a ball of them erupted from between her legs.

Though she must have already died, her mouth kept working as the burrowers emerged, the awful illusion of life through prolonged parasitic vomitus.

If they'd shown any interest in me I would have run straight through the mouth of the cave into nothingness for the fastest way down and away from them, but they had a hive mind mentality that guided them into the recesses of the cave.

To nestle?

To breed?

Tanya lay slack and withered, draped in an ill-fitting skin that seemed partially melted without the buoyancy of those slimy things.

Melted.

My loathing for them, both what they did to Tanya and their sickening existence, pushed me to fire the flare gun after them when it seemed like they had all evacuated their incubator.

The corridor exploded into piercing light as the flare sizzled until the cave narrowed and it struck a shelf of overhead rock. The extent of the progression turned my empty stomach, this lubricated moving carpet pouring down a black gullet. The flare reigned upon the congregation in blistering fragments, and their putrid coating did nothing to stave off the ignition. A large swath of them went up like dry grass in a brush fire and spread the same, illuminating the full extent of the cave.

We'd assumed it led to nothing or that it wasn't large enough to provide us access if it did, but didn't bother exploring because we had no light anyway. Now I saw that it didn't narrow so much; that we could've crawled a mere fifteen yards or so and what seemed to be a barrier at the end wasn't a barrier after all.

Flaming burrowers poured through it and vanished beyond.

I reloaded the flare gun with a cartridge from the case and jammed it behind the waist of my trunks, following while some stragglers allowed me the light to reach the end. The ground became wet and sticky beneath my palms and knees, sometimes bubbling as I maneuvered around scorched remnants. I prayed for no open wounds.

The other side promised more light as the burrowers continued to burn. The barrier was wet and malleable. Like touching a giant eyeball. I winced as I wormed my way through the rubbery coin pouch of its slit.

I only wanted to ensure the incineration of the whole colony, or to fire another flare if need be. I'd hoped they'd do me the convenience of a central location, but I forgot all about that as I beheld the other side of the orifice.

The recesses I'd originally hoped for were here, but not as a network of tunnels with a fresh water source. The ground beneath me retained the same membranous texture as the entrance, the color of human gums. Above me hung organic structures, as massive as allowed by the structure of the hill. One looked like bubble wrap made of flesh and sinew. I saw pulsing sacs bigger than me. The burrowers had been crawling toward a pair of enlarged egg-shaped sacs and had kindly congregated in their death throes to sustain my light source. An enormous structure of tubes, twice my size, hung at the edge of the illumination. They looked to be tied in an impenetrable knot.

Maybe it was a trick of the light, but I thought I saw them moving like a tangle of serpents.

The hill offered more than what hung above us, though. The moist ground beneath me eventually terminated in a ridge, perhaps leading to more organs, tissues, sacs, and systems below.

Wherever we'd landed, it was alive. I didn't know if the rock, sand, and tree were part of it or something it became part of, the way its secretions had made those changes in Grant and Tanya. Maybe it was marooned too and adapted to us as Tanya and Grant tried to adapt to it. Its needs were as unknown to us as its existence, but they seemed unmistakably procreative. If it succeeded, I thought dehydration was probably the best-case scenario for me.

I fired the flare. I aimed at the bubble wrap structure nearest to me overhead. For all I knew the whole cavity could have gone up like a kitchen with a gas leak but it didn't happen that way. A wave of heat engulfed me as it lit up, and one of the nearby egg-shaped sacs caught as I decided if I should reload. I thought I'd hear some kind of deafening shriek but there was nothing.

I crawled back through the oval and on through the cave. I still hadn't ruled out an explosion but I had only fumes left in my reserves, and a tortoise would have blown me off the race track. The susurrus of the ocean continued to call me until I made it past Tanya and out the opening. The waves seemed choppier as if some maelstrom simmered below. Behind me a spark of light remained, like the watchful eye of some creature way back in the darkness.

X.

Grant hasn't returned.

I'm waiting for the strength to drag myself back up the hill.

There's one flare left. I think I can get him and the tree with the last shot if he's still stuck in his feedback loop of trunk or treat. I have to: I don't think he'll be Grant much longer and I don't know what could happen if he worked up a thirst right there next to his preferred sap.

Then I need to make it down to the ocean to wash the residue of the cave from me. I think I'll be doing well to make it to the top, though, and getting down under my own power will be the stuff of miracles.

I wonder if I *do* make it down there what I will see if the current takes me away until I sink like a stone to the depths, the great unknown on the underside of the island.

THREESOME

The digital world is a paradox, in which what we deem as ephemeral is actually eternal. Nothing is ever lost, no matter how much we wish it were so. Like the facility of our consciousness to retain our most humiliating moments and replay them when we are at our most vulnerable, we now find our sins and scourgings preserved beyond the limits of our mortality. Can there be resurrection from this? Are we condemned to deeper mutation? Or is there a third possibility?

—*Transitory Bodies*, Dr. Braedon Obrist

I.

THE SURPRISING THING WAS how aggressively Karla pursued him.

She transferred into his anatomy lab at the start of the semester and walked right up to his table as if he'd called her over, taking the stool beside him. The plain Jane who'd warmed that seat for the past two classes—three hours each—meekly submitted to wallflower mode and drifted off to another table when she saw her place had been usurped. Just like that, Karla was in Blake's group with Trey and some girl with a decent rack whose name he didn't know—and didn't care to know. (The rest of her didn't live up to the promise of the rack.) Three hours passed too quickly, but before the end of the week he was getting much more than three hours with her outside of class. Karla wasn't shy about wanting him. Blake was in spelunker mode with that puss before the Thursday lab. And it just went from there.

Two weeks and three times as many fucks later, she asked him, "How would you feel about making it a little more interesting?"

"What do you mean?"

Blake smiled as if intrigued, but it put him on the defensive a little bit. The implication was this was somehow already stale or lacking. Which for him it wasn't. It couldn't be, at least not for a while. She was a goddess.

We just screwed a minute ago and she's talking about spicing it up?

She shrugged, like she hadn't planned this whole proposal and wasn't sure how to continue. Of course, she did. She always had a secret. Figuring it out became a lust unto itself.

"Oh, I was just thinking...maybe I could bring a friend? I don't *have* to. I just thought you might like it."

The shrug again, like this was all for his benefit and anything other than gratitude would be unreasonable.

She was right about that.

Inside there was an eruption of excitement, magma bursting against volcanic rock. It warmed him up all over and nudged his penis awake, which had fallen over in euphoric defeat after Karla drained it so dry that he was surprised not to find desiccated wood.

Blake had to play it cool, though. This could be a trap. He didn't want to give the impression that he'd been waiting for something like this his whole life. He *had,* of course— what guy hadn't? But he didn't really think it would ever happen and, with Karla, he hadn't been thinking in that direction. She was beautiful. He didn't use that term lightly in his mind, although he could be casual with it in conversation if it proved to his advantage. He'd told many girls they were beautiful because it was expected—even if they were only marginally attractive. He'd never tried the blunt honesty of, "Hey, you're fairly cute. There are about fourteen other chicks in here I'd rather fuck, but I'd feel okay about sticking it in you." He didn't have high hopes for that gambit.

"A friend?" He furrowed his brow as if pondering. "That's...interesting. I suppose." A horrible thought occurred to him. "You *do* mean a girlfriend, right? I mean, not a *girl-friend*, but...like, not some dude."

She giggled. He liked to make her do that, although in this case he was dead serious and not playing for laughs.

"Yes, that kind of friend."

Their faces were level on the pillow in profile. He traced a hand along her hip. He always had to touch her when she was this close with that magnificent body.

"Good," he said, feeling playful again. "You know how I feel about that man-ass."

She broke into another fit of laughter. She still looked lovely when she did. Blake had banged plenty of twats who looked like someone yelled, *Oswald!* and fired a gun in their guts when they laughed. He tried not to be funny around them.

"What's your friend like?" Blake asked. It sounded neutral. Much better than what he really wanted to say and all he cared about: *Is she hot?*

"She's nice." Karla flicked her tongue. "She likes to play."

"You already talked about it with her?"

"A little. She sounded interested."

"How'd you even get on the topic?"

She poked him. "You think guys are the only ones who talk about sex?"

Blake and his friends talked about sex, of course—practically nothing else but how much they were getting or who they'd get it with if they got half a chance—but he could honestly say he'd never once broached the subject of tag teaming some bitch with one of his boys. He had a couple friends who thought those double penetration videos were the shit, but Blake found it creepy. Not much more than a membrane to keep your dick from touching some other dude's—and, of course, the man-ass factor.

No thanks.

She slid over until they were close enough to kiss. Her lips were soft, full. Dick-sucking lips, or DSLs as his friends would say. Kissing wasn't a big thing with him, mostly a boring pre-amble until he could cram his dick in whatever hole they offered him, but he loved the feel of Karla's lips on his. She kissed him now and he stirred against her belly.

"What'd I do to deserve this?" he asked.

"I saw you and I knew I wanted you," she answered simply.

"I meant the threesome."

She giggled again and slapped him. He forced a smile. He hadn't been kidding. He'd really meant the threesome.

"I know you were disappointed about the camera. I wanted to make it up to you."

He held his fake smile. *Oh yes, the camera.* It wasn't too big a deal, at least not yet. He kept hoping she'd come around on that. And, while the hope was alive, he couldn't be mad that she wouldn't do anything on video. It was a shame with the convenience of recording devices these days and it always good to have it. Just in case.

Blake didn't like to lose.

"You may change your mind some time," he said, "but if not, it's okay. This is better."

He kissed her, hoping she'd guide those lips southward and get him keyed up for another trip to V Town.

"Well?" Karla prompted. She coyly lifted an eyebrow, sweeping some blond strands out of her face. Her blue eyes seemed perpetually amused, particularly now when she knew she had him on the line.

He laughed. "Don't I at least get to meet her?"

"One time offer." Her face didn't soften, but he had the distinct sense she wasn't playing with him.

He had so many questions.

What are her tits like?

Does she have alabaster ass cheeks to glaze with my froth?

How's her face compared to yours?

How much does she weigh?

Important considerations, all, but he'd have to take it on blind faith.

"Can I see a picture?"

"You really don't trust me?" She looked less amused now.

"Sure, I do. I'm in. I just want to see her." He tried to mirror her shrug, like anything else was unreasonable.

She slid out of the bed and over to her desk, where she set her laptop. He watched the sway of her ass as she walked.

Don't need those DSLs on me for action now.

He almost called her back to bed.

Karla rented an apartment above an antique store. Way better than his dorm and afforded much more privacy. It closed by 7:00 p.m.

She pushed up the monitor and woke the laptop from sleep mode. Blake padded across the floor to her side and hunched over with an arm around her. She pulled up her bookmarks panel. His stomach flipped at Grudgefuxx. Yeah, no wonder she didn't want to do anything on video. He figured a lot of girls kept tabs on the site to make sure they didn't end up there.

Karla found an Instagram link and his stomach did another flip as the pictures loaded up.

They showed various selfies of a girl with long black hair, doe eyes, lips too thin to be true DSLs—maybe a seven on the ten scale.

No fucking way.

It was Julie. Sophomore year Julie, though they hadn't lasted a full semester. She didn't want to do the video thing either, but he wore her down. She'd been so inhibited last year. A total drag and one of the reasons he thought about breaking up with her. It had almost been comical when *she* broke up with *him*. He would have laughed if it didn't piss him off so much. She'd had the nerve to ask for the DVD he'd burned.

I want the video. You know which one.

He handed over the DVD the next day without arguing, playing it cool. Of course he still had the file on an external drive, Dropbox, and three or four other file hosting sites because he'd known this day would come. And then he went to Grudgefuxx.

He wanted to tell her: *I uploaded the video. You know which one.*

Blake didn't like to lose.

Quite an evolution for ol' Jules, then. The girl who *might* blow you once in a blue moon without having to hold her little brother for ransom, now she was ready to jump into some three-way action, lez out and reopen her storage space for Blake's quim-splitter. Probably with a clause that Karla do all the head-work, but still, impressive. If he'd known such a thing was on the table with her, he might have made more of an effort.

No matter. He'd have dropped her like a bag of shit when Karla came on the scene anyway. He got the best of both worlds the way it had worked out.

"That's Julie," Karla said.

"You showed her pictures of me, too?" he asked.

"She liked what she saw."

He wasn't sure how to play this. Was it a test after all, to see if he'd hold his tongue about the prior relationship? Maybe Julie never said anything about him and this was her olive branch for breaking up with him. An olive branch that would allow Blake to crush two pieces of ass at the same motherfucking time.

"Did she mention that we went out?" he asked.

A voice inside screamed, *What are you doing?* But he decided to play it safe.

"Wow, you get points for honesty. I didn't think you'd cop to it. I'm impressed. Yes, she did say you two went out. Very briefly."

"Oh, yeah, nothing serious," he quickly amended.

Karla laughed. "This wouldn't be happening if it was."

"You two going to do some of that scissors stuff in front of me?"

"Scissors?"

"You know, that cunt to cunt grinding stuff."

"Cunt to cunt? Wow. That's charming."

"Sorry, I didn't mean it like that."

"I know. So you're in?"

"Sure. If you're, you know, comfortable with it."

"Sure. I, you know, am."

Blake reached down to feel the mound of her breast. "I can think of something else I'd like to be in."

She led him back to bed.

II.

Two days later, it was going down.

"Holy shit," Trey said. "What do you even call that?"

"I don't know," Blake said. "Luck?"

They were looking at The Link. It felt a bit weird to watch it with Trey in the room. Checking out porno with another guy was already a bit sketchy and Blake was in this scene, even if he'd thoughtfully put optic censoring fog over his own face. Kind of funny, that: he could upload it for the entire internet to watch with no real qualms, but it made him uneasy with somebody he knew in the room. The first time Blake showed him the video a couple months ago, Trey looked like someone yanked his pants down in front of everyone at a public place. He was a lot cooler about it this time. Obnoxious.

"You put her on Grudgefuxx dot com and you're going to get to hit that shit again ... with reinforcements! Dude, that's not luck, that's like divine providence."

"I'm the Chosen One."

Trey came by to copy the notes from a lab he missed yesterday and somehow finagled Blake into showing him the video again. He pointed to the page views counter. "You broke the hundred thousand mark. You think those are individual hits? Or did you sit here refreshing the page for three days?"

"They're legit."

Trey shook his head in disbelief. "You're a star. An icon."

"Yeah. Can't go to the store without a bunch of girls mobbing me for autographs."

"*Sheeeeit.* For real, though, that's awesome. You gotta send me that link."

"Yeah, man, I will," Blake said. He probably wouldn't. They'd cracked jokes together in anatomy last semester but Blake wouldn't consider them close friends. He showed him The Link because he had to tell *someone;* it was too awesome not to. Let him find it on his own. It was easily searchable by the title anyway: *I'M NOT SURE ABOUT THIS GIRL.* Julie said it about eight hundred times in the fifteen minute clip. Not exactly the biggest turn-on. He meant it like *the* I'm Not Sure About This Girl, but he liked the double meaning by leaving out "the" in the title.

"I gotta be out of my mind, thinking about marriage."

"You are," Blake assured him.

He wasn't kidding. Trey told him he was hung up on some bitch—not his word—he'd never even met in person. The relationship played out long distance, through texts, emails, phone calls, and Skype. They drove themselves crazy talking about doing shit to each other "soon" that Trey could do with about any girl drunk enough at a mixer. (Blake got one who totally passed out once when they snuck off to a bedroom. He immortalized that one with a cell phone clip called *BLACKOUT CHI OMEGA*, though it wasn't very good quality and had only a fraction of the hits of Julie's video.) What a waste when Trey wasn't getting anything out of it but promises written on the flash paper of internet fidelity. He couldn't know if his girl wasn't just reciting a checklist of things she was doing to the dicks of guys all across her campus or town or wherever she could do her hunting.

Small wonder he enjoyed living vicariously through Blake. A fucking oSheath was realer sex than Trey's relationship, especially since you could essentially hack some girl's cunt with one of those, so to speak.

Trey shrugged. "Sometimes you gotta take a chance."

"Just be careful, man. Floor's taking bets on Kendall's roommate, some freshman. He was doing the long-distance thing with his bitch and she pulled the plug. I got twenty bucks on him hanging himself before mid-terms."

Of course Blake didn't really give a damn if he wasn't careful. That girl could eat Trey's heart, shit it out, and mail it back to him media rate and Blake would laugh.

"Kendall thinks dude'll hang himself in the closet. He's already talking about me rooming with him," he continued. "Yeah, right! His last roommate went off to some island with that D-bag rich boy Grant last summer and never came back, now this freshman's about to snuff it. Kendall's like roommate AIDS or some shit. Maybe he can take your place when your girl dumps you and you slit your wrists in the bathtub."

"Nah, bro, we're good," Trey said. "Mostly. I mean, my girl's cool and all, but...probably not down with another girl in the mix, you know. Especially after we get married."

"Wives are funny that way, broseph."

"You gonna try to video this one too?"

Blake laughed. "I wish. Karla's not down with it."

"There's this crazy concept called *hidden camera*. All the cool kids are doing it."

"Eh, I guess. Not worth getting busted when things are cool, you know? With Julie, well...just listen."

He turned up the sound on the speakers. On the monitor, Julie held his dick in one hand and kept looking down at it and then over to where he had positioned the camera for a static shot, as if the camera was going to tell her what to do with this crazy alien artifact she'd just found.

"I'm not sure about this," she said.

"It's cool, Jules," Blake said. Oscar winning performance, no exasperation at all.

She licked it once, tentatively, like an ice cream cone that might be vanilla or might be soft serve cyanide. "I'm just...I'm just not sure about this." Looked once more to the camera for direction that never came.

"You're doing great. You're going to look so hot doing this."

She gamely put him in her mouth. She didn't look hot doing it. He remembered her "technique" well, taking it in her mouth and sort of rolling it around her tongue like a cough drop— always with a facial expression suggesting said cough drop curdled her taste buds. She'd gag and sputter and beg off in short order. He was convinced it was a ploy and it pissed him off, but at least it kept him from having to repay the favor, or *quim pro quo,* as he thought of it.

She gave it the old sophomore college try a lot longer than she ever had before because she knew a lazy effort would be immortalized, but she still gave up inside of three minutes. Then the apologies. Blake was a sport, told her no probs, then suggested she let him mount up from behind. Something else she wasn't fond of, as she apparently preferred for a guy to be stuck with the reality of her face while he fucked her, but she let him do this now because he allowed her to "block" the scene. The static camera shot would only capture her from the side, per her wishes. She didn't want her face prominently displayed. It was a good compromise for her—her disappointingly small breasts could barely be seen that way—and it had been his own suggestion just to coerce her a little bit.

You won't even see much on the tape.

It would have totally worked out that way too, but Blake wasn't totally averse to a hidden camera when he'd been given permission to record: He set up another digital camera on the desk across from the bed, a cheap thing he'd used for still pictures before he got a decent iPhone. He held onto it for just such an occasion. So, Julie was front and center while he drilled her, making some of the most hilarious faces Blake had ever seen. It also allowed a much better view of her tits when he suggested she finish on top of him. She didn't seem curious why he wanted to slip around to the other side of the bed for this instead of stay where he was; she was still in profile view on the known camera and that was good enough for her.

What a waste of a money shot it would have been otherwise because Blake unsheathed and hit her with a monster load. Purposely didn't jack for three days prior to ensure maximal wad blowage.

She *really* didn't like the porn finish and turned away from the camera—now truly in profile on the hidden view—to show her back, ordering him to turn it off. He was a gent and fulfilled her request. She almost did him a favor taking the boring raw footage back. He still had the director's cut. The video was a composite of both angles.

Blake, the porn auteur.

On the monitor, Julie I'm-not-sure-about-this'd again. He'd seriously considered adding a laugh track on an alternate version.

"See what I mean?" he said. "Check out some of the comments."

He scrolled down. Trey leaned forward in the chair.

LOLZ!! If her life depended on suckin that dick theyd of been givin her last rights What up with those faces she make like bitch hooked up to a car battery

Ugh they wud have to pay me to stick my dick in that What IS she sure about??

Cant see her pussy :(I'd hit it.

^^I wouldnt

2 angels? So fake

She's makin faces cuz its not enuff dick like wheres tha beef

Blake scrolled past that one, a newer comment, disheartened by the number of likes.

Ho's kill me "I'm naked on a video with a dick in my hand, better act like I got church 2night"

Like Busta Kapp said Bitchez Don't Be Knowin!

He looped some footage to make it seem like he lasted longer lol you can tell by her identical faces @ 4:17 & 7:22

Blake scrolled past this one too. Jesus, he did the site faithful a favor posting the video and someone had to break it down like the fucking Zapruder film. Yeah, he added about ninety seconds. Big deal.

Five years from now she will be someone's mom stay classy cunt.

Trey laughed tightly. "Oooh. Harsh."

"At least she's *sure* about doing the threesome," Blake said. He gave Trey a second to crack up at the joke, but he missed it. Yeah, he definitely wasn't going to send him The Link.

"Guess I broke her of her camera shyness. I hope so, anyway. It'd suck to get a three-way with one girl totally into it and the other acting like a hall monitor."

Trey chuckled. It sounded weird. "Hey, if they prove too much for you and you need some help, holler at your boy."

Uh huh. What a pal. So selfless.

"I couldn't let you betray your girlfriend, Skype Stud," Blake said. "But don't worry, I'll tell you all about it."

The two seconds of Corpsefrother's "Felch My Beef Broth from Your Sister's Prolapsed Rectum" signaled a new text on his cell.

"Oh, I thought that was mine," Trey said, pocketing his phone again.

Blake crossed himself—*RIP, Giallo Killer*—and checked the screen. He laughed. The magma of excitement burst within him again.

Trey looked at him expectantly. "So...what's the deal?"

Blake showed him the message from Karla: *bring ur cam 2night =p*

III.

He wished he'd had more time to mentally prepare for performing on camera tonight. Now he had to be conscientious about lasting long enough that it didn't seem embarrassing to watch the playback. He could get creative with the editing again, but he'd like to know for himself that he held out fair and square. It was sure to be the most intense experience of his life. He almost hoped Julie still cultivated the "melting cough drop" blowjob technique. He could hold back for hours with that.

Besides, "I'm not sure about this" was dialogue from a movie he'd already seen. Him and more than a hundred thousand other Grudgefuxx surfers.

This was what he wanted.

No question.

They both greeted him at the door. Julie looked almost unrecognizable. Her eyes possessed a hunger previously unknown to her. The only thing that would melt in her mouth tonight would be his dick. She wore a very short red skirt way shorter than anything she'd worn when they dated. A more conservative approach to her shirt since she didn't have much to show off there, but still hot. Karla wore a white skirt of comparable length. Maybe they'd coordinated. Low-cut black top for Karla, Cleavage Central. Two minutes or two hours, this would be epic.

"Hey, sexy," Karla said. "I hope you brought enough for us both." Julie said nothing but smiled.

"Don't worry, there's plenty of me to go around."

They all laughed together. Julie used to be more hesitant, meek, as if waiting for permission to express any amusement. Tonight, she seemed assured, neatly fitted in her skin. It's what he'd hoped for, but still a pleasant surprise. If he played his cards right, this might only be the first time of several.

It also pleasantly surprised him that the girls wanted to get right down to biz. He'd expected a prolonged seduction where they acted like they weren't all here for one reason and hadn't offered him two slices of gash upfront.

Blake unzipped the camera from its bag. A Craigslist bargain, light and effective.

"Where do you want me to put it?"

"Here and here," Julie said, pointing to Karla and herself. Karla giggled.

He wished he'd gotten that on video.

They weighed the options for the best angle. He didn't have a tripod, so they stacked some books on a chair until they liked what they saw on the viewfinder.

A brief silence held sway as they looked at one another. Blake didn't want it to turn awkward so he said, "I still can't believe you're letting me record this."

There was that infamous Karla shrug. "Well, there'll be a lot going on. We don't want to miss anything, do we, Jules?"

"No," Julie agreed.

"And I guess I feel better with the buddy system." She draped an arm around Julie.

"Besides, she told me it wasn't a big deal."

Uh oh, Blake thought. He hoped Julie hadn't discussed the circumstances of her debut.

He figured they wouldn't all be here right now if she had, though. He checked the angle one more time—didn't want to lose a frame of the magic—and pushed to record.

"Okay, then, girls," he said. "Lights, camera, action."

—————

Later, with the camera wired to the TV in the living room, a sated and delirious trio sat down to watch the video.

The static shot captured the bed and part of the computer desk chair to the left. Blake took the middle of the bed and Karla and Julie converged on him. They burrowed into each side of his throat with their lips and tongues, their fingers exploring. Blake's outstretched fingers teased circles on their backs as they tasted him. They wasted little time systematically stripping him down, Karla undoing his pants, Julie helping him out of his shirt. Karla dragged his pants off his ankles and tossed them aside. He lay there naked and erect. Karla slipped a hand down to make sure he stayed that way.

Julie guided the wrist on her side to the bedpost and pulled Blake's shirt taut against it.

"Hey," he said. "What are you..." He didn't sound alarmed at all, though. More like elated.

Julie shushed him. "Let us take good care of you, like you deserve, lover." She knotted the shirt with its long sleeves, securing him to the post.

"Okay, just...slow down if I tell you."

Blake undoubtedly intended to edit this request out in the final cut, same way he'd manipulated the dual footage from the Grudgefuxx video.

Karla slipped out of her top to reveal a black bra beneath. She shrugged out of the straps, unhooked it, and went to work tying Blake's other arm on her side of the bed with the bra.

"You're so hard," she said. "Do you think it can take me and Julie doing the scissors?"

Blake tilted his head back as far as it could go against the pillow, releasing an emotive grunt of pleasure.

"Only one way to find out," he said, almost a gasp.

His heels rubbed against the bedspread as if trying to propel himself backward. His hardness twitched with each beat of his pulse. Karla retrieved his boxer briefs from the floor. She wadded them up in her hand as Julie crouched to reach beneath the bed. Karla stuffed the ball of Blake's underwear into his mouth. He made sounds of puzzlement and surprise, adequately muffled. Karla completed the job by wrapping her top around his face to keep him gagged as Blake thrashed, trying to free his hands.

Julie stood up from the bed with a pair of hedge clippers.

Blake's muffled screaming grew more animated as he saw the scissors. He started digging into the bed with his heels, alternately sliding and kicking out.

"Get his legs," Julie said. "Try to keep low so we get it on the..." She nodded in the direction of the camera.

Karla briefly obscured Blake as she rounded the foot of the bed, grabbed hold of his ankles, and sat down to hold them tight to the mattress. He continued to thrash like a fish with his body in a straight line. He'd lost his excitement somewhere in the binding and gagging process. His penis flipped around in the struggle, totally limp.

"What's wrong, Blakey?" Julie said. "You not sure about this anymore?"

Julie put the tip of the hedge clippers against his sac. Blake stopped moving instantly. His eyes grew to the size of ping pong balls.

"I'll make you a promise. If you don't get hard, I won't hurt you. But if you do..."

She brought the blades back up where he could see them, opened and snapped them shut. Even on the video it was a powerful sound, metal jaws.

Blake looked from her to Karla and back, apparently hoping someone would intervene.

"Okay." Julie set the clippers aside and lowered her head to his crotch. "As boring as you thought I was at this, you shouldn't have any problem now, should you?"

His limp dick vanished between her lips. Julie's head bobbed patiently, barely raising, and then more animatedly. Blake made an *uhhhhhhhhhhhhhhhhhhhhhhhhhhhhh* sound of effort, a man trying to squat-lift the Liberty Bell.

"Uh oh," Julie said, muffled around the meat in her mouth. She pulled away and looked to the camera, hands framing the results like a letter turned on *Wheel of Fortune*. "*Voila.*"

Blake shook his head vehemently, the entire side of his face touching down on the pillow with each turn.

Julie collected the hedge clippers again. "Hold him tight."

The blades of the clippers split apart as Julie guided them to the swaying erection. Blake renewed the *uhhhhhhhhhhhhhh-hhhhhhhhhhh* sound, as if the right frequency of his groan might abruptly defuse his hardness.

It didn't.

Julie snapped the blades shut. They sheared through the head of his penis like the tip of a banana. He bucked against the bed, ejaculating in a crimson geyser. It burst from the stalk in haphazard jets, like someone's thumb blocking a running faucet. It drenched Julie's hands and arms, spattering the front of her shirt.

"Stand back, I'm letting him go," Karla warned.

She disappeared from the frame and soon the lens zoomed to the severed flesh of Blake's cock. Deep red continued to spool from the shredded shaft, the branch of a split artery visible in the close-up. Its buoyancy tapered a bit.

After a little trial and error, Karla zoomed back out. Blood soaked Blake's thighs like he'd just given birth. His shrieks had become mewls, so weak they barely carried past the gag.

"Better make the calls," Julie said.

A moment later, Karla's voice off screen said, "Come on up," followed a few seconds later by a muffled ringing from Blake's pants. When it stopped, Karla said, "Hi, it's me. Guess you can't make it tonight. How about a call next time, asshole?"

"Just in case," Julie said to Blake.

There was a knock at the door. Blake bounced in the bed and grunted into the gag, straining to be heard by the new visitor. He looked like someone receiving an electric shock. It all stopped abruptly.

"I thought you were gonna tell me all about it, Blake," a male voice said.

Karla zoomed in on the bed. Blake's eyes looked a little glassy, on the threshold of shock, but no mistaking his bafflement. He renewed his attempts to talk, though he never came close to saying anything comprehensible.

"I owe you an apology, man," Trey said, entering the frame. "I lied. I have a real girlfriend, not some long-distance bullshit. You know Julie already, obviously. You're probably not too heartbroken that she hooked up with me since you didn't mind sharing her online with all the scum on Grudgefuxx."

"I didn't want to tell him what you did," Julia said. Her assurance wavered for the first time. "But I was scared he'd find out anyway, and then what would he think?"

"It made me fucking sick to have to listen to you laugh about it," Trey continued. "We couldn't let it go. Not knowing you didn't care what it might do to her. No way."

Blake struggling again, weaker now. He looked pointedly in Karla's direction with skin the color of custard.

"Julie and I have been friends since high school," Karla said. She raised a middle finger at Blake when she stepped into frame again. "I'd do anything to help her. Even screw a waste of life like you."

"And you needed a second science credit anyway," Julie pointed out.

"That too."

"You were so excited to get your dick wet after all that shit you talked about her," Trey said. "That's almost the best part.'

"We could have just shot you in an alley or tied you up in the woods to die of exposure," Julie said, "but it wouldn't have been as good. We've been talking about this for a couple months. It had to be something really fucked up, you know?"

Karla waved the middle finger back and forth in front of his face. "Nothing seemed brutal enough for what you deserved. But one day we stopped trying to talk each other out of going this far with it."

Trey said, "If I had any doubts, we'd just read through all those comments on the page. What do you think they'd say about you now?"

"We'll delete that video, obviously," Julie said. "You save your passwords, don't you?"

No response from Blake, of course.

"It's too bad we had to gag him," Karla said. "You know he would have made some good faces."

"He looks like he's going to faint."

"Guess he was wrong about plenty of him to go around." Karla giggled.

"Oh my God," Trey groaned. "He really said that?"

"Really," Julie said. "I wish we got it on tape. Come on, get the other toy."

The video feed cut off. When it came back, Karla zoomed in on Blake's mutilated sex.

They had stopped the bleeding by twisting a rubber band around the shaft, coiling it three or four times to compress the organ. Blake stirred weakly.

"Here," Karla said. A D-shaped metal object with a long row of teeth appeared from the right. Trey reached over to take it. He and Julie moved to the left side of the bed while Karla took her place to the right.

"Picked this up a while ago," Karla informed Blake. "Before I transferred to your class. We came, we saw."

Blake found the strength to kick a little bit, but it was like a possum in its death throes after being crushed by a truck. Trey set the hacksaw down at waist level. He and Julie took hold of their side. Karla took hers. It took a minute to find their rhythm, the teeth of the blade hesitant to carve through the skin, but they finally found a smooth motion at just the right angle, their efforts soon in perfect tandem. They grunted with the effort, like seasoned lovers in an orgy. Flesh separated in jagged ridges. Blake kicked more aggressively, his rubber banded dick flopping to and fro. The red ridge expanded.

"Really bear down," Trey said, winded.

The saw caught on bone, the ribs, the pelvic girdle, the spine. When they thought they had made enough progress, they tried to wrench the lower half away. At one point it looked like he'd tried to roll on his side, but only the waist down got the memo. The trunk of his body stayed in cruciform. Organs spilled from the top and bottom sides, a glistening mound of clumps and coils in primary colors. Trey had to turn away and breathe for a moment.

"Come on, it's not much worse than lab," Karla said, but only teasing him.

When he trusted himself to look at Blake's split body again, they angled the saw into the gap until it caught the spinal column. They resumed the effort with the surreal accompaniment of Blake's buttocks exposed despite him lying flat on his back. The deeply resistant bone could have been mistaken for the grinding of a tree branch, but at last they carved through—Karla urging caution at the end so they didn't accidentally shred the bed.

"Karla?" Trey prompted.

Karla came around to the foot of the bed, seized one of Blake's ankles, and yanked. The lower half came free with a last pop of bone and Blake's knees hit the floor with his arms a good ten feet away. What little remained in his pelvic cavity spilled across the top of his waist into a wet pile as his legs slumped over.

Karla would need a new rug.

Trey stepped over the trunkless legs to take hold of the camera and brought it over to the bed. Julie took hold of the hedge clippers again. Karla removed the shirt around Blake's head and pulled the boxers from his mouth like a magician yanking out a string of colored kerchiefs. Blake's tongue lolled, his eyes fixed on a faraway place.

Trey found the optimal angle as Julie guided the blades to either side of Blake's neck and clamped them. She repeated the cutting several times before they worked deeper through the skin and muscle. Despite his state of death, it still trickled out in steady streams as red grooves opened to expose the muscle beneath, and more bubbled from his open mouth. She worked through the final inches of bone and the head slipped and rolled away from the neck. Trey followed its descent. It bounced off the floor, the meat of the neck flinging droplets of blood.

"No, Blake, we're not done yet," Julie informed him. She picked his head up by the hair. It continued to leak. With the bed a bloody shambles she curled up in the crook of Blake's arm and lifted her skirt. She was naked beneath. She didn't mind the closeness of the camera this time. She centered Blake over the patch of dark hair between her legs and guided his tongue to her clit, sliding him up and down her slickened flesh.

They laughed as they watched this. Blake's mouth gaped in increments like a ventriloquist dummy, but his eyes held that glassy stare.

"I feel like I should be jealous," Trey said, his left arm around Julie. Karla sat on the other side, filling out the rest of the couch. "It's kind of hot, though."

"We really should finish the clean-up," Karla said. The wad of ruined bed sheets and clothes needed to be incinerated. What remained of Blake lay stacked in the tub. Their hacksaw work with him had really only begun.

On screen, Julie said, "He was right. There was plenty of him to go around." They all laughed again, having forgotten about this gem at the time.

"One more time," Julie said on the couch. "He's not going anywhere, is he?"

They laughed again.

They rewound.

DIVINE RED

Mutation is necessary. Stasis in perpetuity is impossible, particularly for growth or evolution. Stasis becomes stagnation. Our bodies are transitory. Progression could mean growing new organs or limbs. Perhaps it may also mean losing some of the old ones through an act of transcendental mutilation.

—*Transitory Bodies*, Dr. Braedon Obrist

I.

HE'D BEEN TO THE building long ago, and he found a compelling symmetry in how it had stood abandoned since, as though awaiting Rob's return as an adult. Back in that distant October, it had been a haunted house attraction. He'd stumbled down pitch black corridors through what seemed like an impossibly deep maze, from one horror spectacle to another.

He remembered a graveyard wedding where the bride lifted her veil to reveal a rotted green face. That stayed with him, as well as a maniac in a bloody apron chasing Rob's group out the exit with a hatchet. He had been scared but elated, and the feeling was not much different now. The place might still be a haunted house, too.

Whatever commerce transpired on the block in the interim surely involved veins, lungs, throats, and cocks, for a soul-rot so deep no one ever razed it to build condominiums.

"Second thoughts?" Alec asked. Rob detected a hint of the trademark smirk he despised.

"Nope." It was technically true—he was closer to the *twentieth*.

In the sickly light of the streetlamps, the structure seemed enormous, with colors and textures of ocher, brick, iron, and rust. It made him think of a diseased organ in some monstrosity. He heard the faintest pulse through the walls, like a heartbeat within the corrupted edifice.

Tattered missing posters for Geisha Hammond tacked to the windowless front in a grid like Andy Warhol's soup cans did little to allay his concern. Farther down hung fresher pictures of the soup kitchen volunteer who disappeared last week.

There were no junkies, pushers, bums, or whores on the block. He almost wished there were, just to make it seem less like it was after the end of the world. Nobody else stood at the door to Painfreak.

"Not a very big turnout," Rob said.

This time Alec did smirk. "We're fashionably late."

Their limited interactions replayed through Rob's mind like the reel of clues in a *Saw* film before the surprise ending reveal. Which in his case would be that he trusted a relative stranger to take him to a mysterious place called Painfreak, only to be stabbed thirty-seven times and dumped behind a building where ironically someone chased him with a hatchet twenty-five years ago. A gruesome end for our Darwin Award nominee.

He believed Painfreak existed, though. Self-proclaimed authorities online wrote it off as an elaborate urban legend where charlatans spun tall tales of impossible depravities. Many more claimed otherwise, detailing experiences hardcore but hardly impossible. Pictures and videos purportedly taken within the club were uploaded online, which skeptics dismissed as artifacts of anonymous clubs or raves. It seemed only too...*convenient* that Painfreak traveled randomly like some decadent circus where people all over the globe could add to its mythos. Like Slenderman and Woodsman sightings, but with more sex and mutilation.

Alec claimed it was all real.

Rob believed frauds nurtured the fantastic element but that a realistic incarnation existed—one he still probably wasn't prepared for.

He'd had to come anyway.

Alec led them to a door which looked black from the street but turned out to be dark green. He knocked three times in slow motion. As the door swung wide the faint pulse hit harder from somewhere beyond the front chamber, like the heartbeat of a beast in pursuit rather than extremis.

A bald, thick-necked wall of muscle in a cream-colored button shirt with rolled-up sleeves stood in the doorway. He looked like he could rip a person in half like wet newspaper. Alec's smirk dropped away in record time. He held his hand out to the doorman, who suddenly grew a third arm as an extra hand reached out of the dark to seize Alec's. It relinquished him a moment later with some prerequisite apparently satisfied.

Alec hooked a thumb at Rob and announced, "He's with me."

The hidden second person leaned out, a man of Asian descent dressed in black pants, white shirt and a charcoal vest. Rob thought he might inquire, "What is your pleasure, sir?" like *Hellraiser,* but he said nothing as he pressed a stamp against Rob's hand. It left no visible mark.

The hulk stepped aside. They walked between him and the Asian to a door at the back of the chamber. As Alec opened it, acoustics changed from a faint rumor of revelry to the mouth of waiting madness. They entered a long corridor lit by cone-shaped lamps, every third or fourth one burned out.

Alec read his uncertainty as the door slammed behind them with resounding finality. The alopecic Andre the Giant safely locked away, the leer returned. "Come on. It's the last night. She'll be here."

II.

Rob first saw her at the building where he worked, which held both offices and medical practices. He and the other office employees—but not supervisors and managers—were ordered to park in the rear lot so decrepit elderly patients could have the spaces nearest the doors. Thus, he was literally running late that morning to the lobby, only to find the cruelty of the elevator gods in the form of an excruciating wait. It arrived completely empty. He muttered, "Well, of course," when he heard clattering steps in the lobby after he pushed for the sixth floor, but he held the door for the late arrival and altered his life.

The elevator gods smiled on him after all when Anna rushed inside with a final staccato beat of her pumps on the tiles. He first noticed her hair, shoulder length auburn against the silk of an emerald blouse. His pulse had settled after his hundred-yard dash but it took off again with the certainty he would like the rest of her too. The door jolted his hand a bit more aggressively than when he first stopped it, as if it resented his first intrusion. Rob yanked his arm away theatrically.

"Nearly lost a limb," he said.

He hoped for a polite smile, but her expression took him aback. It had to be wishful thinking, because for a flicker he saw pure hunger. Then it vanished, like a sequence of frames cut from a splice of film. He rationalized it as a projection of his own attraction—the polite term in his self-analysis, although *crippling lust* held closer to the truth—and understandably so, because it was like the birth of every past crush in his lifetime all at once with a fireworks burst of thoughts which all began with *I must.* He still saw her through the prism of eroticism, and never mind it hadn't really happened, couldn't possibly have. The full lips and bedroom eyes conjured an intensity of desire previously unknown to him. Her black skirt hugged her tight, just above knee length, on a figure some would find too thick, even if they'd be only too happy to see the fullness of her chest uncovered. In his euphoria, he failed to ask which floor she needed and she reached to push for the seventh with a left hand bearing no ring.

Not engaged/married and not here for a doctor's appointment.

By all rights his smile should have broken his face.

He forced himself not to stare at her directly and toned down the wattage of his smile from *escaped mass murderer* to *nice normal guy.* He hoped they would get stuck for about six hours, but the ride lasted only twenty seconds.

As the elevator gods gaveth, so they tooketh away.

Premature evacuation.

As he reluctantly stepped out, he bid her "Good day" with a chagrined smile, an Internet meme lost to the ether. He berated himself the rest of the day for the idiotic exit, imagined her thinking of the old line from *Crocodile Dundee*: *That's not a knife...*this *is a knife.*

God, what a loser.

But that euphoric feeling remained, like he was either still going up in that elevator to the thousandth floor or plunging in free fall.

He had plenty of time in subsequent days to bemoan his limited window for opportunity. For all the imagined conversations and consummations, the divine Red remained more specter than flesh. Seeing her must have been a schedule anomaly because he encountered no further trace on his way up or down, lunch break included. Another chance encounter on the elevator would only afford him the first through sixth floors to forge a connection and asking her out so abruptly could only end in hashtag *creepyguy*. Especially when his most creative opener so far was "You know what you never see anymore? Guys handcuffed to briefcases." He was stumped. He needed an in, something better than the weather, the misery of devoting forty hours per week of a finite existence to pie charts and spreadsheets, and the dearth of guys handcuffed to briefcases.

If not married, he knew odds still favored her having an attachment to another man (unfortunate) or even a woman (also unfortunate—also exciting). All the same he savored the obsession, the mystery of wanting without knowing. His days had already become so indistinguishable from one another in the same way they always did at his jobs, but now simply waiting on the elevator was loaded with potential, like the doors would open on some higher plane of existence. She offered an escape to which he may yet find his way.

Odds and ins.

He could almost appreciate the irony when he found Alec at his desk days later—an interruption in the routine he loathed, but also an intrusion on his favorite new pastime of disappearing within himself in the search for ascendancy with the divine Red. A temp agency dispatched Alec to act as a floater, so Rob's supervisor needed him to show Alec the ropes of his daily responsibilities. The process served to underline their banality. Alec looked on with barely concealed boredom and pity. This all reached its nadir on a visit to the copier room where they found the machine inoperable with a message on the LCD to contact a service technician.

"We'll have to go up to the seventh floor," he said, with a burst of inspiration. "They have a copier."

He hoped they did, anyway. Regardless, he now had an excuse to go up to the next level and wander the Red territory. They took the stairs up and found no corresponding copier room, but Rob knew just the person to ask. He led Alec through the aisles of a cubical maze, painfully aware of their otherness here. He expected someone to stand, point and cry, "Outlander!" He managed to locate the copier at the end of one aisle and fortune favored him—her cubicle stood adjacent to it. He couldn't approach her to ask her about it now—at least not without looking like a complete idiot—but he *would* see her for longer than an elevator ride.

To observe her in such a dull setting seemed somehow profane, but it didn't stop him from feasting his eyes at the profile view of her in a strapless sage dress. It felt like a real video game power-up, restoring his depleted life force. The cubicle bore a name plate, too. Red the divine was Anna. Knowing her true name enhanced the sacred fantasy. He enjoyed a last lingering look on their way back to the stairs.

While she never noticed him in stalker business mode, his voyeurism hadn't gone unnoticed by all.

"That girl an ex of yours or something?" Alec asked on the way down.

Rob answered automatically, "What girl?"

"The only one you were staring at, Captain Creepo."

His aggravation was offset by a darker possibility—Alec fancied her and wanted to test if she might be available.

Before Rob figured out a response, Alec continued. "It's just that if you're interested, I saw her out the other night."

Rob stopped with his hand on the door, frozen by the prospect of his coveted *in*.

"*Where?*"

III.

Painfreak swallowed them, as if the corridor had been its esophagus.

Now—belly of the beast, utter maelstrom—the pulse became a shudder that squeezed Rob's vital organs with each thud. Music lost structure and coherence at this volume, with only an occasional audible lyric for guidance: *Am I not your golden chain?* Prisms of light fragmented the interior into a living stained glass window, the moving tapestry of bodies on both ground and upper levels awash in reds, blues, yellows from overhead in rotational bursts of colored lightning. The carnality

of undulation and abandon seemed like a detail from a Renais-
sance painting of Hell.

Anna was here. Anna was here?

Disparate concepts in the audio and visual bedlam. Not
something conveyable by any cell phone video or selfie.

Rob wondered who the people were, where they came from.
Did they live the sort of sane and measured existence he did,
waiting for this bacchanalian reprieve from the meaninglessness
which buffeted their daily lives with a quiet fervor equal to
the shock and awe on display tonight? It seemed beyond comprehension that he was supposed to go back to work Monday
and be complicit in the madness of an orderly single file walk
through life on the way to oblivion.

Rob tried to follow Alec, the pulse now like rapid fire from
pillars of speakers. Strobes interrupted the flow of color and
the world became a series of still images, each one to match
the throttling beat of the music. He felt disembodied, drifting
past all the faces and their range of expressions. Delight, lust,
loathing, fulfillment. Some were naked, men and women alike.
One man gyrated behind a bent over woman, her breasts dangling and swaying as she bounced her ass around. Maybe it was
dancing, but they were also definitely screwing.

Jizz on the dance floor. Great.

Rob thought of the times he'd been with women in far less
adventurous positions and how he could have superglued his
dick inside them and still managed to slide out in mid thrust. He
admired these precision fuck-robatics with reverence and envy
through a filter of blue light, then red.

He'd lost Alec. He suspected Alec brought him here simply
to enjoy the culture shock, but Rob considered him his guide
if not his friend. He pushed past the bodies more urgently,

hoping to catch sight of him. There didn't seem to be anywhere you could stand apart from this carnival once you abandoned the corridor, but there had to be a bar somewhere. Upstairs, perhaps.

An oasis of normal fluorescent light beckoned from one corner. A bathroom. Rob switched his trajectory. His eyes and ears needed an intermission.

Strange faces blew past in an attention-span deficit simulation like someone flipping their thumb through a thick paperback in about two seconds. Nothing really registered. So how would Alec have noticed Anna? Rob didn't doubt he himself would have, but Alec only saw her as merely human.

If she came, he knew he'd find her. If. He couldn't picture it, but wanted it. Anything to see her, and never mind the impossibility of conversation in this pandemonium. They could save such talk for later, back in the other saner world, because this was the connection that would allow it. It seemed like the entire city populace had crammed themselves inside, but Painfreak was still a curiosity known to few.

After tonight it moved on to parts unknown, not to return for *months*.

Years.

Ever.

She had to be here one last time and she had to see him. She must be into some pretty weird shit to come to Painfreak and it could only help his cause for her to know he knew this and approved.

Cages hung overhead with men and women inside. He'd barely noticed with the challenge of maneuvering through the crowd, but tried to angle himself so he wouldn't be directly underneath the one nearest the bathroom. The rapid-fire pulse withdrew to an insistent steady beat. The woman inside the cage writhed in rhythm. A focused beam of yellow light dispelled all the subtleties. She wasn't naked, but dressed in black shining leather, her breasts exposed, and wore nothing from the waist down. Thin chains from the top of the cage ran between her legs like cables to a power strip. She slumped against the corner bars. The cage shook slightly. Rob took another couple steps to the side as the slack on the chains pulled taut. Her labia were pierced with four or five rings and hooks attached to them from the end of each chain. She slowly slid down the bars until the chains vibrated like bass strings and dropped to the floor. Three snapped away like living vines, pieces of raw, glistening flesh speared on hooks. As the blistering pulse resumed and the strobes reengaged, blood dripped through the bottom of the cage on the heads below. One man stuck out his tongue as though trying to catch the first snowflake of winter.

Jesus Christ...I should have just learned to hack Anna's fucking Facebook.

Maybe she was even logged into that Interdex thing he'd heard about, where one of those oSheath contraptions could simulate actual sex with her. But that's all it was—a simulation. The chicanery of some technologically advanced masturbatory aid. Not good enough. He needed her. All of her.

Rob pushed on, stomach rolling. A new song began on a much quieter note as he reached the bathroom. The volume still hit hard with the open door and poorly insulated walls, but he felt like he'd leveled up in life—he'd entered his first unisex bathroom. Thank God he didn't actually plan to use it given the long line of men hunched over urinals with no dividers, every one occupied. They stood closer than usual, probably for a better illusion of privacy...if such a thing mattered, given some of the things in plain sight just beyond the wall.

One man's head tilted back in a pleasure far more profound than that afforded by an emptying bladder.

Wait a minute...there aren't any urinals.

Another man zipped up and walked out a bit dizzily, nary a glance toward the faucets. Before someone rushed in to occupy the vacancy, Rob saw three holes in the wall, one atop the other, apparently for the convenience of insertion for differing dick heights. Two fingers protruded from the middle hole with long nails, painted orange and black. Unnaturally long fingers that could probably touch their own wrist. As they withdrew, Rob noted the slivers of blood collected below each opening before the sight the buttocks of a man short on shame and shirt alike eclipsed the sight.

The guy nearest to Rob slumped away with a look on his face like he'd banged his thumb with a hammer. The same holes stood revealed, but with shimmering coral flesh packed so tight that some of it pushed through. The semblance of a soggy orifice awaited, the three access holes dripping a creamy runoff. The new arrival literally slid across the tiles on his knees and crammed his mouth and nose into the raw maw.

Nature abhors a vacuum.

Rob sure could have used a toilet to puke his guts out, but he got the fuck out as soon as the bottleneck in the doorway permitted. He moved into the crowd like a man against hurricane winds, looking for stairs. The higher vantage point might help him find Anna.

He followed along the wall as best he could, refusing to be assimilated. It would have been impossible to miss Alec, the one person standing still while the rest of Painfreak shook like a snow globe. It relieved him to see the hated smirk. Rob worked his way over. He'd subtitle conversation on his phone if need be.

Somehow Alec maintained his protected circle. The swarm went on, always maintaining five feet of clearance, as if Alec were an angel showing Rob it was a wonderful life.

He mouthed three words at Rob: *I found her.* He reached down and a door suddenly opened in the wall.

Suspicious as he was, Rob didn't hesitate to go in. More light would have been nice, but a group of people walked up ahead, so it seemed safe-ish. Alec shouldered the door shut and the cacophony dropped from a level that threatened to detonate Rob's cerebellum to a volume akin to elevator music.

"Where'd you run off to?" Alec said it with the feigned ignorance of a swindler working over a rube.

Rob didn't bother to hide his feelings. "Man, this place is *fucked.*"

Alec laughed and clapped him on the shoulder. "I knew you'd love it. I'm glad you came."

To his great annoyance Alec stopped completely. Rob wanted to sprint down the passage shouting Anna's name.

Alec abandoned the smirk for a brief appearance of sincerity. "I guess this is where we part ways, though. This isn't digital anymore...it's all analog now. She's gone."

"Gone? You said she was back here."

Actually he hadn't, now that Rob thought about it.

"She's down there, yes." He pointed. The hall stood empty now, the other people having vanished into shadows. "But much further than last time."

Rob thought of the whispers and rumors of that other side of Painfreak, the one never uploaded to YouTube. The one rationally dismissed from the safety of an empty apartment as a ghost story. The one whose truth he would experience in the flesh if he continued.

"I'd tell you what she watched last time if I thought it would stop you," Alec continued, "because whatever it is now is far beyond your imagination. I'll just say if you were turned off back there, you *really* won't like what you find if you keep going."

Rob considered. No, he hadn't liked it—not Painfreak, but also nothing that came in the decades before it.

Except Anna.

I must.

He kept going. He never turned back, although moments later the music surged in volume as if from an open door before the calm returned.

Soon there was no pulse at all.

IV.

He was certain he'd been this way before, all those years ago. The magic seemed real then and undoubtedly was now. It was almost like he had wandered lost all that time.

The hall wound longer than the building could have possibly held. It curved gradually, almost unnoticeably. He pictured it as an endless spiral drilling deeper into the earth. To either side, he found apertures in the walls with living dioramas of depravity. Their intensity escalated. He saw live sex shows involving gas masks, cat o'nine tails, blindfolds, ball gags, pulley systems, with brandings, bloodlettings, bukakke baptisms. He vacillated between fear she wasn't there and fear she was.

Initially the defilements had their share of onlookers. The participants seemed too intent on the practice of their rituals to notice. There were fewer viewers the farther he went. Only one spectator witnessed a naked man tied down in cruciform to the floor, teased to erection by a dominatrix naked save for thigh high boots. Once his dick pointed to 12 o'clock, she worked the heel of one boot into his urethra. As her slave moaned and writhed beneath, she cocked one leg flamingo-like and stood with her full weight grinding into his stretched organ like she was snuffing out a cigarette. The arch of her foot mashed his scrotum flat. He smiled gratefully through tears of pain. The lone watcher worked his inches.

Past that, a circle of women surrounded a man bound to a chair, head tilted back with a funnel jammed in his mouth. The women vomited into the funnel with the kind of tandem precision rarely glimpsed outside of an aerial show. The recipient bucked in his chair, trying to gulp down the waves of emesis before it blocked his windpipe. The lone watcher worked his inches.

The hallway light ceased, relegating it to the displays themselves. He saw no voyeurs as grislier scenes played out. He'd breached a membrane in the fabric of reality, because now he saw impossibilities; humiliations of the flesh that could never be.

A blonde woman knelt at her seated brunette lover's feet, twisting an old-fashioned crank that gradually extended a furrowed drill segment between the brunette's thighs. The recipient sighed in ecstasy as more and more of the drill penetrated her vaginal canal, which became like a second mouth vomiting blood. Her belly tented as the tip punctured the flesh like some animal burrowing out of the earth. Viscera coiled around the drill bit the way an extension cord wraps around its roller. The brunette looked delighted by this strange new architecture in her body, firmly planted within, excavating her insides as it went. The blonde climbed atop her, grasping the protruding drill bit like a cock she needed to steady, and slipped down upon it with a gasp of pain and pleasure. She bucked, clenching her muscles around it, skewering herself and sloughing something like afterbirth in a crimson cascade that joined with the brunette's own babbling brook of cruor. The blonde could just reach down far enough to grasp the side handle of the crank and turn the drive wheel, alternating it clockwise and counterclockwise, impaling both of them at fluctuating depths.

He intended to bypass each one without registering the depths of depravity beyond, whether or not Anna featured, but his eyes were helplessly, hopelessly drawn. A red latex-suited woman repeatedly fired a nail gun into a man's erect penis, merging it with the outstretched tongue of a hairless, crouching, sexless figure at his feet. The man's eyes rolled back in head as he sighed in rapture. Sensing Rob's spectatorship, the kneeling figure turned its head, stretching the new organ of its tongue. Its eye sockets were filled with nails, like a coffee mug crammed full of pens. Still, it seemed to see him anyway, and through him.

Next, he encountered the semblance of an orgy. To the left a goat-headed man thrust between the spread legs of a woman as she deep-throated the ridiculous girth offered by an elk-headed man on the right. She did this with the bone of her spinal cord visible where her throat lay hollowed out, her head slumped until it rested against her own back, face upside down, mouth agape. Each time the elk-man pumped, the tip of his penis poked through the ruin of her excavated throat like a Whack-a-Mole.

Her cheek bulged as she tilted her head to follow Rob's progress, blinking rapidly as if he were the anomaly. Horribly, unmistakably alive but no worse for the wear.

He suspected the goat and elk heads weren't masks.

Would Anna be a mutilated shell of her former self, unrecognizable as the one who seduced him so profoundly?

He had to believe otherwise to keep going, the thought like a deleted psalm:

Yea, surely I shall not find my obsession in a state of anatomical renovation with an abundance of cocks.

He found her at the next exhibit and could have wept to see her as merely a bystander. He wanted to run up and embrace her, though managed to remember that despite his Odd-yssey, he was still a stranger to her. Instead, he savored her look of unbridled passion at the scene before her, possessed by it so completely she didn't notice his arrival. She wore a white top with an olive skirt, the shortest one he'd seen her wear, as form-fitting as a second skin he would die (had died?) to see her shed.

Rob followed her eyes to her secret fantasy in Painfreak. All thought ceased as efficiently as if he'd been unplugged, but gradually he made sense of it—the *what* of it, if nothing else. He thought he saw naked men of varying sizes vanish into the floor, but, as they crawled, he understood their hands and feet were missing, save for a man who still possessed one hand. Arms otherwise ended above the wrist, legs below the knees. None professionally done; they bled freely from ragged stumps, their faces blood-spattered in a fine mist. Above them dangled a human cylinder, formed essentially by female torsos with shortened arms and legs, their stumps of comparably amateurish quality. They looked turkey-like in the fashion in which they'd been strung upside down, straps around their waists to keep them a foot off the ground—the only foot available to any of them.

One of the crawlers clambered up the body of a blonde woman, awkwardly wrapping its upper limbs around her and planting the point of his shin into the underside of her breast, leaving bloody prints and smears. Scarlet tributaries ran from the jagged stumps at her thighs. He scaled her until he attained the summit. With an eager face and his abbreviated arms clamped around the overhead strap, he worked the point of his shin between her legs. It sank inside her almost to the knee. As if walking on stilts, he extended his other leg over to the body of a larger raven-haired woman, full ass prominently displayed. His other shin sank nimbly in the opening between her legs as well and he boosted himself up and out of the blonde, pulling the bloody appendage up like a boot stuck in the mud. His other stump slid deeper inside the second woman as he pushed to swing his free shin and bounce to the next in line, straining. The resultant hemorrhage didn't seem to bother her. She moaned and sighed in the thrall of pleasure while he landed the other shin within the next crevice. Another man climbed awkwardly atop that initial blonde with the seeming object to circumnavigate in his shin-steps, a *Row, Row, Row Your Boat* of stump-fucking.

In the far rear corner, partially obscured by this amputated configuration, Rob saw a stack of severed limbs. Arms and legs cast off like clothes on a race to skinny dip. Someone volunteered to dismember them. He recalled the crawler who still possessed a hand.

When he pried himself from the morbid display of carnality, he found Anna's passion surpassed the limitations of mere facial expression. She had one hand inside her shirt plying a breast, the other behind her skirt. She slumped against the wall, eyes wide open, transfixed by the interplay of amputated limb with waiting orifice. Even with nothing truly exposed, Rob looked upon her with desperate longing, enraptured by her ecstasy.

This isn't digital anymore...

It clicked for him in that moment, his joke on the elevator *(nearly lost a limb)* forgotten as soon as he made it, while his whole world became her essence. And her brief lust, the merest hint of the one she succumbed to now. One that had been willing to enter the recesses of Painfreak for this moment, maybe conjured for her alone.

Had it been someone else the scene might have been something totally different.

Perhaps it also manifested something from him.

Rob entered the aperture, stepping over all the crawling forms. They paid him no mind as he trudged through the stickiness beneath his shoes, walking through all the blood, searching. He found it back there, obscured by the seeping extremity pile, as he knew he would. He yanked the hatchet from the mound of limbs and carried it back.

He found Anna where he left her, building to her apex, face flushed, beautiful, transcendent. For that, he would sacrifice. He hardly knew her beyond the identity he created for her, ideal in every way, but tonight demonstrated he barely knew himself. He would shape himself to her liking, an endeavor far more meaningful than any he had chosen to leave behind.

I must.

Rob knelt outside the exhibit and drove the hatchet through his wrist with the strength of conviction. His hand came away clean, soon anointed with blood. The pain empowered. He crawled to Anna, a crimson snail trail in his wake, prepared to leave still more of himself behind. Now she saw him, blessed him with that look of infinite desire as he proffered his spurting stump. The smoothness of her pale thighs intoxicated him as her skirt lifted and she allowed him into the sanctum of the divine Red.

DOWN THERE

An accumulation of data is not the equivalent of its essence. For instance, there is a world of difference in the concept of pain versus the actual experience of it. We feel miserable during the malaise of illness, but once recovered, it becomes like fragments from a lost dream we don't particularly wish to recover. Some ideas are coldly and analytically presented, characters solidified from the ether. Their essence could be the difference in conceptual pain versus an outright mutilation of anatomy and even consciousness. As a movie tagline one said, there's nothing in the dark that isn't there in the light—except fear.

—*Transitory Bodies*, Dr. Braedon Obrist

I.

KENDRA DIDN'T LIKE THE woods.

Back home—she still couldn't bring herself to think of Iona as *home* now—they had lived in a neighborhood bordered by other neighborhoods where you could see houses in every direction. She knew the woods only from the school bus ride. They creeped her out, especially mornings with the sun barely risen and so much of the daylight eclipsed by the endless trees.

Russell watched them with the same longing he would show some toy out of his parents' price range, if such a thing existed when it came to him.

Exactly the reaction she'd expect from a total spaz like her brother.

Anything could be back there! he said.

Exactly why she didn't want to go anywhere near it.

Naturally he was happy about the suffocating world of woods so close to their new house.

Kendra suspected her parents even chose this one in part because of the little brat's enthusiasm for all the trees. Another home they'd considered strongly echoed their old one by location if not size. Sure, it would have sucked the big one too by virtue of being anywhere but Clayton, but at least it seemed like part of actual civilization.

Maybe she could lay as much blame on Gwendolyn.

While the real estate agent showed her parents the house, Kendra made the mistake of making eye contact with a girl riding her bike in the street, who took it as an invitation to ride over and ask if they were moving in. Kendra shrugged, bit back the *I hope not* on her tongue, and mentally urged the fact finder to pedal off into the sunset, but her mom and dad locked in and started pumping the girl for information about the neighborhood (liked it but more kids would be really cool; *hint, hint*), the school system (great; she had learned all kinds of neat stuff), even the weather (hot in summer, snow in winter, who knew), and her name (Gwendolyn Marie). With the maximum embarrassment not yet complete, Kendra's mom then introduced her to the girl as if she wasn't standing there in earshot praying for a sniper.

Gwendolyn Marie, that's such a pretty name, her mom said. *Don't you think so, Kendra?*

Sure, if you didn't mind someone losing interest and strolling half a block by the time you spit it all out.

Her parents then shared a knowing look, and Kendra's heart sank. They might as well have stenciled SOLD on the sign then and there.

Two weeks and hundreds of miles later, they moved into the single story home with a sticky-looking brown paint job on Sycamore Lane.

Pros: Summer vacation lasted until Labor Day in Iona.

Cons: Everything else. With the isolation from the blockade of trees, it might as well have been a colony on another planet.

"Kendra, why don't you go out and play with your new friend?"

That was a mom's logic. A girl with a stupid name you talked to one time is automatically your friend because she's your age and she rides her bike past your house in some weird pattern that probably spells out I AM EXTREMELY LAME PLEASE COME OUT AND PLAY.

"You can take your brother out to the woods."

Another mom trademark: *can* as *will* in disguise.

"I already share a room with the little creep. Do I have to take him on a play date too?"

Her mom's eyes narrowed. "Your brother is *not* a little creep, Miss Kendra Jane. It won't kill you to take him out there."

No, I'm not that lucky.

But she didn't say it. She'd edged a toe across the line complaining about the sleeping arrangements and didn't need the whole *your father never asked to be downsized* lecture a third time.

Her mom smacked an animal figurine down on the étagère. "It's either play outside or finish unpacking. How's that grab you?"

Unpacking enhanced the awful permanence of this nightmare. "Guess I'll say hello." Her mom couldn't resist a parting shot as Kendra hurried to leave, anticipating it.

"Honestly! Try to think about somebody besides yourself for a change!"

Oh, you mean like all the friends I had to leave behind in Clayton?

The front door opened seconds later, and Russell followed her out.

Gwendolyn looped around on her bike to intercept them, already smiling, a dark-haired girl with wide eyes. She also had braces, which seemed a little ominous. Kendra didn't want to enter a new school situation befriending one of the kids everyone made fun of since that could put her in the crossfire too, but a new school would be less scary if Kendra made a friend in advance. Gwendolyn didn't seem much like her friends back home, but maybe she would turn out to be cool.

"Hey, Kendra," she said as she pedaled up. "Wanna see the woods?"

II.

The woods swallowed them immediately and utterly, forging its own world with new sights, sounds, and smells. Colors, too—deeper within, some leaves had begun to redden with an early touch of fall. After two minutes Kendra saw no trace of their street at all.

"This is awesome," Russell announced. His head swiveled back and forth as though thinking, *And this is mine...all mine.*

"I love it," Gwendolyn said. "I come back here a lot."

Except when you're riding your bike in front of my house, hoping to be noticed, Kendra thought, keeping a silent rein on her sarcasm, trying to determine boundaries.

The trees seemed endless in all directions until everything began to look the same—much to Kendra's growing uneasiness. It seemed awfully easy to get lost. She would swear they'd passed the same fallen log at least three times. They walked several minutes with the accompaniment of distant sounds—things falling, things breaking, like signals of their approach.

She also thought she sensed someone stepping behind a trunk from the corner of her eye. A couple of times a branch would be waving when she turned to look.

Hi, Kendra...yes, there's someone back here. Come and see.

"It's a little eerie," she said.

"Pretty cool, huh?" Gwendolyn said. "Did you know a girl from another school disappeared here last year?"

Russell's swiveling head stopped and whipped back to her. The woods didn't look quite as awesome to him now.

"You mean they never found her?"

Kendra had no obligation to hold back on her brother today. "Yep, that's usually what they mean by *disappear*. Kind of like how your brain seems to have *disappeared*."

"Shut up."

"She really did, though," Gwendolyn said.

"What do they think happened to her?" Kendra said.

"Well, some kids say she failed social studies and ran away from home."

Kendra saw another waving branch, closer this time. The tree trunk wasn't big enough to hide anyone but she walked faster anyway until she caught Gwendolyn in the lead.

She tried to sound nonchalant. "Do you ever see anyone else back here?"

"Not really. There was some creepy looking guy walking through one time. He had a beard, might have been a bum. I don't think he saw me."

Great.

"Is social studies hard?" Russell asked. He would probably face it in third grade next week.

"It is if your brain *disappears*," Kendra said. It was practically muscle reflex these days.

Gwendolyn gave her the metal smile. To Russell, she said, "Don't worry about it. I don't think that's what happened anyway."

Russell smirked at Kendra like he'd somehow won an argument.

"No," Gwendolyn continued, "I think the Woodsman took her."

"The Woodsman?" Kendra repeated.

Bad enough her parents dragged her to Iona, but was there some serial killer picking off children here too?

She pictured her parents researching on the internet before the move.

Oh, wait, he just slaughters little girls. At least Russell will be okay.

And hey, if anything happens to Kendra, we can cash in her college fund and get Russ a cool car when he's old enough to drive!

Win/win!

"Yeah, you don't know about the *Woodsman*?"

Kendra resented the mild implication that she was uncool for not knowing about a psychotic lumberjack or whatever he was. "We just got here, remember?"

"But he's everywhere," Gwendolyn said. Kendra could see now she hadn't been critical after all, just puzzled by Kendra's ignorance. "I mean, in all the forests."

Kendra shrugged. "No, sorry."

Guess he hasn't opened up a chain back in Clayton.

"He has a lot of names," Gwendolyn said. "Maybe you know a different one."

"Oh," Kendra said. "Yeah, maybe." But she doubted Gwendolyn's woodland boogeyman was operating in Clayton under the alias Steve and she somehow forgot about it.

"But why would he take that girl?" Russell asked.

"It's just a story, spaz."

"It's *not* made up," Gwendolyn said. She looked astonished anyone could doubt it, although *astonished* was kind of a default mode with her perpetual wide-eyed expression.

Russell looked at Kendra hopefully, willing to be called a spaz again if she would just reassure him about the fictional nature of the Woodsman. She rolled her eyes where Gwendolyn couldn't see, but he did not seem comforted. Could she blame him? There was that Agent Orange *thing* behind the walls of Morgan and Sandalwood that she tried not to think about. Her parents' reassurances about how far away they were from those towns rang hollow.

At one time, Agent Orange would have seemed like a ghost story.

If he existed, what else could?

The Woodsman?

"I'll show you where he is," Gwendolyn said. "Come on."

She led them without any noticeable change in direction that Kendra could see. It had probably always been the girl's intended destination from the moment she took charge back by the house.

The foliage grew thicker in the following minutes, taking away the brunt of midafternoon sunlight.

Shadier, Kendra thought, but the word hiding behind that was *darker.*

The distant splintering of branches which had become almost subliminal to her gradually intensified. A strong wind which had not been in evidence at any earlier point in their exploration stirred the boughs. Pinecones and acorns clattered through a maze of limbs in a circle that seemed to be closing in tighter on them.

The whole thing had to be made up, of course, right down to the missing girl, but understanding this couldn't quite make it actually feel that way to Kendra. She wanted to suggest they turn back but there was no excuse that wouldn't seem like she was freaked out. She wasn't, not quite, but feeling so cut off from everything here, it was a little easier to accept that Gwendolyn's story could be real after all, the way monsters seemed a lot more believable in the dark.

"Here." Gwendolyn pointed.

She'd led them to an arch of trees. It couldn't be an accidental formation. All the others on their outskirts had sprung up independently with no sense of proportion. The branches intruded on one another and the spaces between their trunks varied between a few feet to several yards.

The arch stood perfectly symmetrical, gnarled ash-colored trees with no leaves and strange growths that made Kendra think of tumors. Some of those protrusions looked to have formed around human heads. A perfect three yards spaced each tree from the next. The column extended for twelve trees on both sides with just enough space for Kendra, Gwendolyn, and Russell to walk side by side until past the halfway point. Gwendolyn stopped them there. The trees ahead grew closer together until they left a space for one person at a time.

It's like a doorway, Kendra thought.

"If you go through there," Gwendolyn said, gesturing to the end of the column, "you'll see him."

A few yards past the last two trees, there was a hole in the ground.

"He comes up from the dark, and if you don't bring an offering, he takes you back with him."

"That's why he took the girl?" Russell asked.

"Probably."

Russell took a step forward, searching through his pockets. Kendra's hand instinctively went to his shoulder to stop him. She shook her head. He gave her a look that said, Now *who's being the spaz?*

This was silly. Nothing would happen if she let him walk through the doorway, and she wouldn't see anything if she followed him, either.

And we definitely won't see him if we never walk through it in the first place.

She studied the hole closer, standing tiptoed and leaning forward. "That's not even big enough for one of us to get in there. How could a man do it?"

"But he's not like us," Gwendolyn explained; slowly, as if to someone feeble-minded. "He can be anywhere in the woods, or anything. He could be as tall as the trees if he wanted. And he can fit down there too."

Kendra thought of something vaguely human shaped contorting, breaking itself down with collapsible limbs to slip deep into the earth. The shade grew much colder on her skin.

No, he wasn't real, of course not...

...but if he was less unreal, was he poised beneath them now, ready to emerge from the deeps if one of them took another twenty steps forward, crawling along in some spidery fashion in an ebb and flow of crackling shifting bones?

"Have you ever seen him?" Russell asked Gwendolyn.

"I...I'm not sure." Gwendolyn frowned. "I thought once, maybe, over there."

The tree she indicated stood well away from the arch. A knothole gaped in its trunk like a porthole for someone to observe their archway.

"He was inside the tree?"

Kendra meant for it to sound skeptical—and not more than a little mocking—but it came out wrong and nearly sounded declarative, as if part of her mind understood and believed even if the rest resisted.

"It was a face," Gwendolyn said. "I think." She stared intently, like it might still be there to help her find the words. "Not how it'd look if one of us was looking out, though. More like the pattern inside the tree had a face you could see if you looked at it long enough. I know I saw its eyes. They were...they were *moving*."

Kendra silently urged Gwendolyn to snort sudden laughter. *You should see your faces!*

Oh, man, I really had you guys going! By the way, nobody at school likes me!

Instead, she shook her head, still solemn. "I don't know. I walked over and it didn't look like anything by then, but until I got really close, I could see that face."

She sounded disappointed for its loss rather than frightened by its appearance.

Russell frowned. "Hey, what's that?"

He took off running toward the oak with the knothole. Kendra followed, mainly to get away from the arch. Apparently, there was no hard and fast special Woodsman protocol about cutting through the arch of trees since Gwendolyn tagged along too.

Russell knelt and picked up something from a mound of leaves.

It was a child's doll. It had taken a beating from the elements, the white dress damp and filthy. The plastic girl with curly blonde hair looked stoic about her predicament, a smudge on one cheek like a bruise and deep red lips to form a small heart-shaped mouth.

"Is that yours?" Kendra asked Gwendolyn.

"No, I've never seen it before."

"Let's give it to the Woodsman!" Russell said.

Kendra doubted a homeless girl would condescend to rescue this battered thing from the trash, but Gwendolyn nodded and said, "Good idea." She took the doll from him, in the lead once more, and let it dangle from her hand as she walked.

They worked their way back to the entry of the arch rather than cutting between its trees again. This time they walked beyond the halfway point, eventually falling into single file with Kendra in the middle. She kept her eyes on the doll to avoid the approach of the doorway. Its blue eyes returned her stare, blank and soulless.

Gwendolyn stopped four trees from the end. The snaps and crunches of the surrounding forest continued with the occasional call of a bird, but it all sounded somehow muted from within the column.

"Have you done this before?" Kendra asked when Gwendolyn didn't move after five seconds.

Gwendolyn shook her head, not turning around. The doll gazed at something unseen behind them. Kendra wondered if the face in the knothole watched Gwendolyn so impassively.

There was no face!

She didn't doubt Gwendolyn saw one, though, if only a trick of light and shadow. If she looked back now, would she see it too?

"Just toss it into the hole," she suggested, an easy compromise which wouldn't require Gwendolyn actually stepping through the passageway.

Russell made an exasperated noise behind her.

"But we won't know if he took it." Kendra's stomach flipped. They would have to come back here again, just to see, wouldn't they?

Like her dad joked about washing the car—you do it once, it means you'll have to do it again someday.

Gwendolyn advanced carefully as though walking to the edge of a cliff.

"Great Presence of the Woods, we offer this to you," Gwendolyn said, loud enough to carry. She delicately set the doll down before the threshold, then turned and hurried back to Kendra and Russell.

"We'll come back tomorrow to see if it's gone," she said, softly now as if they were in a church. She and Kendra walked back through the arch with more haste. When Kendra turned to chart Russell's progress, she saw him casually walking backwards, as if hoping to see some gnarled, emaciated hand extending out of the dark of the earth to claim their offering.

III.

Neither of them slept right away that night.

After several minutes waiting for sleep, Russell said, "Do you think he took the doll?" It was the first they had spoken of it back in the house.

"Of course not."

"Why not?"

"Duh, he's not real."

"But Gwendolyn saw him!"

"Think about it, Russ. If she really saw his face in that tree, why would she keep going back there all by herself?"

Kendra had pondered that question all night, though instead of comforting her as evidence of a hoax, she'd found herself thinking, *Because it's making her come back...because it wanted her to bring us.*

Russell stayed quiet long enough that she thought he'd gone to sleep, but at last he said, "He's real. I bet he's coming out of the ground right now."

IV.

"It's still there," Gwendolyn said the following afternoon, clearly disappointed.

It was right where they left it, a flash of white at the foot of the passage where definitely nothing would happen if they were to walk through to the hole beyond.

Aw, man, the terrifying thing in the woods is just a story after all. Bummer!

Kendra could finally loosen up. Her chest felt tight all morning, especially when the walk here already seemed impossibly familiar despite the lack of distinguishing landmarks. She was sure she could find the arch without Gwendolyn now, not that she would ever want to. Still, this awareness worked its way out of the tangle of her thoughts for safe keeping.

The three of them approached the apparently rejected offering. Kendra made it a point to find the tree with the knothole. Nope, nothing there, why would there be? She let Gwendolyn spook her yesterday, that was all. The only scary thing now was starting a new school with a friend who saw faces in tree trunks and left broken dolls for the *Great Presence of the Woods*.

Total freak show. And probably known for it by everyone at school.

"Hey, do you see that?" Gwendolyn asked.

She sprinted the rest of the way to the doll. Heart heavier in her chest, the tightness settling back in, Kendra hurried to catch up. Russell ran around her to get there first.

"Look." Gwendolyn pointed to the doll. Its dead eyes and ruby heart-shaped mouth looked no worse for the horror of the thing in the earth. Not so for the dress itself. They'd left it behind damp and grimy yesterday, but its moisture held a distinctly crimson cast now.

Russell reached down to yank its dress up to the neck.

"Oh God," Kendra said.

Gwendolyn's hand flew to her mouth. She looked away in a hurry.

The doll's chest gaped, hollowed out, the resultant cavity filled with blood of a similar shade to its lips. It held other things inside too, islets of glistening tissue. Kendra thought it a trick of light shimmering in the red reflection but realized something moved inside after all. Tiny whitish-yellow slivers writhing in the hole.

Maggots.

Kendra looked away too, eyes watering, gorge rising. She took deep breaths until the worst of it passed, vision in and out of focus as she searched for distractions. A falling leaf, a sycamore tree, the bushy tail of a squirrel like a sail as it dashed between a cluster of trees.

"What does that mean?" Gwendolyn kept a hand close to her mouth in case the urge to puke returned.

"I don't think he liked it," Russell said. He continued to peer into the cavity as if to see his mirror image, a blood shadow.

"Come on, Russ, you don't need to be looking at that."

He shrugged at her, as if to say *Just because* you *can't take it...* But he abandoned his vigil.

"Did you do that?" Gwendolyn asked.

Kendra thought she meant Russell. And then realized, even more absurdly, Gwendolyn meant Kendra herself.

"You're asking if I stuffed that doll with *gore* and...and..." She couldn't get the word out but she saw them in her mind, the swarm of grubs. "No! Did *you*?"

"No, I swear!"

There hadn't been enough pieces for identification but someone obviously dissected some small creature and tossed the stuffing into the doll.

Either that or a woodchuck threw itself on a grenade.

Gwendolyn seemed sincere in denial, her face curdled. Kendra couldn't picture her coming back last night to do something so sick as darkness spread over this secret world. The arch was the last place in the world she'd want to be in the dead of night, though there was an undeniable fascination at the prospect as well. A desire that didn't seem to belong to her any more than her familiarity with the path here, to feel the caress of the night air with a prism of bone-shaded moonlight glowing through the gnarled pillars in a land cast in shadow.

And him waiting to bestow his favor beyond the arch, down there.

"Oh, cool," Russell said. He had wandered back to the doll.

She and Gwendolyn turned, careful not to look at the ground, though Kendra would swear she heard the moist sound of those slivers squirming in the rot anyway.

Russell examined one of the trees at the threshold to the hole.

"Don't you go through there!" Kendra said.

"Duh."

A knife protruded from the tree trunk on the left. Its handle shared the weathered appearance of the doll, something potentially lost back here for months. A dark stain shadowed the trunk around the groove, like the tree bled from the stab wound.

The blade stuck at an angle where its handle pointed to the ground. At the doll.

Russell reached for the knife.

"Don't touch that," Kendra said.

He made the trademark *uh!* sound she despised. "Why not? He gave it to us!"

"Then he should have asked Mom and Dad first. You know they'd never let you keep a knife."

Russell turned up his lip in pout mode. Kendra almost preferred to look at the doll instead.

Gwendolyn's eyes popped. "Do you think he really left it there for us?"

"No," Kendra said. "Come on, it was probably that creep you saw with the beard. I bet he's watching us."

She didn't believe it, though, not at all, and was too shaken to appreciate the irony that some nut spying on them and leaving mutilated trinkets would have been a relief.

Gwendolyn and Russell didn't appear to buy it either.

"Okay, then why give us an offering? Russell's nothing special. He doesn't even brush his teeth half the time."

"Yes, I do!"

"It's not an offering," Gwendolyn said softly. "You know it's not."

"Did that girl really disappear last year?" Kendra asked, desperate.

"Yes, I swear to God!"

Kendra sighed. "Come on." She grabbed Russell's shoulder to coax him away from the knife and the passage, toward the mouth of the arch.

"What are we going to do?" Gwendolyn asked.

"There's nothing *to* do," Kendra said. "We just need to stay the hell out of the woods."

"I'm telling Mom you're swearing!"

"But we didn't do it right," Gwendolyn said. "If he's giving us another chance and we're just walking away…"

"We didn't walk through the last trees," Kendra said. "And you never have before, right?"

"Never."

"There you go. We don't owe him shit."

Russell renewed his threats. Kendra ignored him. She did not glance back at the arch, and absolutely would not look in the direction of the knothole where Gwendolyn saw his face.

V.

"You suck," she told Russell when their parents sent him to bed—a full hour after her own imposed bedtime since the little creep tattled on her about the profanity. She would also have the pleasure of being grounded tomorrow.

If he hears you talk like that, he's going to think it's okay to do it too, Mom said. *You need to think about how you influence him.*

Kendra answered with token nods, remembering her dad's colorful phrases about the bosses from his old job, and how those *cocksucking fucks* would rue the day they told an asset like him to hit the bricks since they *couldn't find their own assholes if they followed the big rubber dick.*

Nothing she'd ever repeated, so maybe the whole influence thing was a bit overrated.

"Sorry," he said now.

Though she kind of wanted to smother him with a pillow while he slept, she didn't mind sharing a bedroom with him tonight given what they'd found today.

Her bed faced the large windows above his, which had yet to be outfitted with curtains or blinds large enough to cover them. Their panes opened on the trees, but the blur of darkness seemed less threatening with the periodic flicker of fireflies. At least until she noted how a couple of glows seemed synchronized at eye level, drifting closer and closer. Russell would be first in line if something crawled out from the woods. It would have served him right, too, the little tattletale, and she almost told him so, but soon lost herself in thoughts of how they could open those windows and slip unseen into that eternal kingdom of shadow. She knew they could find the arch blindfolded.

And he would be there: *come and see.*

Kendra awoke an unknown time later from a dream of falling endlessly. She sat up in bed. A leaf became stuck to the window while she slept. The backyard glowed in the moonlight, the front line of trees visible at the border of the woods. Past them several black shapes seemed to move as clouds rushed past the night sky.

Another leaf settled on the window.

Kendra squinted. Were they actually leaves or some kind of insect, like a butterfly?

She slid out of bed and crept to Russell's side of the room, unknowingly adopting the same pose with which she examined the hole beyond the arch. She decided the black shapes were leaves after all.

As she looked, leaning slightly over Russell's bed, others began to float to the window, as if propelled by a leaf blower. Though concentrated in a specific pane of glass, they did not land in a scattered fashion where one covered up another. One would land apart from the others, followed by another and another beside it, gradually obscuring the pane in an oval shape. It was like watching the formation of a vertical jigsaw puzzle with pear-shaped leaves. When they settled to complete the shape, they all moved en masse, like something tilting its head to see at an angle, amidst a flurry of scraping sounds against the window.

Kendra jerked back, twisted, and dove into her bed, yanking the covers over her head.

The bristling sound continued, like the head or face sought every corner of the room, periscoping to higher and lower panes and shifting from left to right to evaluate the room. She thought she heard more of the things lighting on the window too, perhaps providing additional shape. A neck, shoulders, chest, arms. She knew if she were to turn on the bedroom light, she would find an assembly of multicolored leaves, able to effect eyes, a nose, a mouth in a crude, horrible fashion.

She stayed under cover, shaking, heart bouncing this way and that like a ball tethered to a paddle, filled with an urge to scream—anything to drown out those seeking, whispering sounds which she feared would become actual words if she heard them long enough.

After untold seconds, a great whooshing sound consumed the night, like a giant snake slithering through the woods to shake all the trees from here back to the arch.

He could be as tall as the trees.

"Kendra?" Russell called, sleepily.

"Go back to sleep," she said. "You're dreaming."

She stayed with the covers pulled overhead the rest of the night.

VI.

She awoke early to find her mom in the kitchen sipping coffee, the sun bright through the windows and the world sane.

"Oh, getting an early start on going nowhere, I see."

Kendra smirked without much enthusiasm.

Russell wasn't far behind, joining them in the kitchen before she'd finished her breakfast. When their mother went back to her bedroom to work on more unpacking, Kendra took hold of Russell's wrist.

"You can't go back in the woods today."

That *uh!* sound again. "Why?"

"It's not safe."

"But I'll go with Gwendolyn."

She thought of Gwendolyn wringing her hands. *We didn't do it right...if he's giving us another chance—*

She tightened her grip. "*Especially* not with her. I mean it."

"Ow!" He pulled his arm away, rubbing his wrist. That damned pout again. "You can't make me."

"I'll tell Mom you're swearing," she said.

An empty threat since even if she wasn't making it up, Kendra would probably be super-grounded for putting that filth in his head in the first place, and never mind their dad saying far worse during fix-it projects this week.

It seemed to do the trick, though. His shoulders slumped.

"We'll go tomorrow," Kendra said. She meant it to be a lie, but found the idea agreeable.

Yes, they could go back there and get the offering right this time. The knife would still be there...

Russell left the kitchen with exaggeratedly heavy steps.

"I'll be watching," Kendra warned.

She did, too: Per Mom's orders she worked on unpacking her room, but every few minutes she went to the front of the house to make sure Gwendolyn and Russell stayed on the street. They rode their bikes, sometimes trading. Kendra filed that away to tease him about a pink bike for his birthday.

They kept an eye on the house and caught Kendra at her vigil several times until resigned to the fact they'd go nowhere today but in circles. Even then she kept watching.

They talked, but Kendra couldn't hear any of it even with the window cracked. She wondered what Gwendolyn said to him, what they planned.

They stared at the woods.

VII.

Russell insisted they talked about school and people in the neighborhood, nothing at all about the Woodsman. He stuck to that story when pressed.

Me and you don't talk about it, so why should she?

A logical question—and probably one Gwendolyn coached him on this afternoon.

She got nothing from him.

After dinner, their father finally set up the computer they all shared so that evening Kendra did some searching in the paltry thirty minutes they gave her. They acted like this was some amazing privilege since she was technically still grounded. She didn't argue because she suspected a trap. They wanted her to complain so they could strip it from her. She wouldn't give them the satisfaction.

A whole half an hour? Heck yeah! You guys rock!

Her searches confirmed the Woodsman had many names, as Gwendolyn said, and was believed to be many things: demon, shapeshifter, Wendigo, spirit. The lore went back decades, predating Agent Orange. Some called him the Stickman, Daimon, Amduscias, the Dweller of the Deep Woods. Accounts of his appearance, origins, powers, and objectives varied. The lore said nothing about a mystical arch of trees. The subject of blood sacrifices received little coverage in the articles she found, though she wasn't sure what she expected. A how-to guide?

There *had* been a disappearance last year, too. A bit farther off than Gwendolyn swore, a neighboring county, but a girl named Sarah Putnam vanished near the Cedar Bluff Woods while playing with her doll. Pictures showed a redhead with a wide smile interrupted by two missing teeth in the top row. Just a year older than Russell. No description of her doll, but Kendra could guess what it looked like. Maybe a boy with a buck knife went missing another time.

It wasn't only children, though.

One website maintained the Woodsman claimed a news reporter named Geisha Hammond. She did a piece about this woodland boogeyman, and she vanished six weeks later, never to be seen again. It almost relieved Kendra to expand the search and discover that bodies found in woods thirty miles away had merely fallen prey to a human sicko. Speculation ran that this serial killer loser "messed around" with the corpses. The ick factor of doing that sort of thing with a living person already seemed too gross to bear, but with a dead body? That was grody enough to make her puking-sick.

Perhaps the most disturbing thing about all Woodsman lore came from the idea that those taken by the Woodsman didn't simply "go to their reward," as Kendra's mom was fond of saying. He kept them for some unfathomable purpose—she'd had to look *unfathomable* up on the Merriam-Webster site to be sure of the context—but one popular theory held that he drew power from their souls. The horrors like she had seen with the leaves, those came courtesy of some child husk withering deep in the earth, maybe a little girl forever separated from her doll.

Was it originally human?

Was it hungry?

Was it evil?

No one knew, beyond that it just was.

What she didn't find before signing off was any sort of solution—a ritual, a spell, an incantation, *something* that would make him go away.

Kendra doubted she would sleep with the uncertainty of tomorrow looming and the memory of last night's horror at the window, but she nodded off soon after Russell turned in. If not for the breeze on her face, she may have slept on through the night.

She expected to find a monstrosity comprised of leaves hunched over her bed, blowing the breath of early fall into her face, but the room lay empty of anyone else—including Russell.

The chill air of night found her through his open window.

She clambered out from under the covers, quickly trading her pajamas for clothes in her hamper.

She thought of Gwendolyn leaning over to confide in Russell while they played this afternoon.

Come out tonight after everyone's asleep, Russell. Meet me at the trees...you know which ones. And you can't tell Kendra, okay? We'll get it right this time. Something small. I know what to do.

She used the illumination from her cell phone to find an older pair of shoes in the closet, rather than risk waking her parents by going to the front door for the ones she usually wore. Her mom wouldn't so much as entertain the idea that a new school might possibly suck for Kendra, so the existence of some unholy leaf demon living in a deep hole out back in the woods probably wasn't going to fly.

She crawled through the window and dropped to the grass, then ran in a crouch to the cover of the woods. After stumbling where moonlight didn't give her enough guidance, she soon felt far enough away from the house to use her cell phone as a flashlight.

Terror and exhilaration consumed her, the feeling she'd entered a forbidden place contrasted with a sense of belonging. The trees past the moonlight were black towers, artifacts of a dead world. All around her, sounds of rustling, snapping, cracks, collisions. She saw faces everywhere now. Anything she saw in the pale light of the moon or the blue glow of her phone—moss growing on one tree, a fallen bird's nest, a collection of fallen pinecones, the whirls in the bark of a trunk—took on vaguely humanoid (or inhumanoid) features.

Eyes everywhere.

Glimpses from which she wished to avert her eyes, but the caricatures dissolved almost as soon as they formed, to recede into the deeper darkness ahead and await another spotlight.

She yelled Russell's name. It didn't matter to announce her presence. The Dweller already knew and Gwendolyn would see her light anyway.

No answer. Only the scuttling, knocks, and sighs that had followed her the whole way, the breathing of the forest.

She reached the arch. The tumor trees regarded her, as though curious how she'd proceed. The moonlight revealed most of the column, but only a void waited at the end of the path.

"Russell?" she called into the darkness.

She heard something in the black. A whisper of movement or maybe just a throat accustomed to a different idea of language.

Kendra advanced. Every part of her screamed to run, but that other influence held her to the path. It wanted her here, and something inside her that wanted to be wanted responded to it eagerly.

As the trees drew closer to her on either side, the darkness ahead continued to deny her like a living black drape, concealing its secrets. Past the arch, a ray of moonlight found the hole. It seemed to stop dead at the opening, revealing nothing.

"Answer me, Russell, you little asshole!" Kendra shouted. She'd take the grounding tomorrow and be glad, if he'd just respond.

Heart straining in her chest, she revived the light from her phone. Its glow revealed the knife last seen embedded in the trunk, now bloodied from tip to hilt as though dipped in the doll's gory chest. Farther up in the path of her light, she found shoes and legs in a pair of jeans.

Russell.

Another step showed the upper half of the body, the arms stretched out in cruciform. Like a human reflection of the doll, the skin of the chest had been removed in an imperfect circle, displaying the organs beneath. Rather than the hodgepodge of anatomy, though, everything remained in its proper place here with mushroom-colored ropes of entrails still neatly tucked within the abdomen. Above those, an assortment of shimmering sacs and tissues to which Kendra could initially supply no name, although the single beat of one darker-shaded structure announced itself as the heart.

She clamped a hand over her mouth, nearly fumbling the phone. Her haste to take the light away from the grotesque sight afforded her a view of the rest of the sacrifice.

Gwendolyn's face did not suggest the blank expression of the doll. The wide eyes appraised Kendra as though she were responsible for this humiliation of the flesh from which Gwendolyn somehow had not yet succumbed. Blood bubbled from a puncture in her throat.

Whatever her plan, Russell had surprised her.

"Hel..." Gwendolyn managed—a sound so slight as to be the wind.

Kendra turned the light away toward the arch, where a large, misshapen oval of skin hung. She dropped the phone and merciful darkness absorbed the nightmare images once more, save one—that of an impossibly tall and gangly shape maneuvering past the gnarled pillars in silhouette. Its movements were shuddery as it came to the edge of the arch, between Gwendolyn and the hole in the earth. Its size diminished as it slipped through the threshold to claim its sacrifice, a shadow sinking within a shadow. Gwendolyn's body slid across the grass through the portal of the trees. Kendra thought she heard the faint beat of the heart.

"Great Presence of the Woods, we offer this to you," she shouted.

The shape sank once again, into the hole. Clouds rolled past to emit more moonlight, which revealed Gwendolyn hovering above the entrance. Her limbs flailed as something manipulated her in impossible directions with a series of grueling snaps. Something splattered, like a bucket of wet sponges poured out on the ground. The earth accepted her, Gwendolyn the shape of some boneless sprinkler toy both tucked and poured into the abyss.

Kendra found her phone, searched briefly with its light, and a moment later began her walk home.

The leaves and the moss were now just leaves and moss.

No faces.

She thought of Russell's eagerness to provide the offering, the first among them to try to take the blade.

Was the face at the window even meant for her?

Maybe it wasn't a warning at all, but a blessing.

Russell had left the window open for her when she found her way home. She pocketed her phone and as quietly as she could, she twisted the knob of the spout in the back of the house to wash the blood off the knife in her other hand.

Perhaps the Dweller would remain sated and not call either of them back to the arch. If the day came when another offering was necessary, though, Kendra would take her mom's advice and not think of herself for a change.

JUNK

We associate our world with contagion, with disease. When we all see and hear something trending in popularity through social media, it is said to have gone "viral." Will this always pertain exclusively to ideas, images, scandals in the digital realm? Or is a viral concept awaiting its evolution, like the first species to forsake the water for land?

—*Transitory Bodies*, Dr. Braedon Obrist

I.

NICK DIDN'T KNOW WHERE the impulse came from, but he followed it with vigor. It seemed to have been there as long as he could remember, like a post-hypnotic suggestion. Those moments were the only ones that mattered in his life. All the rest was simply preamble and postscript to the thrill.

He didn't remember when he first found out about the InterphaZ website. Nick thought of it as some kind of glory hole for casual conversation, a way to meet new people from all walks of life and forge a friendship or perhaps even a relationship. A complete waste of time, in other words, but it hadn't taken him long to realize its potential for his own needs.

That's when the fun began.

And it hadn't let up in the past four months.

Virgins were the conquest—the noobs who just signed up on InterphaZ who were more likely not to have yet had the random chat experience spoiled for them. New arrival HellKat99 looked promising, an attractive blond with hair tied up in two twists on her avatar. *Like horns*, he thought at first, but then realized they were supposed to affect cat ears. She must have liked what she saw from his avatar and profile—expertly crafted to present a charming and unthreatening persona after weeks of trial and error—because she accepted the chat request. Her webcam feed sprang up in the left corner of his screen.

He had it down to a science. As soon she accepted his request, he bolted up from his ergonomic chair and hit his mark like a consummate pro. The view of his maroon shirt and plain face—eyes too close together, nose too thin as if compressed by the nearness of his eyes, his fingers curled over his chin to suggest a pensive harmlessness—vanished in a flash, a smash cut leaving HellKat99 with a window to the bearded thatch of his scrotum. He lifted his shirt to allow her the unhindered view.

And, of course, he was rock hard.

How could he not be?

This was the pinnacle. He could have run dick-first into a brick wall and crashed through like the Kool-Aid Man.

"Ugh!" HellKat99 grunted over the computer speakers. She recoiled from the image, eyes squinched shut like he'd proffered a photo of children blown to pieces in a drone strike rather than a pulsing boner. The resolution on webcams always left much to be desired, so it wasn't as if she could see Rand McNally tributaries of veins spreading the good word about his arousal through the length of his girth. But if she wanted to act like it was the first time Cinderella went to the ball, Nick was all for it.

This was the kind of reaction he relished best.

HellKat99 finally realized she had the power to disconnect this live feed to genital horror, and she groped for her mouse with one hand. The other she kept in front of her eyes to block him, like he could glaze her face through the computer screen. E-facial, the next stage of human evolution.

"Sick bastard!" she shouted.

HellKat99 has disconnected this chat.

Nick sat down again, grinning ear to ear.

Would she report him?

It wouldn't be the first time. There were always ways around banishment.

He went ahead and blocked her. The prospect of a sequel down the line was amusing in theory—*just when you thought it was safe to InterphaZ...*—but it gave them time to process the encounter and reflect on what they should have said for maximum damage, a tirade against him and his ilk. He learned that lesson the hard way with user anellasyst. They could run these little mental fire drills and assure his surprise reappearance, with a new name and profile, displayed the law of diminishing returns.

Better to hit and run.

"Cock and awe, bitch."

This had been a good night with consistently satisfying reactions—disgust, horror, anger. Some nights were less fulfilling, prompting only indifference, boredom, and sarcasm.

Is that all you've got? My webcam doesn't have a microscope feature, little man.

Not tonight, though. They cringed, they shuddered. One even shrieked. The cross in her avatar suggested big time Christian beliefs. She was probably kneeling in broken glass and flagellating herself in penance. Nick's personal project tomorrow during the misery of the call center would be to craft a more religious-friendly profile. That would be fishing with dynamite, something he should have considered long ago. Few were more predisposed to be forever haunted by the specter of Nick's throbbing gristle.

It was funny to think he would never have done something like this in different circumstances. On a crowded bus or in line at Starbucks, never. There were real world penalties for that, jail time from the cops, pepper spray, and sharp fingernails from the civilians. Doing it online in the privacy of his own apartment, though, it may have been unwanted, but it was tolerated, the same as someone texting at a movie.

You go to a theater, you expect to see the glowing screen of a smartphone during the feature presentation.

You go online, someone's throwing a dick in your face.

That was just the way of the world now.

He hadn't been thinking of doing it when he bought his webcam. He just expected to chat with different bitches who would get naked on their own cams every week if not every night—law of averages—but it hadn't worked out that way. When the familiar disappointment shadowed his latest attempt to escape his incessant boredom in life, he became inspired by a new idea with a different objective.

This one was working.

He was winning.

A chime played through his speakers. New email alert. He clicked over to the tab.

Another InterphaZ notification of his latest expulsion. *Failure to uphold community standard...conduct unbecoming...violation of membership agreement...blah, blah.* It meant about as much as dying in a video game. It was a fine paid with Monopoly money.

He frowned at the subject line of another new email: SAVAGE YOUR PENIS B4 ITS 2 LATE! That was a far cry from the usual promises of genital size enhancement and aphrodisiacs. Maybe it was supposed to pique his curiosity enough to read it. (Fail.) It must work on someone out there, maybe the sort of person who thought they'd been personally selected to play cash mule for the Prince of Nigeria.

Nick marked the junk mail as spam—for all the good that would do—and closed the tab.

His preferred notification of a chat request from InterphaZ—the quaint sound of a ringing phone—brought him back to the mission at hand. This was surprising since Nick was supposed to be locked out again and expected to switch to a new ISP and profile, presto-change-o before another chat encounter. The notification came from user nerXam83, the avatar a photo of some primo jailbait. She might have handled more dicks than a porn set fluffer or maybe the only cramming she did was for the SATs.

Or as a popular meme once said, *Why not both?*

It was hard to tell these days. The 83 seemed questionable, but it didn't necessarily mean year of birth. If it was just some creepy guy, he could pull the plug easily enough.

Nick accepted. The window appeared in the same sacred place where so many InterphaZ users of yore found themselves blinded by a wall of his junk.

Nick's eyelids vanished in comical surprise. NerXam83 was definitely a man, a man who had bested the master of Cock and Awe at his own game. There was a twist to his version of surprise scrotal maneuvers, however. NerXam83 was *afflicted*. Like something out of a medical textbook passed around in a macabre parlor game to see who puked first. Pustules spread across the shaft of the dick filling his chat window in a bubble wrap formation. Perhaps the flicker of the feed created the illusion, but Nick would swear the fleshy growths pulsated as he watched.

Unfortunately, the resolution of this window to repulsion seemed mysteriously like Blu-Ray level quality to better disgust him with its palette of moist reds and yellows. Some nodules were blood blister-like, while others oozed with a custard syrup in milky tributaries he could see gradually advancing between protuberances of inflamed skin. NerXam83's presentation front and center on the world's sharpest webcam had cracked open the coral reef of penile rot currently festering inches away.

In Nick's shock he looked far longer than reason dictated, both grossed out and engrossed by this abomination the same as he would have been by an animal with two heads. Perhaps more so because this person hailed from the same species...someone who even shared the same pastime.

"Ugh!" Nick finally groaned and disconnected the chat without looking directly at it another second, lest he turn to stone. He needed his own eye wash station.

Some distance from the computer seemed like a good thing, so Nick made his way to the bathroom down the hall. An afterimage remained. What could have caused that? Did he bang some leper whore with syphilis near Chernobyl? Nick didn't think he could have shown his face to the world after contracting something so hideous, much less the spoiled genitals that were part and parcel of it.

It had to be fake. Dude could just be some special FX wizard looking to freak people out, that was all.

Sicko.

Mystery solved, he intended to relieve himself and then get back to the business of flashing his junk in the faces of unwary women on InterphaZ.

Another bone strike of Cock and Awe. That's the ticket.

He unzipped his pants, then forgot all about his special FX theory and plans for scrotal domination at the burst of pain ignited by the release of his bladder.

"Ow, fuck!"

He twitched like a frog hooked up to a car battery, the entirety of his world condensed to an inch of blazing fury at the tip of his organ. It was like pissing napalm when he had failed to fireproof his dickhole. His keening wail accompanied this slow eternity of urination, unself-conscious about the thin walls between him and his neighbor. Right now, this geyser of molten lava was all that mattered—the only thing that existed. The last drops singed as well, as if they sprouted claws to slash through his membrane on the way out.

Nick had shut his eyes tight against the onslaught and now opened them to a world blurred by tears of pain. The spasms turned his aim all scattershot, leaving splashes of red across the seat of the commode, the roll of toilet paper, the floor, the wastebasket.

That's blood, he thought dumbly, cold sweat beading in his scalp. *All of that was blood.*

He tenderly shook off, grimacing at the wetness on his fingers. He already dreaded a couple of hours from now when the call of nature forced him through this excruciating torture again. The first time might have only been a warm-up—

His train of thought derailed.

Wetness on his fingers? Despite all the cringing a moment ago, he didn't believe he'd sprayed himself, but now expected to see the same bloody excretion when he examined his hand.

He didn't, though.

It still had traces of blood, but the fluid seemed far more suggestive of pus. A runny wax not unlike what he saw on the computer a moment ago.

He laughed with barely suppressed hysteria because the cause and effect was so impossible. Even if nerXam83 whipped his rotting manhood out one apartment over instead of another state or continent altogether, it made the theory no more logical. Nick had only looked at a computer screen.

It went viral, he thought and almost laughed again. It made an ominous sense, however crazy, especially when he considered the circumstances. Banned by InterphaZ but still able to receive that one request from the site. Now this.

Nick's guts double-and triple-knotted as he stood before the mirror and examined his penis. Now that he'd confirmed the infection, his shaft felt tingly and hot, as if he could sense new pustules forming on a microscopic level. He held his length gingerly by the head, inspecting the column with mounting horror. Several sores had already burst in his tightened grip during the throes of anguish. A cobweb of stringy flesh dangled from the underside, having peeled off from the base, revealing raw layer of crustacean red.

Nick met his own stricken gaze in the mirror, mouth agape, his sickly pale reflection commiserating: *Are you seeing this?*

Unfortunately, he did, and no reset from a universal do-over restored the integrity of his genitalia.

He had some gauze in one of the bathroom drawers. He didn't know what to do, except wrap himself up. Smear the bandages with some triple antibiotic—assuming quadruple antibiotic didn't exist—and pray for a miraculous return to its pristine state while he went through life in the meantime looking like a stunt dick for Claude Rains.

He reached for the drawer...and that was the point when the corona of his cock adopted the texture of a sponge. His index finger and thumb pushed trenches into either side instantaneously. He shrieked and withdrew his pincer grip, but the caverns remained. A piece dislodged within the crumpled pillar and dropped to the counter.

Nick looked around frantically, as if a bottle of Acme Dickhead Skin Regrowth Ointment^{TM} would magically appear somewhere.

It didn't.

The impulse loomed to call for an ambulance, but what would he say?

My dick is rotting before my fucking eyes because some freak flashed me on a webcam. Hurry!

When they finally accepted it wasn't a crank call and actually sent someone, what could they do?

SAVAGE YOUR PENIS B4 ITS 2 LATE.

Yes, that was what the strange email said. It seemed no more coincidental than nerXam83's request. He gingerly walked back to the bedroom, stripping off his shirt so it didn't catch his groin and exacerbate the damage. He launched his email again, heedless of the rancid juices left behind on the mouse and keys and the pitter-patter of his sores upon the carpet, like melting icicles. The nausea in his stomach churned with greater urgency.

He found the email in his spam folder and opened it. The sender name contained the word InterphaZ. And "no-reply." No text, only an embedded .GIF file of a man with his sex organs on a flat table surface as he swung a meat cleaver at the scrotal pouch, an unsettling smile on his face. An animated balloon obscured the actual hit, filled with the word THWACK!

That was savage, all right. Not exactly the most tempting prospect for a potential cure. B4 ITS 2 LATE.

2 late for what?

He looked forlornly at the disgusting thing attached to him, which had been perfectly normal not ten minutes ago. The disease progressed like an old school werewolf transformation with superimposed special FX.

"No," Nick said. "Oh God, no."

The sac of his scrotum showed burgeoning, bloated pearls emerging between the furrows.

Hundreds of them, like mutant spider eggs primed to hatch an adipocerous offspring. The burning, tingling sensation erupted in full, with tiny needles prickling every millimeter of skin.

There could be no doubt—the maddening sensation was spreading. It had already done this much to him within minutes. What would happen by the time the paramedics showed up?

B4 ITS 2 LATE.

Nick staggered to the kitchen, the droplets of his gangroin spattering the linoleum. As he reached for the electric carving knife, he comforted himself with the countless miracles of modern medicine. People lost body parts all the time—with practical advances in technology, they could basically spin straw into dick, couldn't they? He wasn't out of options—so long as he survived this. The solidity of the carving knife handle reassured him. It featured a slide button rather than a trigger, so it would keep cutting if he passed out.

He called 911 first for an ambulance, reporting massive blood loss from a carving knife mishap. He claimed it was his fingers since they probably wouldn't get here any faster anyway. They assured him help was on the way and he hung up, his eyes blurry again.

He revved the carving knife as he took hold of everything in his other hand, cupping beneath his testicles with the palm, his fingers and thumb forming a C-shape. Any doubts about the necessity of his course of action were neutralized by one last humiliation of the flesh. The patchwork of pustules slipped beneath his fingers like some kind of revolving cylinder, both on his dick and the sac beneath. Skin barely adhered to the organ now. It pulled loose from the stalk with ease, lasagna-colored meat beneath. The loose rope of dangling flesh slid away, abracadabra. It sloughed as a shed snakeskin, popping and bursting in the few places still attached, liquid tendrils stretching like taffy to reveal shimmering tissue. The underside tore with it in a burst as if something detonated beneath. The sac detached in tandem like a wet rubber glove in his palm.

The testicles and cords dropped like dead jellyfish, oysters in a Jell-O mold upon his quivering hand. The emptied pouch hung limp, the penile skin like the empty husk of some insect draped in his palm. It all clumped wetly to the floor. He watched it go like a soldier unable to hold in his own intestines. There was curiously no pain, other than the trauma of the sickening sight, the nerve endings perhaps jellified now. Clinging contents of the pouch sagged like syrup, halfway to the floor. His actual penis was but a strange glistening tube apart from the head, which retained its skin and something of its shape save the trenches from his fingers.

Otherwise, he beheld something virtually skinless, corroding.

On the plus side, he had much less he'd need to cut now.

Nick engaged the carving knife again. Whatever whimpers he made were drowned out by the whirring blades. He locked in on his target, a miraculous sliver of pale flesh at the base of his organ. There was pain at the root where the true skin remained, but far less than he expected.

Perhaps that was the silver lining to an impromptu session of unlicensed surgery to rid yourself of your liquefying fuckmeat. He screamed anyway, for this insanity that had dethroned the natural order of his life. The blades shredded through the tissue effortlessly, an explosion of crimson giblets blown across the kitchen counter and sink, the refrigerator, his stomach, thighs, and feet. He held up his other hand to block the blowback.

In seconds it was over—barely longer than his webcam session with HellKat99.

Nick left the carving knife grinding, the circuit breaker in his mind so overloaded he couldn't remember how to turn it off at that moment. He looked at it as if he'd never seen such a thing before and didn't know how it wound up in his hand, but finally connected enough dots to see the slide button and remember its function as *on/off*.

Simple, sane.

He had just placed his thumb over the button when the awful tingling suddenly lit up across the fingers of his right hand—the one with which he'd held himself in the bathroom. Even amongst the streaks from his operation, he saw the blisters forming like islands in a bloody ocean, felt them shifting beneath like tectonic plates.

B4 ITS 2 LATE.

His 911 call would be truthful after all.

Unsure if he heard an approaching siren or it was just the grinding serenade of the blades, Nick withdrew his thumb and guided the carving knife to his fingers, trying not to think about all the places covered in his fluids, already tingling like a fresh bed of sores.

ANGELBAIT

It is indeterminate whether the fractured nature of reality and consciousness argues for or against a so-called higher plane of an afterlife. I do think it would be so alien and unfathomable as to render "higher" a misnomer, however. We seek to perpetuate our existence through other means—biologically, by legacy, fame, or infamy. There can be no saints now, only adherents to a Promethean discipline whose livers regenerate day after day, endlessly torn out and eaten.

—*Transitory Bodies*, **Dr. Braedon Obrist**

I.

SHE AWOKE TO VOICES in the darkness and a rattling sound.

"Hello?"

"Yes, I'm here! Hello!"

"I can't see anything!"

Two others besides her crying out in the void.

"Who's here? My name is Michael." A nasally voice in front of her.

"Isabella." Hispanic accent, also across from her but more to the right.

"I'm Tilda," she said.

Thirty-four, divorced, and blessed with a vision of horror—mustn't forget that.

That was something that always waited in the dark, rather ironically.

Don't you see the light? she'd asked Lydia.

But her sister and all the others only saw the blood that day.

The rattling returned.

"Can anyone move?" Michael said.

Tilda tried to stand but didn't get far before something caught her wrists.

"I'm chained to the wall!" Isabella said.

"How did we get here? I don't remember any—"

"Wait, do you hear that?"

"Shhh!"

Tilda listened. Before she heard anything beyond the clinking of their chains, she first noticed a smell: musty and putrid, but beneath that, an almost pleasant sweetness. Not quite rewarding enough to endure the overarching reek.

Far off to her left, a sound between an exhale and a groan, like the impression someone would make of a ghost at a campfire story. Her imagination filled in the blanks with something unspeakably horrifying, so easy to conjure when she couldn't see her hand in front of her face.

Anything could be over there.

"I hear it," Michael whispered.

Overhead, a large bolt slid through its metal catch and a door nudged open, amidst the squeaking of haunted house hinges. Weak light bled through the opening upon a stairwell, and the dying sun revealed the nightmare chained down here with them.

Tilda almost wished it better reflected the phantasms of her imagination after all.

II.

It was a man, or at least had been once upon a time, his deformities apparent in the dim pool of light even before someone flipped on overhead fluorescents. He sat with his arms folded around tented legs, no full fingers to clasp together. They were like bulbous sausages snipped off at random lengths. The flesh had peeled back from the knuckles as if not elastic enough to seal them up, opening a large divot to coral-colored tissue beneath. Where there should have been toes, he instead had gangrenous, oozing ridges, which surely accounted for the sweetness amongst the rot. Between the hands and blocks of his feet a network of sores traversed his legs, some like gigantic hives about to burst, others which already had. His face looked rubbery, malleable, with shapes imprinted across the forehead as if sculpted with fingers which never smoothed out the skin again. The nose retained no cartilage, reduced to two caverns into the sinuses like one might see on a skull. Each tortured wheeze of air created a tiny whistle, and a bubbling response on exhale from mucus dribbling out of the openings.

Tilda supposed he couldn't be bothered to wipe himself when he had so many leaks. One eye looked out impassively, the other permanently slit from a swollen lid.

An overload of repulsion prevented her from contextualizing his presence—who he could be, what made him this way, how he factored into any of this.

The light also showed her in a maroon shirt and faded jeans she only wore around the house. She recalled them as her wardrobe during the contentious call with Lydia. She hung up on her sister first this time, and shortly after that, the memories stopped until the dark.

Footsteps clumped down the stairs. If Tilda expected any big revelation about the identity of their captor—*hey, that's the janitor from the community center!*—he disappointed her when he drew near enough to see his face.

She didn't know him; had not seen him skulking around the block the night she disappeared. He looked strong enough to crack a tree trunk in a bear hug. Carrying her to a van would present no problem. Ditto breaking someone over one knee for trying to stop him.

Were further intimidation required, he also carried a spear ornate enough for the gates of a bourgeois neighborhood.

He nodded at the living monstrosity in passing, just like any fellow passenger on an elevator, then walked over to Tilda and her group. He smiled at them and closed his eyes, as if savoring the ambiance.

Tilda took her first look at the others and the immediate surroundings. The walls were concrete, bare but for the shackles, and the oval of a drain in the floor. Had this nutcase stashed them in a bomb shelter? A basement?

Across from her, Michael bent forward like he could rip the shackles out of the wall. His bookish appearance—gold-rimmed glasses, curly hair, scrawny—suggested more time logged in the library than the gym, so just as well for him the chains held him fast. To his left, a younger woman than Tilda with dark hair and a flowery dress tried to stand to confront their host, but settled for a seat on the floor after discovering the shackles were bolted too low and offered too little slack.

"Who are you?" Isabella said. "Why are you doing this to us?"

He ignored her, but finally spoke. "I can almost feel the holiness radiating from you." Tilda and Michael frowned at each other. Whatever they'd expected him to say, that wasn't it.

"From all three of you—Michael, Isabella, Tilda," he continued.

The blood drained from Tilda's face. He hadn't chosen them by accident, and he wanted her in particular.

Why?

"I guess you already met Simon over there. That's not his real name, but he doesn't talk anyway. He might have eroded his vocal cords."

A louder wheeze came from behind him, as if the malformed man were trying to answer roll call.

"Who the hell are you?" Isabella shouted this time.

His smile held, untroubled by the spike in volume. "All in time, Miss Isabella. I promise. I'm not important anyway."

"What do you want with us?"

The man held his hands up for quiet. "I'm Otis," he said. "And I need all of you."

He twisted the spear in his fingers as he talked. Its massive head may have been longer than his hands from wrist to fingertip. He had enough of a walkway that he could move between Michael and Tilda with neither being able to touch him.

"Michael, you organized missionary groups to bring the teachings of Christ to South American and African tribes, while serving as a medical volunteer. You vaccinated their bodies and souls. Whacked off a few foreskins too, yes?" Otis chuckled. "Oh, I'm sorry, I should have put that more delicately."

He turned to Isabella now. "And you, Isabella, volunteering down at the soup kitchen almost every time they open the doors, leading food and clothing drives for the poor and hungry."

At last, he came to her. "Tilda, you were present at the Miracle of St. Mangum, the only one to see something besides the stigmata. It has to mean something, doesn't it? All of you with your holy deeds and experiences, living within fifty miles of one another?"

"Otis," she said. "Why did you bring us here?"

He grunted, as though it were so obvious he couldn't believe she had to ask. "You're all saints," he said. "And I need you to help me kill an angel."

III.

Later, once Otis returned the room to darkness.

"Should we talk at all?" Michael said. "He might be listening in somehow."

Isabella scoffed. "He thinks we'll be on our best behavior. We're *saints*, remember?"

"He may already be listening to too many voices as it is," Tilda said.

He didn't outline his plan, only indicated the spear had been "specially made" for its fulfillment.

"I've seen him before," Isabella said. "He came out of the laundry at my apartment building a couple weeks ago. I figured he was a pervert. You know, a panty thief or something. I bet he scouted for cameras. That's where he got me later. Never knew he was there."

"Maybe they caught him on a security cam somewhere," Michael said. Otis had grabbed him from a parking lot. "A SWAT team could be on their way right now."

Tilda considered this. Could anyone disappear now even if they wanted to? When she signed into Facebook again, she expected to see an ad for chaincutters.

"They didn't even find that Sarah Putnam girl," Isabella said. "And everybody was looking for her. What chance do we have?"

The wheezing and bubbling continued. Why did it sound so much closer in the dark? She pictured Simon slipping his shackles through a combination of malnourishment and the lubrication of sores on his wrists. She'd attribute the sounds to a trick of the mind while he crawled ever closer to her in the dark, reaching out with those infected hands.

She spoke so she wouldn't have to hear the sounds of his breathing. "Why do you think he has *him* here with us?"

"Simon?" Michael said. "I don't know. Didn't call him a saint."

"Maybe he's part of Otis' plan to catch Bigfoot," Isabella said.

"But what's wrong with him? Why does he look so...sick?"

"I think he might be a leper," Michael said.

Isabella cleared her throat. "Is it...is it okay to call someone that?"

"Oh God," Tilda said. "We won't get it, will we?"

"Michael, do you know anything about it? Did you see any of them in Africa?"

"Wait, you're worried it's not politically correct to call someone a leper, but you think I must have seen some while I was out running with the lions?"

"Sorry."

"I think you have to be around them a long time to get infected, Tilda."

But he could keep us here for weeks. Or longer.

Simon didn't sound like he'd be sticking around too long, though, so they had that in their favor.

She almost laughed. Otis thought her a saint, and here she'd started a dead pool.

"Maybe he's right about us being like a miracle version of the Avengers," Michael said. "So let's pray our asses off for the police."

"Sorry to break it to you," Isabella said, "but I'm not on the team. I go to the soup kitchen hoping my brother will walk in someday. And I only got *that* idea from serving a shitload of community service first."

"For what?"

"Vandalizing a church."

"Oh. Why didn't you say anything?"

"The guy wants to kill an angel. He won't drop me off at a bus station with a pinkie swear not to tell anyone what happened. He might just go grab someone else."

"Why'd you do that to the church?" Tilda said.

"My brother. They knew what was happening to him there, and they didn't do shit. They sent the guy off to do his buttfucking at some other house of God. But, hey, sorry for smashing a few stained-glass windows and hanging a blow-up doll on their cross. They're the real victims."

"I'm sorry," Tilda said.

"He ran away because of them. So, I did that. Now my mom has both of us missing."

"We'll get out," Michael said simply.

"You're right, this kind of thing doesn't happen to good people, like, all the time." Tilda lowered her voice, not wanting Simon to overhear. "I know it's bad to say, but...if Simon's hands fall off, he'll be out of the chains. He could get out."

Michael laughed. "Leprosy doesn't work like in all the jokes. *Keep the tip* and all that. Even if it did, how would he open a door with no hands? Or dial 911? Someone would probably swerve to run him over if he got out on the street...but he wouldn't blow apart like the guy in *Robocop.* That'll never happen. Let's just hope the cops are headed here right now."

"We don't even know when now is," Isabella said.

The weight of nothingness pushed in on Tilda. "If we don't get rescued, what's he going to do when he doesn't get what he wants?"

IV.

Days may have passed, maybe only minutes. It amounted to the same in the void. At one point Otis brought buckets down for all of them as a sanitation system but gave them no water, no food. It couldn't have been more than three days—the human body couldn't survive much longer without water—but it seemed like it. He also gave them no indication how they factored into his plan, presenting himself only as formidable and unknowable.

No overtures toward rape, though, thankfully.

Simon expanded his repertoire from wheezes, whistles, and bubbles to slurping and sucking. It went a long way to dispelling the worst of Tilda's hunger, but the torture of thirst remained. The dryness of their throats leveled off the conversations of hope, despair, and strategy...then more despair. They were grimly contemplating drinking from their waste buckets when Otis returned.

Tilda's hopes see-sawed when she saw him carrying a bowl.

Only one? And why the surgical gloves?

"It might surprise you that there's still leprosy, but would you believe there are actual leper colonies, too?" Otis paused and knelt by Simon. "I got him from one. No one really makes a fuss, as you can imagine. It's not like stealing towels from a hotel."

He examined the wounds. Though within striking distance, Simon made no move. He could do little more than dribble on someone in his wretched state, but maybe Otis would be so careless with one of his alleged saints, who wouldn't hesitate to choke him out with their chains.

"I went to that island to hunt. It was the first time I didn't enjoy it. The first eight or nine times I hunted people, it was pretty intense...but then it wasn't. If I didn't lose, it was just the same thing as before. I needed something else."

"If you need a challenge so bad, why don't you let us go and try your luck with Agent Orange?" Isabella said.

Otis chuckled. "And are you so sure I haven't?"

"Hey," Michael said. "What are you doing to Simon?"

They could all see *what*. Maybe a better question would be *Why?*, though no answer Otis gave could possibly satisfy them.

He continued as if Michael didn't say anything. "The lepers gave me this idea in a roundabout way, is the funny thing. I did some research because of that colony and learned some fascinating things."

Otis pinched a sore on Simon's arm. The pustule burst, and milky white fluid dribbled into the bowl he held at the ready.

"It got me thinking about the role of debasement in sainthood. Did you ever think about how everyone does the same religious rites now? The same ceremonies and lines, like Shakespeare plays with different actors. Maybe we don't see the same miracles now because of that. Everything's sanitized and rote, pageantry without meaning. Even leprosy is treatable these days, though I guess wherever Simon came from, they didn't take his HMO. He probably panhandled until they shipped him off to the island so they didn't have to look at him. I guess beggars can be oozers."

He repeated the process again and again through the monologue—found a pregnant ulcer or boil, squeezed it, drained it in the bowl. Alarmingly copious amounts. Simon sat patiently as Otis used him as a human pus nozzle.

"I think we have enough." Otis stood up and carried the bowl toward Tilda, careful not to slop any contents over the rim.

"In the thirteenth century, Angela of Foligno drank the bath water of lepers. She compared eating one of their scabs to receiving the holy sacrament. Looks like we have a couple of those in Simon's offering today, Tilda. You'll have dibs."

She burrowed against the wall, but the bowl hovered closer to her face. She gagged at the pungency of the concoction. Through the film of her tears, she saw those scabs buoyant in a custard of pus. She longed to slap the bowl away, but he'd purposely bolted their shackles where they couldn't lift them high enough to interfere.

Velociraptor arms for all.

"I'll give you water only if you drink it. You get nothing if you don't."

Tilda turned her head away. She'd rather die of thirst than play his sick game. She meant to stick with the plan too, but Otis pinched her nose shut. She shrieked at the thought that the gloved fingers which had just milked a leper dry were touching her bare skin. Ever ready with the bowl, Otis set it to her lip and tilted it. The rancid sauce of Simon's boils spilled over her tongue like the milk from a cereal bowl. She closed her eyes for sanity's sake then wondered if she should look to be sure she didn't accidentally ingest a scabrous wafer of this abominable communion. The taste fulfilled her prophecies of disgust. It was no holy sacrament, this curdled brew of excreted sludge. She would have spat it out, but Otis kept her nose clamped and tilted her head backward to encourage her to swallow. Her pinched nostrils did not alleviate the taste. The putrescence coalesced into a bolus of leper effluvium that slid down her throat in slow inches.

Tilda expected to vomit all of it the second she opened her mouth, but it seemingly sealed the passage on its way down. Simon's living rot slopped through her digestive tract as she sat there dry heaving.

Otis stood again, checking the bowl. "And blessed be ye, Tilda. You got at least one of those scabs. If you want the other, Michael, you better drink deep."

V.

Unknown hours passed, maybe a day. She sobbed at least half the duration.

Did her tears seem thicker, perhaps from pus?

She felt infected: Tilda, the patron saint of burst sores.

Conversation flagged among them, demoralized by Otis' misguided purification process to bring them closer to God—or whatever he hoped to achieve. Tilda had never been farther from salvation. They crawled deeper into some sewer of Hell.

In the ensuing silence, Simon treated them to a carnival of sound effects of a disquietingly masturbatory nature, particularly when someone maneuvered their buckets for use in her group. The incessant whistling picked up its pace as The Little Engine That Could strove for the top of the hill. Tilda hoped the dribbling on concrete emanated from his wounds and not his loins.

Otis eventually brought them water, as promised. He used Styrofoam cups— environmentally unsound, but safer for him. He also brought down sandwiches on paper plates. They had to force themselves to eat after so many hours reflecting on Simon's revolting bounty and its rancid aftertaste. They'd all vomited into their buckets immediately following lights out, except Tilda, who worried Otis would force her to drink it again along with whatever else she excreted.

Now however, as the door opened again, Otis brought them replacement buckets. Isabella had threatened to soak him with hers, but she behaved herself for the time being. He carried the old buckets back upstairs, ignoring all the usual petitions for freedom.

The expected darkness did not come. Instead, he returned moments later with his bowl.

"Oh, come on," he said good naturedly at their cries of protest. "St. Catherine of Siena starved to death. At least I'm not asking you to do that. Catherine could rarely bring herself to eat, but she once drank a dying woman's pus. She said, 'Never in my life have I tasted any food and drink sweeter or more exquisite.'"

He found a few virgin pustules to milk, but the prior communion required the lion's share and left the seepage field somewhat barren. In lieu of this, Otis implored Simon to forcefully exhale, somehow coaxing him through an obvious language barrier, whereupon he collected the foamy discharge with his trusty bowl. There seemed no bottom to this mucoid reservoir. While collecting the overflow, Otis suddenly took hold of Simon's hand and pulled the brace of the shackle back and forth.

"Hey, when did this happen? Oh, this is glorious." He worked a key from his pocket and slid it into the shackles, freeing first one wrist then the other.

Tilda, Michael, and Isabella shared looks. Would that key work for them, too?

"Come on, Simon. Try to stand. We're going for a little walk."

Discolored bands circled both wrists from where the shackles wore away his skin. He'd surely compounded the problem with his fist pumping endeavors, and were there any doubt of *that,* a closer look at his groin area dispelled the notion. The tatters of his wardrobe revealed the blistered, suppurating protrusion of his member, from which dangled a flap of glistening skin partially sloughed with his machinations. It swayed uncertainly as Simon staggered toward Tilda, revealing puffy red tissue beneath.

She screamed. One thing for him to seep and gasp several feet away with a courier for his ooze, quite another for the festering source to mobilize. He left a snail trail of gangrene smears as he lurched. When his legs gave out, he crawled the last ten feet to her like a wounded dog at Otis' feet. She saw movement in those abraded patches of his wrists, writhing yellow slivers.

"Saint Mary Magdalene de'Pazzi was a self-flagellator," Otis said. "But I guess she had a better appetite than Catherine, because she licked the open sores of lepers and chewed the maggots of infected wounds."

"Leave her alone!" Michael shouted. He made far less of a show yanking on his chains, though, no doubt dissuaded by his front row seat to the results of infection.

Otis knelt to eye level with Tilda. "I'll tell you straight up, nasal fluid is a really good way to contract leprosy. That's what most of this is."

He proffered the bowl to show her the collection of mucinous fluid.

"You don't have to do that if you do this instead." He nodded toward the maggots flopping in the trenches of Simon's wrist. "It won't hurt him any. They're eating him and he can barely feel it. They're even rich in protei—"

Tilda seized the arm and sank her teeth into the wrist. She tried to do it fast, eyes squeezed shut as she licked the trench of the open wound. The reek of putrefaction made it difficult not to vomit upon the limb like Jeff Goldblum in *The Fly*. She'd hoped to chew and swallow the maggots before she felt them moving, but she couldn't seem to work up the saliva. They squirmed on her tongue until her teeth scraped something on his wrist that burst, filling her mouth with the vile discharge. Awful as it was, it provided the momentum to swallow everything and free her from this decomposition rehearsal.

She vomited this time, as much from the lingering odor of Simon's rot as its taste. She held off until the others choked down the bowl of mucus and Otis rechained Simon, but reached for the bucket before he fully made it back up the stairs. Tilda heaved as quietly as possible.

Before the mercy of the void settled upon them again, she saw the grubs she'd swallowed whole squirming in the emesis.

They sounded like fallen teardrops a moment later in the dark.

VI.

"How long can he keep doing this?"

"When leper boy hangs up his dripping jock, we'll be free and clear," Michael said.

Isabella laughed. "Are you kidding? There's probably some hot-shit holy pervert who went ass to mouth on a corpse, so Otis'll drag the dead fucker over here and we'll weep for the good old days of pus and snot. I don't give a shit if you call them the patron saints of sporks and hand jobs, these people were *sick*. It's like *Two Girls and a Cup* centuries before the internet...but they did it for God, so it's okay."

"Don't forget maggots," Tilda said quietly.

"Yeah, but he only let you have a crack at those."

"Lucky me."

Michael said, "She's the only one of us to have a holy vision. I bet you anything that's why."

Isabella laughed again. "Sure. The vision."

"Big surprise, you think it's made up."

"I need better evidence than a hallucination."

"Hallucinations don't bleed."

"Okay, fine. But don't tell me because it was some holy statue that it couldn't be fake."

"You weren't there."

"And we have that in common, don't we, Michael? But you'll believe it because there's no burning bushes or old men parting the Red Sea anymore. You have to buy into tabloid stories of bleeding statues and Jesus in tapioca pudding. It's all you have left to convince you of *God's mysterious ways*. So all your suffering means something."

"It's not supposed to be a hayride."

"I never went for those either." Isabella changed tack. "So, what about it, Tilda? You've barely said anything. Tell us about your miracle or prank or whatever it was."

She hesitated. Michael would see it as an unequivocal blessing that made no sense to fear, same as Lydia. Isabella wouldn't believe it at all.

But what better place for the tale than this purgatory?

"My sister and I went to the St. Mangum Cathedral in Ledney," she began. "They have all these statues out front. Mary, Jesus, apostles, saints. Tourists take pictures with their iPhones. They pose and clown around in videos. Maybe Otis is right about that, at least. Sacred, empty things."

She expected rebuttal from Isabella, but the others remained silent. She could have been speaking to an empty room. Even Simon curtailed his self-gratification endeavors...either that or he just couldn't produce the *whap* sound with half his penile skin molted.

"We were at the statue of St. Francis and this...this *radiance* beside us started reflecting off it, like it was glowing. But Lydia didn't seem to notice at all. I thought, *Am I having a seizure?* I turned to the light and saw the Mary statue. It was like there was a small sun on the other side, with all these shafts of light breaking around it. Except from its...from her eyes. Her eyes glowed too, and that's what lit up St. Francis before. I couldn't hear anything. I don't know when that started, but I'd stopped hearing Lydia, all the other voices, the street noise, my own breathing. I was about to start screaming.

"Then Lydia grabbed my arm and I could hear her and all these other cries. Like someone turning a volume knob, real quiet at first. She got louder and louder saying, *Oh God, Tilda, her eyes are bleeding, look at her eyes!* The radiance was vanishing. And I was thinking the whole world would go dark too if it went away. When it left her eyes, I finally saw the blood too, trickling down her face. Lydia and the others seemed so thrilled. They didn't see the light...only the blood. I thought I saw something behind the statue. Just for a second. Then it was gone."

After a pause, Michael said, "Still think it was a hoax?"

"Of course," Isabella said.

"No one else saw the light but her."

"Yeah, I heard. Wasn't distracted looking out the window."

"It sounds like a miracle to me," Michael said.

"The others thought so," Tilda said. "None of it seemed very holy to me."

"Why? Mary, Jesus, and the saints, what else would you call it?"

She thought of the presence behind Mary. Obscure, but she'd seen enough to know whatever it was had been smiling at her with nothing of benevolence.

"Terrifying," she finally said.

VII.

Otis returned with the spear and said simply, "Time to hunt some angelcunt."

Tilda assumed she'd be force-fed more carbuncle extracts. Cold horror replaced her despair. Most saints led altruistic lives without stomach-churning sacraments, but Otis had not made them his study; it followed that his research would overlook any who passed away peacefully in bed, emphasizing far more grueling final hours.

She, Michael, and Isabella would probably all die today, without any semblance of the grace from painted depictions of martyrdom.

He remained deaf to their pleas and protests as he scrawled cryptic symbols on the floor with black chalk, reciting a language Tilda did not recognize and periodically tossing handfuls of powder though the air.

Multiple trips up and down the stairs followed. He left the door open the whole time, unconcerned about the volume of their shouts and screams.

Otis whistled as he brought down an extension cord winder with nothing on its reel and a clump of thick metal strands bearing several barbed pieces, like something police would roll out to puncture the tires of a vehicle in a chase.

"This won't work!" The cords in Isabella's neck stood out as she berated him. "There are no angels! No gods, no devils, no heaven!"

Michael tried a different approach. "If you let us go, we couldn't tell them where to find you if we wanted to."

"No, you couldn't," Otis said, setting down the winder and strips several feet from their reach, where he'd also leaned his spear on the wall. "I'm not in their mug shots. I'm not even online. Just believe me when I tell you I want you to be rescued. That's what all of this is about."

He trudged back up the stairs.

Michael looked to Tilda and Isabella. "What does he mean?"

"He's crazy, you already know that," Isabella said.

"He'll have to get close to hurt us."

Tilda kept an eye out for his return. "We can't get our hands high enough to go for his eyes."

"We can go for his throat if he gets close enough!" Isabella said.

"That's right," Michael said. "Don't hesitate. If he gets close, latch on to him with your teeth, tear the son of a bitch wide open. Any luck, we'll tear a major artery and bleed him out."

"That's way better than the other shit we've tasted down here!"

"What if he doesn't have the key?" Tilda said.

"I guess one of us will have to chew off a hand."

"Shhh! Here he comes."

Otis returned carrying a quiver of arrows over his shoulder with his thick arm looped between a bow and its string. Had he used these on his island prey?

"I'm not a saint, you sick bastard!" Isabella shouted. "I don't believe in any religion!"

He set down the quiver, withdrew his arm from the bow, and pulled on a pair of work gloves from his pockets. "Don't sell yourself short. You've suffered in someone else's place this whole time."

"Well, I'm through with that shit! Let me—"

He moved fast, snatching his spear and dragging a spike strip with him, sprinting between Michael and Tilda to slash down the front of Isabella's shirt to open the fabric. The torn ends of shirt and bra hung to either side, leaving her bare beneath. He'd opened a thin line of skin with the maneuver and, before she could reunite the clothing to cover herself, he sliced her with quick motions, creating a bleeding symbol in her flesh similar to the ones drawn on the floor. Her mouth gaped from the pain and surprise as he lunged forward with the spike strip. Any intention she may have had to tear out his throat vanished as he led with a fist that found its way down her throat.

The strip clattered on the concrete as he forced his arm deeper and guided the spikes in like a feeding tube.

Isabella choked, spitting blood down her chin to pool in her lap with shredded tissues from her throat. He extracted his arm and ripped the strip out like a lawnmower cord. Barbs rattled on the ground, dotting the floor with crimson spatters. The chains stopped her from grabbing her face, the scream silent, pouring from her mouth as fragmented syrup.

Tilda and Michael screamed in her place, in terror for her and themselves.

"When St. Eulalia was martyred," Otis said, positioning himself in the menial space between Isabella's back and the wall, "they removed her breasts. This was after they'd rolled her in a barrel and pierced her with knives and broken glass."

He crossed his arms to drape the spike strip beneath her breasts like a jump rope, then looped its length to encircle both mounds. As he worked his arms back and forth, the barbs ate through her skin in uneven circles, clacking against one another like percussion to the sound of ripping meat. The crude mechanism left more of the left side than the right, but most of both breasts separated from her chest when the loops snapped shut on themselves. Jagged strips of flesh formed petals around florets of bloody tissue and fat. The teardrops of excised mammaries became oozing islands in a blank concrete ocean.

Otis draped the strand around Isabella's neck like a noose as soon as it shrugged free below. He alternated with his left and right hands between the barbs, coaxing the tiny blades into her neck deeper and deeper with each slide. She gagged, face deathly pale, no strength to raise her arms, crimson seeping from her mouth and the excavations of her chest.

"They finished Eulalia by cutting off her head." Gouts of blood burst from her throat suddenly, then fluently, like the spray catching from a shower nozzle. Her head titled forward as Otis sawed through the rest of her neck, the spikes grinding against vertebral bone. "A dove was said to have flown from the stump."

Tilda almost expected to see something so impossible as Isabella's head dropped off. It landed lopsided upon one of her breasts, the face rolling mercifully away from Tilda. Nothing departed from her stump except final currents of blood in a weakening fountain.

"Disappointing," Otis said. He stepped out from behind her and made his way back up the stairs once he accepted there would be no miracle bird. He left the spikes like a necklace of garland, but even stretching and reaching with his feet, Michael couldn't get enough leeway to snatch hold of them.

"Go for his throat if you can," he whispered. "Or even the back of his leg. Or his balls! We have to cripple or kill him!"

Otis brought down a large iron bowl in a pair of gloved hands. It looked like something found in a blacksmith's shop, casting his face in an amber glow. Steam curled from within. An instrument they couldn't see poked over the rim.

"St. Lawrence was cooked alive," he said as he set down the bowl. The thing inside turned out to be a small fireplace shovel. He drew an arm across his sweaty forehead. "Not everyone believes that, but he's the patron saint of cooks, so close enough for me."

"Otis, come on, you don't have to—"

"Oh, don't let that bother you, Michael. I don't have anything big enough." He reached down to pick up the extension cord winder and hang it from a bolt set overhead. He fed its power cord into an outlet beside the bolt, probably intended for a handheld work light. "We better get this show on the road before the coals cool off, though."

Michael crouched open-mouthed, poised to sink his teeth into any vulnerable place he could. Once again, it didn't matter. Otis retrieved his spear and plunged it into Michael's belly, keeping his throat, balls, and Achilles a couple of feet away from any potential bite wounds.

Michael's scream gurgled, bright blood dribbling between his lips. Otis hiked the spear, opening a deep groove from the initial puncture. He put a palm to Michael's forehead and knocked him against the wall, preventing any biting in extremis as he shoved his other hand into the groove. It disappeared to the wrist and emerged with a fistful of rubbery rope. Otis hoisted it, unraveling from Michael's stomach until he fixed it to the cord winder. He flipped a switch and Michael's intestines wrapped around the device, spiraling from the cavity until it strung along his stomach too, like a chair lift made from his alimentary canal.

Michael had enough reach to clutch at his organs but lacked the strength to seize them.

They oozed through the other side of his fingers like handkerchiefs in a magician's act.

Otis held Michael's head again as he tore aside an abdominal flap to increase the opening. He scooped up a shovelful of glowing coals and upended them into the cavity. The remnants of entrails sizzled over the sound of Michael's screams. Steam drifted from the tear in his belly and some of the innards drawn up from the extension cord winder, like smoked sausages. His pancreas squirmed out to slither in his lap, hissing from the basting of gastric juices.

Perhaps the worst thing for Tilda, even beyond witnessing Michael's suffering, was the grumbling from her stomach at the scent of cooking meat. Her gorge rose, but her mouth watered all the same.

Something snapped and digestive fluids trickled across the concrete as the last of the organ trail joined the winder. The coils bulged where they draped lopsidedly over one another and the obstruction of the stomach. The last strip flipped over and over until Otis turned off the motor. Juices hissed and bubbled from Michael's abdomen, the only sounds he could make now. He lay slumped against the wall, glassy eyes fixed on Tilda, as though to assure her that now it was her turn.

Tilda sobbed. She'd seen what she'd seen at St. Mangum and it meant nothing. She would endure the same humiliations of the flesh as those who had not beheld that statue, would meet her end not knowing why only she saw the light.

Otis set his spear against the wall. Red trails snaked down the concrete from its tip. "So now we come to it, Tilda." He picked up the bow he'd brought down earlier and notched one of the arrows.

"What about him?" Tilda nodded her head toward Simon.

"He's already served his great purpose to humble you all."
He assumed an archer's stance. "When they tried to drown St.
Philomena, angels cut the rope to her anchor."

He released the bowstring. Tilda tried to move but from ten
feet away, he couldn't miss.

Fire erupted from her shoulder. The arrow cracked her collar
bone.

Otis reached for his quiver. "So, they shot her with arrows.
Again, the angels came to her aid, healing her wounds and even
sending arrows back the other way."

The next arrow struck her other shoulder. The third hit lower, in her pectoral muscle. The fourth hit the opposite pec. Tilda
shrank from the pain, barely able to breathe. The contraction of
her chest caused the arrowheads to gouge her deeper.

Otis looked around expectantly. He found nothing but a dim
basement with a wheezy leper, a gasping Tilda, dripping organs
from a cord winder, and two shackled bodies in spreading pools
of blood. He withdrew a screwdriver from one of his pockets.

"You're going to let me do this? She's one of your saints!
Won't you help her?"

No cavalry appeared, heavenly or otherwise.

He approached Tilda with the screwdriver. She prepared to
defend herself, only to pass out when he nudged one of her
arrows. She awoke seconds later minus half her hearing, and
barely had time to acknowledge the whirlwind of agony swirling
in her ear when he punched the screwdriver into the good side
and punctured that drum as well.

The beginning of her scream was the last thing she heard.

VIII.

Just like her sister at St. Mangum, Otis did not see the light. His mouth moved in Tilda's new world of silence, hefting his spear toward the absent forces he'd hoped to conjure; berating them for letting their champion suffer, perhaps willing them to heal her. It must not have worked for St. Philomena. Martyrdom offered no do-overs, after all.

It seemed too little, too late for Tilda as well. Why now, after she'd been stuck full of arrows and rendered deaf? It wasn't something she wanted to survive, and she wished Otis took her eyes instead so she wouldn't have to see this awful manifestation again.

She looked despite herself, now screaming for reasons beyond the pain. Something materialized beside Isabella, a being in flux, as though Tilda's naked eye understood only a mere fragment of its substance one second at a time. This had been the shadow behind the light of St. Mangum, passing through her line of sight mostly unseen, like dust motes. Worse, the familiarity she saw in its barely humanoid face and asymmetric features exuding madness, pleasure, vengeance. It offered nothing holy, and blood from stone would be no blessing from its derangement. Its body likewise displayed a disturbing incongruity, gangly limbs almost again as tall as a person, its trunk in the shape of a question mark that put its face at chest level.

Otis' awareness came belatedly, like Tilda's delay seeing the blood at the cathedral. He had time to lift the spear—just.

The thing shouted with its warped mouth. Air rippled from the cacophony and Otis evaporated like a ground zero bystander of a nuclear strike with accompanying red shadow. He exploded from within, blasted to instant red mist and sundry pieces of flesh, tissue, and fabric in the blink of an eye. His spear hit the ground and rolled through the blood tide. The wave hit Simon with the same incendiary velocity and obliterated him an instant later in thrown-bucket crimson cascades, reducing him to puddles of skin, blood, and pus. He sluiced from the ceiling.

The celestial illumination vanished even before all the pieces from the audience to the shattering symphony had fallen to the ground.

With no one left to hear her screams—not even herself—Tilda stopped. She remained shackled, pierced, and punctured, but intact.

Because I couldn't hear it.

Had the being not intervened until its shout wouldn't kill her too? She wouldn't call that a benediction, any more than those deemed saints once upon a time should have considered torture and execution a privilege for their charity.

If that was the favor of the heavens, she'd sooner walk alone.

Something glinted in a trail of blood spreading closer and closer to Tilda—a key, still intact. If the scarlet stream continued to flow, she could reach the key with her foot and slide it within grabbing distance. She wasn't yet sure she wanted to try, not for a life imprisoned in the silence of her own thoughts, still able to see the manifestation of light.

She looked at the spaces so recently evacuated by Otis and Simon. It hurt, but she laughed. The arrows stuck inside her shook.

Otis and Simon left scarlet silhouettes across their respective walls, widest toward the tops. Like arms outstretched to hug the blast that undid them.

Or wings.

Tilda waited for the key in a dead world, watching the steady drip of the blood angels.

Orificially Compromised

*Consciousness is as malleable as flesh. The world
of the mind is its own reality and supersedes that
of material existence. The narcissist sees triumph
in ruin, the triumphant overlooks the spoils for the
specter of failure. Our existence may be a simulation where nothing is real, with only the man-
ufactured sensations of programmed impulses accounting for what we perceive as the tangible. We
could be, in effect, dreamers inside of a dream,
but on every plane, nothing is immutable—not the
carnal or the immaterial. Even our own desires
could become the instruments of mutation with
flesh colliding in the vortex.*

—*Transitory Bodies,* Dr. Braedon Obrist

I.

PORTER RETURNED FROM WORK to find Ella in the lobby of their apartment building, sticking pushpins into a notice on the bulletin board—a quaint carryover for those residents who didn't *do the internet*, though he knew she herself did. She lived two doors down from him in 1511. They had exchanged pleasantries in the elevator, something he strenuously avoided with everyone else when possible.

For her, he made an exception.

Perfume filled his head as he drew nearer, something jasmine-scented.

Ella stood a few inches shorter than him. Late thirties, brown hair parted in the middle which fell past her shoulders, gold-rimmed glasses. She always wore business professional attire with skirts and dresses that promised to slide up past her knees if she sat down. No ring.

She brightened in recognition. "Hi."

"Hey, Ella. Emergency meeting?" he joked.

"No, but something important," she said. "Or I think it is."

Porter agreed—and read the flyer aloud to see with what exactly he had agreed: "EphemaSpect presents Dr. Braedon Obrist, author of *Transitory Bodies: Anatomy in the Digital Age*, Friday, August 15 at the Keller Center...our changing reality and the threat of InterphaZ."

Ella looked at him expectantly.

"InterphaZ?" he repeated.

"You know of them, don't you?"

He nodded. "I've seen the name around."

Not untrue, and he had her to thank for that.

"Mega conglomerate. Medical research and technology, social media, weapons systems, foreign interests...You name it, they're in it."

Porter made the sign of the cross with his fingers. "Social media, now there's an evil if I ever heard one."

Ella offered an indulgent smile. "Yes, they have a video chat site to meet new people." She leaned in conspiratorially. "I lasted about five minutes before I'd seen enough dicks to last me a lifetime."

He laughed, deciding not to ask her familiarity with certain other InterphaZ products.

They'd kept their prior conversations PG-rated, but now she had ventured their first profanity—a most special occasion. Knowing she relied on the tram system also provided him the ideal opening.

"Sounds like there's a lot I need to hear about InterphaZ and this other..." He pointed to the flyer, searching his thoughts for an impressive word. When none came, he settled for, "Stuff. So you're definitely going to this on Friday?"

"Eight o'clock, if InterphaZ doesn't shut it down first. You should come."

He nodded like he'd only just begun to seriously consider the idea. "You know where this Keller Center is? I could drive us, if you like."

II.

Porter cautioned himself against expectations in the interim days. Ella clearly didn't consider it a date, as there had been no discussion of plans outside Dr. Obrist. He started to give her his number in the lobby. She waved him off, saying just knock on her door Friday at six-thirty. He'd have to hope she liked his company enough to consider meeting up somewhere that didn't involve a self-proclaimed technological prophet in the role of cockblocker.

Porter picked her up on the dot—if that could be said of walking down the hallway to knock on 1511. She answered in a sleeveless dark blue dress he hadn't seen before, slipping through a narrow clearance and closing the door behind her in a practiced fluid motion.

Inquisitive meowing bled through the other side.

Nola, the Persian cat.

Porter complimented the dress as she locked up, inhaling jasmine and relishing the allure of Ella's smooth legs and the carefully painted toes revealed by single strap heels. She thanked him without looking at him or acknowledging his own wardrobe, a white button-up shirt and black slacks he'd actually ironed for the occasion.

"Would it be okay if we stopped at a bookstore first?" she asked. "The mall's on the way."

"Sure," he said.

"I only have the ebook of *Transitory Bodies,* and I'd love to get him to sign a copy."

The humble beginnings of their deeper rapport from Wednesday weren't easily fortified.

She talked plenty, but more at him than with him and rarely about herself, mostly just Dr. Obrist. It was about as interesting to him as sitting through a presentation on a timeshare opportunity.

"Such a brilliant, brilliant man." She held up the hardcover of *Transitory Bodies* with gold letters on the cover and spine as they walked back toward the mall entrance. "It's just articles from his blog, they're all online, but I had to have it. Have you read any of them?"

"Not all of them just yet."

Or any of them.

He hadn't been inside the mall for years and the lack of foot traffic surprised him. It seemed more like a library now, with hushed conversations and a few homeless-looking types shuffling around.

"Aren't they fascinating?" Ella asked. "The way technology has not only changed our lives, but our bodies too, our psychology."

One of the men he assumed to be homeless fidgeted on a bench up ahead, a scraggly guy in an army fatigue jacket with jangling dog tags. He avoided eye contact, staring at the ground as they approached. Maybe he wasn't so destitute after all because he had something to eat in his lap. He reached into the bag with one hand while the other held a hamburger to his face. Poor guy must have some neurological condition, the way both his limbs shook, lettuce sloughing from the burger like pencil shavings.

Yeah, the mall was really going south.

Would it even be here in another two years?

"I keep thinking about Dr. Obrist's case study of the child who created an avatar of his father for a boxing game," Ella continued. "Well, with the brutal realism of the sport, the avatar was beaten to a pulp. And the boy sobbed uncontrollably, because in his undeveloped mind, he'd just seen his father pummeled right in front of his eyes."

Porter turned his snort into a believable cough as they emerged into the parking lot.

Ella said, "These weren't traumas a generation ago, but now the mindscapes of these children will be reshaped in ways we've never seen by new confusions of experience. That's just one facet of this."

He nodded, thinking, *Maybe don't put a controller in the little bastard's grubby paws until he knows how to use the block button.*

"That's like some of the weird stuff going on in Morgan and Sandalwood now," Porter said. "The Sandalwood Syndrome thing, and all those kinks they keep coming up with."

It felt almost scandalous to make this observation, knowing how both their thoughts were directed toward sexuality—and aberrant forms of it.

Porter held the car door open for her. Her skirt drew back about four inches above her smooth knee as she settled into her seat. He decided he could happily tolerate the endless Braedon Obrist exaltation. Maybe that was its own new kink.

As he dropped into his own seat, he dared to say, "Anyway, I can see why that would interest you. You told me you were in therapy, didn't you?" He laughed. "As a profession, I mean."

She'd never told him that and seemed puzzled that he knew, but shrugged it off. "I'm a counselor, yes. I work with women who have histories of horrible trauma. I moved here to work with the Raglan Group. I don't think you told me what you do."

He indeed told her when she first moved in, hoping she'd share the same. "I'm IT at the Somafree building. Basic troubleshooting, but we also write programs for the website and go through the grind to test them. So, if you get a virus or anything like that, feel free to ask for my help."

Ella laughed humorlessly. "It's changing our language, too, isn't it?" She patted his arm. "Well, thank you, I'll keep you in mind when I have a virus. I bet if I ever do, it will be called InterphaZ."

III.

Hoping to score some points, Porter dropped her off in front of the Keller Center while he drove off to find a parking spot and regroup. He'd spent more time with her in the past forty-five minutes than the last six weeks combined but if anything, he felt closer to Braedon Obrist. He'd known little about him, beyond being mouthpiece and research director for EphemaSpect, a rival to InterphaZ positing themselves as some gluten-free alternative to corporation dominance. Now he knew about the eye-glazing articles too, which somehow earned Obrist enough cachet to assure a good turn-out for speaking engagements like this one, making the most of his fifteen news cycles of fame.

Porter found Ella in the atrium introducing herself to a couple of fellow guzzlers of the Obrist Kool-Aid named Hart and Rose Trellan, recognizable by their shared copy of *Transitory Bodies*. She only provided a first name, though of course he knew the last too—InterphaZ identified her as Ella Geller.

"This is Porter," she said upon his arrival. "He's from the same building."

They shook his hand, but he quickly found himself sidelined with nothing to contribute to their Obrist discussion. They waited to place their electronic devices and keys in plastic containers before walking through the metal detectors. Handheld scanners traced anyone who failed the first pass. Standard procedure at all the doctor's engagements, some onlooker claimed.

Ella made him sit with the Trellans once inside the auditorium, and soon it was time for the man of the hour...an hour Porter glumly suspected would last the rest of the night.

IV.

Dr. Braedon Obrist took the stage to enthusiastic applause, an average-looking man at best—at least in Porter's assessment—closing in on fifty years old.

All that deep thinking evidently cost him some hair follicles too.

Ella leaned forward in her seat, smiling more radiantly than she had any point in the previous hour. Porter made a note to look up *Transitory Bodies* at home; there had to be some one-star-reviews to enjoy.

"The next pivotal stages of our evolution will be quantified by technological innovations. The latest have already dictated our diminished attention spans, where even as we are more connected, we also become more disconnected from our world and each other...from our own identities."

Several heads nodded with murmurs of agreement, including the seat to Porter's left.

"We tailor ourselves more than ever to an ideal of how we hope to be perceived digitally. It is becoming more important than the reality of this room, of everything beyond it. Someday soon we could see a new variation of identity theft which changes who we are even to ourselves; a future InterphaZ may lead us to."

Mutters of condemnation for the hated entity spread through the audience.

"While the claims are unsubstantiated, some believe Inter-phaZ's medical implants are a Trojan horse for nanotechnology—additional implants of mysterious purpose. To track the recipient? To manufacture disease their products would be needed to address? Something unthinkably worse? Even their so-called line of pleasure enhancements—"

VenEros...isn't that right, Ella?

"—records and stores the measurements of its users, male and female. This is no secret, either...what they call the Interdex is a selling point for their brand."

Porter's mouth went dry. Ella's face went flush.

"With so many streams of income, there is no shortage of policies they'd love to influence for their benefit. How comfortable can we be with these unethical and anatomically unsound practices from such a powerful company?"

V.

Dr. Obrist finally wrapped the speech up an hour later, though he could have surely stroked that InterphaZ hate-boner until the janitors were sweeping up the aisles. Another hour of Q&A followed with Obrist offering the floor to Ella at one point, who gushed over his book and asked if she would have the chance to get it signed. Unfortunately, he replied *yes*, so later Porter tagged along as Ella shoved her way against the tide to the stage. A decent line had formed by the time they made it up, but they didn't have a long wait. A security entourage stood close at hand.

As Obrist's pen scrawled across a page of her book, Ella turned to Porter to say, "Do you think you could get the car?

I really need to talk to him for a minute." She swiveled back to Obrist to reiterate, "Just a minute, I promise."

Following this disappointing dismissal, Porter exited stage left to play valet. She really must not have taken long because she stood waiting outside when he pulled up, reading the inscription in *Transitory Bodies* like a schoolgirl poring over yearbook signatures. He wondered what it said.

INTERPHAZ SUCKS! HAVE A NEAT SUMMER. BRAEDON "THE PROPHET" OBRIST.

They switched roles on the way back where he talked more, trying to draw her out but Ella gave autopilot replies and stared pensively out the window as if replaying sound bites from Dr. Obrist to drown him out. She'd recorded several minutes on her phone and maybe had a selfie of him now, too. If that were the case, Porter would surely see it on one of her social media accounts.

In the elevator ride to their floor, he noticed a business card sticking from *Transitory Bodies* like a bookmark, enough for him to see handwritten print reading *obrist1@*. Personal email?

As they stepped out on their floor, Ella patted his arm and said, "Thank you so much for the ride tonight, Porter. I hope you're glad you went with me."

"Oh, of course." Looking at her, he even kind of believed himself. "It was a real eye-opener."

"Brilliant, brilliant man. He's giving another talk next week, if you're up to it."

Somehow Porter held his smile. "Sure, if I don't get stuck testing one of those program launches or something."

But he had a strong feeling he'd miss out—whether his company had one scheduled or not.

"Great! Let me know." She waved as she walked away from him, calling back, "Good night."

"Night," he echoed and stood still a moment to watch her arrive at her door—the same spot where he'd seen the package from InterphaZ last week.

VI.

At that time, he'd known only her first name. So, when he spotted a package propped against her door that Tuesday afternoon, he "dropped" his keys to take a closer look at the address label.

From InterphaZ VenEros, for Ella Geller.

The full name led him to a Facebook page and various networks connected to it. Her pictures were not so revealing, sadly—selfies tended to favor the same angle, rarely full-bodied—but he still relished a deeper look than the one provided by their hallway and elevator banalities. She liked her Persian cat Nola, wine ("redder the better"), binge-watching, and freedom from the burdens of a relationship ("intentionally, ecstatically single!").

Much as he wanted her, he found it easy to imagine needless complications arising from their proximity, to say nothing of the stigmata if he creeped her out with his interest in the first place—admittedly the likeliest scenario.

Still, Porter had identified a few potential bombs in his time and done nothing to defuse or evacuate the situation, opting instead for further study. True to form, he researched InterphaZ VenEros and discovered with growing excitement, of both figurative and literal sorts, that they involved "personal pleasure enhancements." A different brand handled fairly simplistic vi-

brators and compact instruments; VenEros did the exotic, inva-
sive stuff exclusively. Knowing she'd bought something new for
this express purpose and would probably try it that very night
escalated his idle fantasy to a more obsessive level.

Before the Obrist talk, he hadn't considered a satisfying alternative until the doctor apprised Porter of one tonight in the
zest to besmirch his pals at InterphaZ. Now he had both that
and an opportunity to support EphemaSpect's competitor out
of good old-fashioned spite.

VII.

*The oSheath: This pleasure enhancer from InterphaZ will
change your life! Simply plug the corrugated sleeve into your USB
port and let it do the work for you! Adaptable polyamalgamatic
fibers conform to your erection while a self-moisturizing membranogel lining simulates the feel of* TRUE INTERCOURSE.
*Easily detachable reservoir piece for convenient cleaning. Easy
come, easy go! Complimentary 16 oz bottle of Depuramase steril-
izing agent with every order. PLUS: All registered oSheath users
will have access to the Interdex. Submit image files of your crush
and the Interdex will apply its highly advanced algorithms to
recreate her inner contours in your oSheath. If she happens to be
a customer of the InterphaZ VenEros line, you are guaranteed an
exact replica! (Click* HERE *for a list of confirmed celebrity and
adult entertainment endorsements.) It's not reality...it's better!*

USER REVIEWS

Camvale: Amazing! U won't know the deferens!

DarrylR: its like a dualshock controller for your d**k 5 stars
cant stop using.

VIII.

The oSheath arrived late Monday afternoon.

Porter hurried home from Somafree to wait for the delivery guy and prevent anyone from making the same connection to him that he had of Ella.

That was fine for *her*, but a guy purchasing some kind of space-age jack-off sleeve, well, there was no salvaging that humiliation. He'd have to move out.

"Porter Drazanian?"

"Yes."

"Sign here please."

Moments later he slipped the oSheath cable into a USB slot and his computer installed the drivers. The device possessed a pod-like appearance, thickest in its covering of black ridges at the middle which diminished toward a trapezoidal apex like a biomechanoid outline of the intended organ—ridges that could adjust accordion-like to accommodate varying girths. The oversized entry slot underneath would automatically adapt to the user's base.

Porter impatiently clicked his way through the copyright, registration, and user agreement screens. He had made his peace with the notion of the sleeve adding him to the Interdex database while he exploited it to experience Ella's exquisitely recreated contours. It made a solitary pursuit uncomfortably global, but you couldn't jump in the water without getting wet. He doubted anyone would program some malleable VenEros dildo in his mold, then laugh and call a Johnny Wadd-ible pronto.

He imagined Ella trying him out of some strange (and remote) curiosity, but she probably gave her VenEros apparatus up for Lent in her anti-InterphaZ hysteria. Perhaps she only learned the Interdex database caveat after the fact, then stumbled on Dr. Obrist's accusations of their unethicality in her outrage. Such medicine had to go down easier than failure to read the fine print.

With the oSheath in place on him—disconcertingly unlifelike after all the hype and a hundred ninety-nine bucks—Porter performed a drag and drop operation to supply the Interdex one of Ella's selfies. Facial recognition could correlate it with her online profiles and registration info. In seconds the sheath stirred to life, the clearance around his organ vanishing as the inner sleeve conformed.

He wasn't so impressed so far, could definitely tell the "deferens"...

Then the sleeve cinched around him solidly, and he would have sworn its interior had been replaced by living flesh...flesh with escalating, dripping heat. It squeezed and shuddered along his cock the way Ella undoubtedly would, grinding up and down on him. He found her picture from Friday. She had indeed tweeted a selfie (@anellasyst) with Obrist which he retweeted, and Hart and Rose "hearted." Porter groaned as he fought to minimize the JPEG so Obrist didn't get to horn in on the fantasy. He had to hurry, totally bereft now of the cognitive ability required to click the InterphaZ icon and find a slower vibration setting. Maybe he should have run the tutorial after all. The tight wet grip sealed him, simulated the clamping of her inner walls in frenzied abandon. Ella's picture smiled at him, pleased by his invigoration.

In less than a minute he jolted in the chair as if electrocuted, then sought the complimentary Depuramase bottle.

IX.

By Friday morning he found himself in need of a different doctor than Obrist and begged for an emergency appointment.

"I think I have something," he said, somewhat unnecessarily given the evidence on display. The professionalism of the windowless room, papered-over exam table, and posters for mental health ("Do you remember the last time you were truly yourself?") and diabetes awareness couldn't entirely alleviate his discomfort.

As if it would stop Dr. Vinokur from crouching down for a closer look, Porter amended, "Yes, I have something."

Do I have to close my eyes? Will that help?

He didn't want to watch this scrutiny of his anatomy but he had to monitor her expression for any flicker of disgust or disapproval. Doctors would have that, wouldn't they? Like a teacher with aspirations for a star pupil who crashed and burned on the big exam.

Porter, I had high hopes for you, but gotta be honest...this sickly-looking penis? Total letdown.

Her fingers felt cold through the surgical gloves as she palpated. Did each touch trigger a pulse of slight burning? Or did he only imagine it after three days of this abnormality?

"It's not what it looks like," he said.

"No? You didn't have one of those illegal operations in another country, did you?"

"I just mean...it's not a *disease.*"

"Don't you want me to be the judge of that? Or in your indelicate way are you just trying to say your affliction is not of a sexual origin?"

Porter's face burned. "Right. That."

"No change in laundry products or cosmetics of any kind?"

He shook his head.

"Is there a family history of skin disorders you haven't mentioned? Maybe an undocumented latex allergy?"

"No. I break out in hives from aspirin, but..."

He left it unfinished rather than say, *I haven't fucked a handful of crushed pills lately.*

She pulled his member upright to examine the ventral side. The affliction encircled the whole organ in a spiral of raised flesh, as though a large, heated corkscrew burned its pattern along his member. Except it didn't hurt and the device responsible inflicted the opposite of pain.

She could be forgiven if she thought it intentional. It looked that way.

It began like a contact or heat rash, but by Thursday night evolved to this disconcerting sight.

"What aren't you telling me, Mr. Drazanian?"

Porter sighed. Though he mentally rehearsed how to divulge the information, he'd hoped she'd prescribe some sort of cream on sight without deeper inquiry. Ideally they'd both shrug like, *Well, that was weird but totally random!* and leave it at that.

"I used something," he said. "For...gratification."

Dr. Vinokur raised a palm. "I need to know...did this coincide with use of an InterphaZ product?"

He considered lying, but meekly said, "Yes...the oSheath."

It was like a DualShock controller for my d**k...I really couldn't stop using. Even after Saran wrapping my junk to keep the membranostuff from directly contacting skin, it still felt like heaven.

"I'm not going to be able to help you."

"What are you talking about?"

"I mean I'm not *allowed*. I'm not licensed. I think your device may have introduced an untold number of implants into your system."

Porter blanched. "Implants? From a *sex toy*? That's ridiculous, they can't do anything like that!"

"It's InterphaZ. They can do anything you authorize."

"But I never consented to anything like that!"

Dr. Vinokur looked at him sympathetically. "It would seem nano implantation is the new fine print of user agreements. You'll need to be referred to an InterphaZ-approved provider if you want to pursue this...but I wouldn't trust them not to simply initiate more implants."

Porter stood there dumbfounded, lacking the wherewithal to pull up his pants.

"I fear that in the years to come, Mr. Drazanian, orificial integrity may be compromised in ways we can't begin to imagine."

X.

Porter had heard of parasitic fish that entered the urethra. InterphaZ had apparently done one better, programming microscopic nanotechnology to lie dormant in a protective seal of membranogel until the catalyst of use. Then these tetanus seeds could implant themselves in Porter's fertile soil.

Would this feeling of infection become a genuine disease process?

He sat in the parking lot, searching the phenomenon on his smartphone. There weren't many alleged cases, and the only ones anybody credited were from medical procedures.

InterphaZ steadfastly denied any implant accusations about their specialty products, dismissing the damning user agreement verbiage as *content error*. They insinuated the complaints came from hoaxers seeking an easy payday.

This info was available to him and Ella all along, but you didn't know what you didn't know, especially with access to too much in the first place. Insidious details could creep past undetected like...

Nano implants.

No way Porter could face a shift at Somafree. He called out for the rest of the day and drove back home. At some point on the way, his thoughts shifted back to Ella.

The puzzle pieces all fell into place. Defecting from InterphaZ support so soon after her purchase, her admiration for Dr. Obrist and need to talk to him alone, a retweet about his new exposé on InterphaZ—she'd been a victim of the implants, too.

XI.

He walked to 1511 from the elevator, not expecting her to be there but hoping she would in the wake of his revelation. They could commiserate about their condition, a disease support group without an actual disease, at least not yet...the Orificially Compromised.

Ella answered after all. He hadn't considered how he would explain what he had to say— the language was still new to him...the implications largely unexamined...her involvement mere speculation—but she stood aside and urgently beckoned.

Desire enveloped Porter instantaneously, the full body seal equivalent to the rapture triggered by his first use of the oS-heath. Sex had been nowhere near his thoughts but over-whelmed him anyway. She looked exciting in a cream skirt and jacket with a black top, though that wasn't why: the inferno seemed born of nothing and everything.

More incredibly, he saw the same need mirrored in Ella's face. She'd shown no hint of it before but now she reached for him, tilting her chin up to lock her mouth to his, slipping her tongue through his parted lips. She melded their bodies together, nudging her groin against him. Her warmth seeped through the fabric to find where he'd become rigid as he crossed the threshold.

This only furthered the illusion of the day's dream-like impossibility. He'd wanted this since she moved in.

Ella led him to the living room section of the open floor plan to a black leather couch where she slipped out of her heels and scooted all the way to the far end, undoing the single button of her jacket at waist level. She braced herself long enough to slide her fingers under the hem of her skirt and pull it up to her waist. The silk cream fabric of her underwear whispered down her thighs.

Porter fumbled with his pants to offer her the same access, even as he said, "I don't think I can. I'm…"

He started to say *infected*, but she waved him off.

"Yes, you can, with me. I know you can."

She spread her feet apart on the cushion, knees out, and between them, he saw he'd been correct about her. Where she wanted him inside her, there were indentions in the membrane like the furrows of a cone-shaped drill, sure to match the ridges encompassing his sex. Had this eventually become her template in the Interdex after implants, with the oSheath shaping him into the ideal fit?

She helped drag his pants down and guide his erection inside, paying no mind to its new mold. The connection brought startled gasps from them both as their contours alternated between friction and symmetry. Where entry would have been a grand sum experience previously, their new flesh consolidated to create deeper levels of immersion.

A pleasure the equal of the need.

Ella soon pushed him to an upright sitting position and settled onto him, grinding up and down with greater urgency. The oSheath had trained him for this in a way. She finished just ahead of him after a minute, clamping tighter and bringing him along. He seemed to ignite inside her.

She soon unseated herself and stood up, smoothing her wrinkled clothes. Porter tucked himself away. He still didn't want to look at what became of him.

Nola meowed inquisitively in the recesses of the apartment, safe from the incursion of strangers.

The spell had passed. Did the implants allow InterphaZ to manipulate their pheromones to trigger this meltdown? Did his and Ella's close proximity activate them? It had used them, unmistakably.

"I know about the implants," he huffed, still breathless.

She nodded, rebuttoning her jacket. "I'm in contact with Dr. Obrist. He wants EphemaSpect to create nano antibodies. It might be the only way to purify us."

"Do you know what they're even for?"

Ella paused as if seeking a specific word. It went unfound. Porter jumped as her stomach and chest exploded, shredding the fabric of her shirt in numerous places like hot shrapnel from a bomb. Moist tissue clumps spattered the couch, borne on a gust of wind strong enough to stir his hair. The button from her jacket struck him in the forehead and bounced away. Blood and offal spattered his face. A misshapen mound of organs burst from the blown cavity, flailing tentacles in a whirlwind. The spinal cord looked crustacean-like behind the wall of toppled anatomical integrity.

Ella slumped to the ground, glassy eyes fixed on Porter from the floor.

He bolted up from the couch, mouth agape. He tried to spit out the salty clumps of her that rocketed into his mouth, an internal French kiss. Bloody fragments dropped from his hair as his head swiveled, seeking cover from what could only happen within. He finally stopped and looked down at himself reluctantly, waiting to see and hear his own detonation.

Instead, he heard Ella.

"Porter." Or a halting approximation of her voice. Her body remained motionless except for a fluttering in her throat—not a pulse—and the slightest shift of lips and tongue, ventriloquist-like. "You have to go all the way through it, Porter...all the way through it to the end. Assemble the weapon. Eliminate Braedon Obrist."

XII.

Determination to complete his mission drove him, as irresistible as the previous display of desire.

He arrived at the Keller Center by seven, showered and casually dressed, wanting to assure himself a front row seat. He crossed the metal detector without incident, holding a copy of *Transitory Bodies*. It did not completely shut, but no one noticed. He spotted Hart and Rose but didn't acknowledge them, and once admitted he commandeered an aisle seat in the middle section.

When he cracked it open, the cover of the book shielded the instrument sequestered in its hollowed-out pages from the people to his left. They'd never have known what it was if they'd seen it, though.

Dr. Obrist emerged to enthusiastic applause once more. When Porter stood up, others followed his example for a full-fledged ovation. The gun made from Ella's organs felt slippery in his hand, its body formed from the ruin of her pancreas, like a melted corncob, and the grip a conglomeration of her kidneys. A spleen remnant formed its trigger. Porter squeezed it, unsure of the ammunition, only the certainty whatever implants he'd exchanged with Ella would assure the function of the apparatus.

Obrist's delight over his reception quickly dissolved into distress at the sight of Porter extending the impossible contraption. It retained its form enough to allow proper aim, and when Obrist flinched, Porter knew he'd hit the target. Security converged from both sides. He fired at them too, and although nothing resulted from it, someone with a clear line shot him as if he wielded a pistol.

Shrill screams soared around him.

Porter sank to the ground, bleeding out from a bullet in his chest. Obrist stood far above on the stage, puzzling over the sequence. As if the revelation—

InterphaZ

—took physical shape in Obrist's mind, his head abruptly exploded in a shower of blood, bone, and brain fragments which seemed to suspend in the air for multiple seconds like lazy dust particles in a sunbeam. A cloud of mushroom fragments tossed heavenward, the mind of that brilliant, brilliant man a gyre of expanding gore. The vibrant assassination worthy of

JFK, though less *back and to the left* than back, forward, left, right, and all points between.

A crimson Rorschach blot splashed the beige curtain behind him: Flowers to some, upheaval to others.

Porter turned the Ella-gun toward his own head and squeezed the spleen tip once, twice. The second time, the whole thing seemed to melt like taffy in his fingers. Empty.

Horror dawned on a security team member's face. A delayed gut-shot manifested itself literally as a bouquet of entrails erupted from his belly in a heap on the floor. The impact burst through his back as well, blowing him in half. The trunk canted and slid off the waist, collapsing onto its back while the rest dropped forward. This was the embodiment of EphemaSpect, an organization broken in half, the organs detonating in bursts of confetti.

Someone else raised a hand to the Fates, imploring a stop to something that had no end. Porter smiled and waited for his turn.

TEMPLE OF AMDUSCIAS

We live in myriad realities—the unfettered lives of our minds as well as the practiced personae of our digital selves and "real life." These are amalgamations of a truth ultimately unknown—even to ourselves. Consider how easily we perceive the lives of others, able to identify the patterns and the paths of destruction to which they commit themselves. The minefields of relationships, careers, and vices we can so easily negotiate for them, but somehow never for ourselves. They are pointillist paintings we glimpse too closely to see the finer details. Digitally this all manifests as ones and zeroes, but it seems like you could quite easily see it superimposed over our aforementioned "real world" with the proliferation of emptiness in our existence. Where could a one go in such a maelstrom of voids?

—Transitory Bodies, **Dr. Braedon Obrist**

I.

Olivia sought the absences, the lost worlds sometimes so near to the known. Before it brought her to a gate to Hell, this search allowed far more earthly explorations, always with a touch of the surreal and the forbidden.

If not lost, Naughton was well on its way. Without a college or an essential industry, at its best it offered a convenient commute to the busier cities in a forty-mile radius and a slower pace of life. Eventually, those other places became more alluring, somewhere to escape *to* rather than *from*. More and more of Naughton's populace abandoned it over the last decade. Nobody wanted to live in the shadow of Morgan or Sandalwood these days, and the crash of 2008 only hastened the pull of its life support plug. It still breathed on its own, but haggardly. You could find extensive sections of forsaken businesses and homes, like frostbitten limbs whose cells could never regenerate, allowing for the desolation that awaited her on Maranatha Trace.

Traffic thinned considerably after five or six miles, as if most of the populace gravitated toward the interstate turn-off and the assurance of evacuation at a moment's notice. She found formerly main arteries of town clogged with stagnant blood. She lost count of the going-out-of-business signs and untold strip malls with empty parking lots and grimy shop fronts. Every other gas station had the tanks removed from their islands, and oceans of weeds blowing up through cracks in the lots. In residential areas, for-sale signs stood in leaf-strewn yards of houses with overgrown grass and bushes, empty driveways, and windows without curtains. No children to be found on the swing sets and slides in the park on a pleasant, unseasonably warm October Saturday.

The decay appeared to have taken deeper root since Olivia's last trip here several months ago. She rationed the visits, approaching them like the bibliography of a great author whose books she wanted to savor, so the day would never come when she had no others to look forward to. The excitement also came with an undeniable wariness she tried to suppress.

"In a quarter of a mile, turn left onto Maranatha Trace," the GPS voice instructed. A moment later, Olivia did.

II.

She parked where she could see the mouth of the road as well as the splendor of the withered business district.

Two-story buildings stood on both sides of the street. Sun glinted off windows coated in dust, some of the panes shattered with rocks, probably thrown by people who left Naughton years ago. Railroad tracks bisected the end of the block between the two-story structures and a church, though Olivia wondered if any trains actually came through anymore. The buildings were both brick and stone, some of them hemmed together like impacted teeth. A few alleys stretched between them to other streets with a more spacious arrangement of properties, mostly warehouses with similarly broken windows.

She'd charged the phone to full battery power through the eighty minute drive. Full-service bars. A text came in from Jiro: *Ghosting...really???* He worked for a fantasy football operation. He knew when to sit a star receiver but not when to give up on scoring any points in his own life. They both worked with numbers, a point he belabored as some kind of profound connection. She liked the simplicity of 1's and 0's in a binary system, but accounting work sadly didn't accommodate her. Neither did Jiro. A useful distraction two weeks ago, a growing regret since.

She blocked him. Clean slate.

She left her heavier flashlight on the passenger seat, opting to only bring her phone. Between the sun and her flashlight app, she would probably have enough.

Olivia gently shoved her car door closed to preserve the sense of stillness. No passing cars, landscape equipment, voices. The emptiness sounded tidal, with the slight interruptions of wind scraping through the broken windowpanes in an almost melodic hum, and the tap of water spattering a concrete block. The shriveled husks of leaves like desiccated insects scraped and crackled across the crumbling street in a halfhearted gyre. It fascinated her how these places deteriorated, as if seeing no point to the effort of preserving their structural integrity with no one watching.

She could relate.

She crossed the road, skirting a red marking that looked suspiciously newer, perhaps from a city crew still making the rounds. She didn't look too close, like someone in a dream trying to protect the spell by not thinking about waking up.

Farther down the block, a sign said RED CIRCLE INN. A smaller one beneath read VACANCY. She wondered how a motel sustained business even before the exodus began.

The street terminated past the line of disused buildings at the church. Five years ago, it probably raked in more profit some months than all the businesses on the block. Paint peeled from the triangular shape of its entryway. A bell tower soared above with ports on all sides and a steeple. On the marquee out front, someone failed to remove all the magnetic letters, leaving behind a black oval from a name in a book of the bible or the number of a verse, or maybe just the time of Sunday service. Technically, the latter was correct.

Some of the businesses retained lettering on the windows. She could read ANTIQUES on the first in line. The proprietor apparently hit the road without removing a lot of stock: displays were visible through windows on the top and bottom floors. Best of all, someone already shattered the glass on the front door. Usually, she could find a way in wherever she wanted to go, even if she had to help make it herself, but this was more convenient.

This might end up being the pinnacle of the whole block, but she wouldn't deny herself any longer.

She went inside.

III.

The owners undoubtedly took the most valuable items and citizens of Naughton helped themselves to some of what was left, but quite a bit remained. The sickly fall sunlight bled over cabinets near the street-facing windows. Dust motes hung lethargically in the rays. The shelves contained various knick-knacks, figurines, clocks, and statuette things whose continued availability seemed understandable. The remaining volumes on a bookshelf were noticeably bleached by years of sunlight.

That was a pretty stupid place for these, she chided, then wondered if bibles lay in the darkness of nightstands all throughout the Red Circle Inn.

Deeper in, a lot of furniture, mostly chairs and tables. More clocks, more cabinets. Ceramic dishes, ornate plates. So much random detritus, relics of a barely bygone moment.

Everything seemed both alien and strangely familiar to her in these shunned sites. She often felt like they allowed explorations of her own mind, as if its mysteries and contours were projected onto a landscape that she could access in a kind of living dream. It wasn't uplifting, nor did it offer some sort of communion with existence. Instead, it emphasized her feelings of disconnection, of some nameless spiritual decay within that answered to these areas. It once comforted her in a way beyond explanation or her own comprehension.

For all the allure of this place with its tangible atmosphere and furnished curiosities, though, she couldn't feel much of anything now.

A few years ago, this place would have been pure euphoria. At some point, a gangrenous familiarity seeped into the pursuit. It became less like her own lucid dream and more like the stammering account of someone else's. It reached nothing within her, played only as a random phantasm. Whatever this once gave her, the returns gradually diminished over time, not unlike the population of Naughton. She still sought to absorb this specific feeling only conjured by the convergence of something left and something lost, but it stayed hidden now, even in hidden places.

She didn't care to speculate what this apathy meant long term. What was left in the absence of absence?

Olivia worked her way to the back of the room, ignoring the stairs for now. The light met too many obstacles to reach her, with no windows on this side of the building. Old mirrors hung on the wall with ornate bronze frames, the glass layered with dust. Could any of that come from skin cells with the perpetual absence of skin in here? It turned her reflection into a faceless shape.

She pulled her shirt sleeve up over her palm and wiped away a swath. The mirror hung in the right place to reflect the entrance to the shop, and a blonde woman stood there now, reaching inside.

Olivia coughed from her sudden intake of breath and dust.

So much for any element of surprise or chance to hide.

The woman twitched too, like a living mirror.

Olivia whirled. Two others stood behind the blonde now, a man and a woman.

She got her cough under control, lightheaded from the intrusion of these strangers and the chagrin of feeling like they caught her in some embarrassing private moment. Also, she became acutely aware of how far from help she was if these three meant her any harm.

How had she not heard them?

"Aw, man," the blonde said, downcast. "Did you already find it?"

Olivia looked around as if she'd know "it" when she saw it. She hadn't noticed any obvious treasures in her initial pass; quite the opposite. "Find what?"

"She doesn't know, Angela," the man said. "You're okay."

All three were younger than Olivia, mid-twenties at the most. The guy kept his hair close-cropped on the sides, thicker on top. The other one might have been his girlfriend, a fair-skinned woman with dyed black hair. He kept his hand on her back.

"I haven't found anything," Olivia said. "I'm just looking."

It seemed a funny thing to say in an abandoned store.

The one called Angela stepped deeper inside. "So you're not geocaching?"

"No." Nothing about their appearance belied anything sinister, but unmistakable relief swept over Olivia.

"Oh, cool."

"Why are you here, then?" the guy said. "Picking up some free antiques?"

"No, I...": She stopped, embarrassed.

"No judgment," the black-haired woman said.

"I'm really not."

She'd never encountered anyone on one of her explorations, never had to come up with an excuse. If asked about her weekend at work, she would merely say she went hiking. People thought they understood that, and it rarely required any follow-up inquiry or embellishment.

She finally added, "I just wanted to see."

"It's kind of cool," he said, looking around the store doubtfully. "I guess. Is that your car across the street?"

Olivia made a noncommittal grunt and said, "You're local?"

"God, no," the other woman said. "Iona."

"Woodsman territory," the guy joked.

Olivia recognized the town name, much closer than hers. Some little girl disappeared there awhile back, #prayforgwendolyn trending locally. Olivia had found that notion almost alluring: vanishing into nothingness. She chose to see it that way, rather than anything supernatural or some maniac or the girls' parents.

She opted not to volunteer how far she came, twice as far they did. This already seemed weird enough. She wished she'd stayed there today, and wondered if she'd ever feel like coming back here now. In this moment, the already fleeting enticement of Naughton seemed effectively spoiled altogether. She'd been brought all the way out of herself, from some kind of guided unconsciousness to pure self-consciousness.

Hell is other people, as the saying went.

"Do you come to Naughton a lot?" Olivia asked. She didn't care, she just hoped her questions would deflect any they might want to ask her.

The man scoffed. "First time. Last time, too, with any luck."

His girlfriend said, "I kind of like it. It's so..." She trailed off for want of the right word.

"Shit?"

She rolled her eyes. "No. Wrong."

"Mya, it's all junk."

"Okay, yeah, but it's still great. Hey, I call dibs if we find any taxidermy."

Angela glanced at them disapprovingly and addressed Olivia again. "You haven't seen anyone else, have you?"

"Not a soul," Olivia said.

Angela walked deeper into the store, eyes glued to her phone. Her friends tracked her, and for a moment Olivia felt gloriously forgotten.

"Don't think it's here," Angela said. She tilted her head back. "Must be upstairs. Were you already up there?"

All eyes returned to Olivia. She shook her head, wanting to vanish.

"Okay, we can all go up together and check it out."

Or not, Olivia thought, but she felt hopelessly caught in this unexpected current.

The mouth of the staircase opened right beside her. The exit seemed a long way off.

"Just hang back from Angela," the guy advised. "She'll mow you down to get there first."

"Oh, shut up, Noel," she said, laughing, but she angled past Olivia to get to the steps ahead of her. "I'm Angela, by the way."

They exchanged names as they followed, Olivia as mystified as ever by the notion that everything inside of her could be summarized in six letters. The risers took her to a quarter-space landing, then back around for another six or seven stairs to the top. Noel and Mya clumped behind her.

"Is this your first time geocaching?" Mya asked.

Olivia answered something affirmative. She only knew a little about it. You downloaded an app, which gave you the GPS coordinates to hidden containers other players left behind for you to find. It struck her as more of a group activity, and while it might have been convenient with some of her destinations, it held no interest. The concept of any sort of *intent* within the ruins would have spoiled the endeavor for her as efficiently as this unexpected meeting.

"We're mostly just tagging along with Angela," Noel said. "She's big on the whole FTF thing."

"FTF?"

They reached the top in time to see Angela veer around a display case, out of sight.

Mya said, "First to find. All the stuff in this store is probably way cooler than whatever's in the cache—"

"Doubtful," Noel muttered.

"—but sometimes they'll leave something special for the first person that you're allowed to take. So when Angela gets an alert about a new cache, we have to drop everything and go, just in case."

"What have you found?"

"That the shit we dropped was usually a lot better," Noel said.

Mya elbowed him. "It's fun if you actually let it be. Like an adventure."

"Yeah, *Tomb Raider: Antique Store* was the best one."

Mya ignored him. "There was a gift card once, that was probably the best thing."

"We split it on stuff like here, except, you know, actually good."

They tracked Olivia through the clutter of the second floor. Glass cabinets, chests, lamps, glasses, desks, rolled carpets, rugs, toys, posters, coat racks, radios, records, magazines. Stronger sunlight came through the windows up here. They heard tired hinges somewhere in the maze, but hadn't seen Angela since she disappeared in the labyrinth.

"Angela," Mya called.

No answer.

The hinges groaned again.

"Angela?"

"Over here!"

They worked their way toward the rear of the building and found her. A clear walkway spanned the length of the store at the back. Olivia spotted a water tower through the windows, could see the ladder up one of its arachnoid legs.

"You find it?" Noel asked.

"No, I thought it was in here..." She pointed to a door in front of her. "But it must be the men's room." She walked farther toward the rear corner.

"Wait up," Mya said. "You don"t know what's in there."

"Mya, it's a bathroom. Pretty sure I do," Angela said, but she waited for them anyway.

"Is it okay to go in now?"

Before anyone answered, she twisted the knob and pushed her shoulder into it. The door scraped against its frame and creaked open. Darkness backed up into the recesses as faint illumination from the front windows spilled into the entry. The room branched off to the left where no light could reach.

Angela held her phone at the ready with its flashlight app. She stepped inside and peered around the corner.

"Oh, this is weird," she said, moving out of the reach of the sunlight.

IV.

Olivia activated her own flashlight app. The blue glows of their phones hit the wall like misaligned headlights. Mya and Noel flanked them. A mirror to their left reflected the light and a hint of their guiding shapes, as well as the lone stall to their right.

Someone had dragged one of the display tables in here, sliding it against the wall. A small notebook sat on top beside a ceramic sculpture, the design so strange, Olivia needed a few seconds to even see it for what it was. It looked like a human head, but at forehead level its gray solid shape turned into something suggesting liquid, with several black strands unspooling above as though the head melted into the sky. The artist sculpted the mouth as a silent scream, and something about the empty eyes of the face suggested terror at its dissolution.

Above the table and sculpture, someone drew a circle on the wall in chalk. Inside it, two more circles with letters running clockwise between both, though they didn't spell a clear word or phrase she could see. Within the second circle, a configuration of connected smaller symbols, most notable for two more circles. In the larger one, the post of an uneven cross terminated in an oval at the bottom, forming an uneven line with two other ovals below the serifs of the crossbar. The other circle appeared to contain the Roman numeral III.

"What is that?" Mya asked. Her voice echoed with the acoustics. "What does it even say?"

"Looks like some satanic shit," Noel said. "*Am...du...cias*, maybe?"

"So this isn't at all the kind of thing you're supposed to find?" Olivia asked.

"No," Angela said. "There's supposed to be an actual container, like a box or something."

"You're sure that's what they left here?"

"Yeah." Angela took the three steps needed to grab the notebook off the table. "This is the logbook."

Olivia pointed to the head. "Are you supposed to take...that thing?"

"No. Most of the time you don't take anything."

Olivia nodded like any of this made sense, but she did not understand the object of this at all.

"I think we should go," Mya said. "Forget about the other two."

Noel put his arm around her. "Someone probably just found this on the wall and said, *Oh, it'd freak someone out if I left a cache here!* I bet there's twenty dolls they could have used instead that look like they'd steal your soul and shit."

Olivia frowned at Mya. "Wait, what other two?"

"There's two other caches on this block."

Angela pulled a pen from the spiral of the notebook. "And three chances to be first."

"And there wouldn't be a logbook if it was just some trick," Noel said to Mya.

Angela made an *uh!* sound. "You've gotta be kidding."

"What?"

"It's already signed! Steve and Brianne."

Olivia took her eyes off the sculpture, the apex of the dissolution. "Maybe they live here."

Angela shook her head. "No, we know them."

"They're from Iona, too," Mya said to Olivia. "She has a not-so-friendly competition with them."

"They must have been ready to go the second they got the alert. Unlike *some* people." Angela glowered a little at Noel and Mya, who rolled their eyes. She trained the phone on the logbook. "They both wrote *1st* beside their names with smiley faces. Ugh, I hate them."

"Pricks," Noel agreed. "Bet they already posted a picture to Instagram."

Angela scribbled her name unhappily. Olivia considered the irony of how each of them had their expeditions to Maranatha Trace spoiled, both by other people they hadn't expected.

"Make sure there's nothing in it," Angela called over to Noel.

"Way ahead of you." He'd picked up the ceramic sculpture. A loose piece clattered and nearly fell from the head. Noel slapped his hand over it and gently pinched the piece in his thumb and finger. "Bring the light over, there's something in it. Maybe they missed it."

"No way they didn't look in there," Angela said.

She and Olivia brought their phones over.

Noel held the head out under the lights. He almost dropped it.

Mya screamed. She turned to the sink under the mirror and vomited.

Olivia backed away until she struck the stall door. It ricocheted and struck a handicapped rail.

"Bullshit," Noel said, visibly shaking. "They've gotta be fake."

They didn't look fake to Olivia. Maybe the low lighting influenced the group's imagination to run wild, but what she'd seen looked like genuine human eyeballs—four of them in a soupy red gravy, with the vestiges of optic nerves still attached.

Angela's light swept past Olivia, then shifted back. "Oh, God."

Olivia hurried from the stall before looking back to see what she'd unknowingly stood so close to. There were fingers on the wall, a nail driven through each one to keep them in place, fresh enough to have bled down the wall. Two index and middle fingers formed a line vertically, with four thumbs creating a parallel bar near the bottom. These all formed an inverted cross. Strange symbols such as the ones above the table were scrawled around the fingers, drawn in blood rather than chalk.

Mya hyperventilated behind her palm.

All the fingers looked to have come from two people. That would also match the four eyes in the sculpture. Maybe nothing more than a convincing prank, but Olivia wanted to get away from this room, back into the natural sunlight.

"We need to go," Angela said. "Now."

"I said that five minutes ago," Mya grumbled between breaths.

They shuffled around the corner to the front door. Olivia expected them to be locked in, but the door swung open. The expected reprieve from the darkness of the men's room did not come. It was still dark.

V.

"What the hell is going on?" Noel said.

It looked like nighttime through the windows, though with a warmer tinge than moonlight.

"We were only in there for a few minutes," Angela said. "There should be hours of daylight left!"

"I lost service," Mya said.

Noel checked his phone. "Me, too."

So had Olivia.

"Come on," Angela said. "Follow me and try to keep your flashlights in front of me."

Noel and Mya added their phones. The glows reflected off mirrors, glass cabinet cases, windows, giving the constant impression of someone walking beside them or trailing them. In the constantly shifting shadows, too many objects looked like a person standing up or stepping out of hiding to intercept them. Angela glided swiftly through the obstacles of furniture, end caps, and table displays, and Olivia brought up the rear since the trio moved so much faster. She pushed herself to keep up, waiting for a hand to clamp down on her shoulder. At last they veered around a wardrobe and found the stairs. It seemed a greater relief than it should have; not just because they could get downstairs to the exit, but that the stairwell still existed at all.

Maybe all of the strange occurrences of the past five minutes could be rationalized, but it felt to Olivia less like explanations were forthcoming than more mysteries.

The flashlight beams shuddered at the base as the four of them rattled down the steps.

Angela turned to the exit, angling her light into the flotsam and jetsam of the ground floor. This would be the last chance for someone who wanted to stop them from getting out and could track them by their lights.

Up ahead, the exit thankfully looked the same as before. Everything did—other than the stubborn refusal of the exterior of Maranatha Trace to provide the sunlight it was supposed to. A long counter flanked the wall on their right, likely the checkout. A sign Olivia missed before in part read: NULL AND VOID. She swung her own phone at the displays she'd investigated before, which seemed so different now, misshapen and alien. Between two bookcases as tall as she was, she found another eye. This one floated in the space between cases in a vertical strip revealed of a pale face, the width of two fingers.

Someone screamed, maybe Mya, and the eye dropped away into the darkness. Furniture shifted as he or she scurried past the shelving units, moving with them through the maze. Angela burst through the front door with Mya and Noel close behind.

Olivia emerged on the street last, thinking this nightmare had to end now with the return of October daylight. Reality chose not to capitulate. Something enveloped the immediate block like sheer black drapes, obstructing the parallel street she'd seen before with the defunct warehouse. It bisected the street a block to her left. She couldn't see where she'd parked her car now. Through the darkness surrounding them, something like liquid fire churned in the distance in red and orange bursts. Its faint glow reached the street like embers through a pile of ash.

Amid her uncertainty, she could nearly appreciate the isolation, a more extreme variant of her purpose for coming here.

There were lights on at the end of block, in the church, but Angela led them past an empty building and into an alley on the same side of the street as the antique store. They ran toward the parallel street Olivia spotted earlier but stopped short at the end where something like a scarecrow waited.

"It's Steve," Angela said.

VI.

Someone had planted a pole in soft ground beside the asphalt and mounted part of Steve's body.

Dim amber lit the bare flesh of his torso and the thin slices carved into it to recreate the symbol from the antique store, right down to the clockwork arrangement of letters. The double zeroes of hollow sockets stared back from the eyeless head, arms hanging limp with fingerless hands.

No sign of his bottom half.

A couple of yards past the body, the ribbon of blackness ran the length of the whole block like a curtain around a hospital bed. It shifted like some living thing.

So far, the stretch of alley remained empty with no sign of whoever tracked them in the shop. No one approached from the back of the antique store either.

"We parked through there," Angela said, pointing at the swirling wall. "Should we try it?"

Olivia looked at it doubtfully. "Maybe we can find a break in it somewhere else."

"We need to get out of here, now!" Mya said.

"Hang on, let's try something." Noel searched the ground and found a bottle. He launched it at the veil, where it vanished instantly. Something shattered an instant later.

They all regarded each other hopefully, surprised by this concession to cause and effect in the face of a mystical unknown. It was like hearing sounds from the real world while dreaming.

"Come on!" Noel said. "This is all Mysterio bullshit, just some illusion!"

He forged ahead, tugging Mya's hand as he passed. Within five feet of him reaching the wall, the orange glow in the recesses barreled to the front and coalesced into a whirlpool. The back alley took on a brighter shade of flames. The whirlpool deepened to a concave shape.

Mya stumbled back toward Olivia and Angela, and they kept reversing to put more distance between themselves and the vortex. Noel seemed rooted to the spot. He strained to turn around, twisting his head toward his shoulder as if pushing against invisible hands. He tried to drag his foot in an arc to turn himself around, but he tilted back on his heels, pulled by the force.

Mya reached out to him as if she stood anywhere close enough to lock hands and pull him to safety, shouting his name. His unraveling began at his scalp, pulling loose in bloody threads with the skin unraveling like an Ace bandage. Ruby streams, islets of tissue and bone, and shredded fabric spiraled through the air, gradually erasing him where he stood as the whirlwind ground him up. He screamed until his mouth and vocal cords dispersed to the void, constellations of flesh and blood consumed by the black hole.

Mya wept, but Angela shared Olivia's awe of the display, a barricade to any emotion as formidable as the wall enclosing them.

Shadows settled over the street again as the whirlpool receded into the nebulous dimension of nothingness, sated for the time being.

In the faint light afforded by the embers in the swirling wall, she saw the shadow of the man from the antique store gliding across the alley walls back by Maranatha Trace.

"Your friend is one with Amduscias," he called, walking unhurriedly. "He is truly blessed. You are all welcome to give him your souls."

"Mya, come on!" Angela snatched her friend's arm and they sprinted up the back alley without looking back.

VII.

Olivia let them lead, not wanting to run three abreast, especially when she'd be on the far right and nearest to any potential whirlpool. She didn't want to feel *truly blessed*.

Angela stayed as near to her left as she could, and Olivia fell in behind her, their shoes scuffing on the pavement. It sounded like Steve and Brianne's murderer took flight as well, but didn't pursue them down the back alley.

The backs of buildings passed beside them. They slowed when they reached an alley that could take them back to the main street, but it might only lead them to the man with the malevolent eyes. Something they couldn't see hissed in the darkness, accompanied by grating sounds in its throat. Heavy limbs thudded upon what might have been asphalt, but sounded higher up than that—maybe the stone or brick surfaces of the building walls. A human pursuer would have been far preferable.

They kept going.

"There were lights in the church when we were back on the street," Olivia said between breaths.

"The church? It's abandoned like everything else," Angela said.

"We need to go *somewhere*."

"It won't help," Mya said, still sniffling. "I don't believe in any of that stuff."

"You better believe!" Angela said. "You've seen for yourself. Whatever this is, it's *evil*."

Olivia wanted to dismiss it, but she'd seen for herself too. The strange symbols, the mutilations, what happened to Noel, it all suggested black magic. The man with the devil eyes sealed them in here. He'd transposed them to Hell or some near-enough netherworld. She wondered if that had something to do with so many people conveniently showing up to this forsaken spot at once.

"Look," Angela said.

The darkness loomed ahead of them like a tidal wave of black. Angela pointed to the juncture where the black ribbon rounded off in the direction of the church, spitting out the teeth of railroad ties to intersect with Maranatha Trace. Probably etched in blood, the symbol carved in Steve's torso appeared again. How many sigils would they find circumnavigating the block? She flashed on the red marking she'd seen when she arrived. Was that another anchoring point for the black veil around them?

"If we could erase that..." Angela trailed off, perhaps visualizing the possibilities.

"With what?" Olivia said.

If someone left behind a bucket of paint in one of these buildings, maybe, but right now they didn't even have access to bottled water.

She had left *that* in the car, too.

Mya shook her head. "You can't get so close, or..."

She left it unsaid, maybe seeing Noel's disintegration again.

They couldn't keep going straight, so they followed the railroad tracks. In the drape of so many shadows, the façade of the church stood out with the clarity of light at the end of a tunnel. The man could be waiting to intercept them either somewhere in the shadows or around the corner, but they didn't have many options; reversing might bring them face-to-whatever-the-fuck with that thing from the last alley.

As she ran with them, Olivia wondered if she might not be better off on her own. Even though the same thing would have still awaited her on the second floor regardless, she felt more sheltered by the idea of hiding away by herself at the Red Circle Inn, not dependent on the whims and theories of anyone else.

They found themselves at the edge of the church's illumination. The doors hung slightly ajar, a bar of light peeking through. The stretch of Maranatha Trace stood empty past the railroad tracks, still no sign of the conjurer, but there were many sounds to which no comforting images could be assigned, and a sour smell in the air.

Angela led the way inside. The doors appeared unharmed from the intervening years, and they were even able to lock them as well as the interior door beyond. It provided only a faint illusion of safety, but better than nothing.

"Should we call out?" Olivia asked.

"That's why we're here, isn't it?" Mya said. "Someone might hear us."

"That's what I'm afraid of."

They whispered in the vestibule, but still heard echoes. The light in here came from candle sconces on the walls, but they found it bare otherwise. Two doors on either side would take them deeper into the church.

They allowed themselves a minute to orient while their breathing slowed. After the panicked flight of the last ten minutes, it was nice to have a clearly demarcated area with no obvious threat. Mya shook as she dabbed her eyes.

They jumped as one at a sound beyond the doors—the strange sounds they'd heard by the alley were now only a few yards away. Something large and mucilaginous slid across the face of the building.

The three women looked up as if they could see it through the walls.

"This is a holy place," Angela said. "It can't come in."

Olivia heard a phantom *can it?* at the end of Angela's assurances.

They waited several tense seconds for what the thing would do next. It sounded like multiple misshapen mouths strangling at different octaves. Something slapped the church wetly, but the thing made no attempt on the exterior door itself.

"We better get the hell away from the doors," Angela whispered.

Olivia nodded. Closest to a narthex entrance, she slowly pushed the door until sure no immediate threat waited behind it. Some offices and a couple of closed doors flanked the walls, but nothing stood between her and the next set of doors to the sanctuary. More sconces lit the narthex, with candelabras stationed on tables. The interior lacked the obvious signs of disuse she expected. The light hinted at desks and chairs in the offices.

Had it not been abandoned after all?

The soft gleam reached a rail and the first couple steps of a stairwell leading below. Though another step and another waited beyond the stretch of the luminescence, it gave the appearance of some yawning chasm.

"Long as that thing out there doesn't try to barge in, we might be okay," Angela said.

"We can't get out, but that psycho can't get in, either."

"Maybe not the front," Olivia said, "but I'm sure there's a back way."

"He'd still have to get there without being seen and, for all we know, there's something even worse back there."

"This isn't a very holy place if there is," Mya said.

"Whatever's by the doors doesn't care about consecrated ground either," Olivia said. "It was touching the walls, even with that huge cross up there."

Angela threw her hands up. "Okay, I don't know! But we're better here than out there."

Olivia examined the door back to the vestibule. It locked, but only with a key.

"Someone lit the candles in here," Angela said. "Maybe they'll help us."

Olivia gestured to the walls. "Should we check behind the doors?"

"I think those are bathrooms."

"No!" Mya said. "I'm not going into any more bathrooms around here."

"What about the stairs—"

"I'm not going down those either!"

Olivia wanted some kind of weapon. If the steeple cross up top wasn't getting the job done, she didn't hold out hope for the handheld version. There might at least be something useful in a maintenance closet.

Angela creased her forehead. "Do you hear anything?"

They were silent for several seconds. Faint sounds outside continued from whatever horror followed them to the church, but Olivia heard nothing from inside.

"Okay, let's try the sanctuary," Angela said. Olivia hoped that name still held true.

VIII.

They approached a set of double doors. The congregation would have filed out through here, shaking hands with the reverend. Angela gently pushed it in a few inches to test.

"Everything's still in there," she whispered back to Olivia and Mya. "Maybe they never shut down."

Olivia had her doubts. Were they trying to save on the electric bill with all the candles?

The grass didn't look well maintained this afternoon either, not to mention the sign with one letter. Even if they did find any clergy, it wasn't like they'd been instructed on how to repel black magic at divinity school.

She hadn't been inside a church in over a decade, not since a cousin's wedding. She found the beliefs archaic, but more than anything she avoided it because of its communal nature. She hated the thought of being a drone in the overbearing hum of one grand voice in its prescribed hosannas. It struck her less as a call to heavens than the hopeless cry of something sinking to the depths.

The sanctuary presented everything Olivia would have expected from a typical house of worship and a bit more. Rows of pews stacked in two columns with aisles between, hymn books jutting from the compartments on their backs. Two doors up front, one on each side of the carpeted stage. A piano or organ sat to the right. The aisle between the pews led to the center of the stage and the pulpit, behind which were rows for the choir as well as another raised platform with a clear water tank, presumably for baptisms. Gold curtains flanked the font.

The windows betrayed nothing outside, stained-glass depictions of biblical events involving martyrdom, death, resurrection, salvation, judgment. Upon the wall between two of those windows hung an enormous, life-sized wood carving of Christ on the cross, stained a dark walnut color. The meager candlelight cast its features into shadow, a hanging void observing them in cruciform on the opposite wall.

Olivia watched the windows uneasily, such delicate layers between the sanctuary and the deformed world outside. Whatever slapped the wall out front could easily shatter the glass, as could anything else out there in the night.

They slowly advanced, listening, footsteps padding lightly on the carpet. Despite the signs of life, they hadn't seen or heard anything within the building.

"Maybe we should try the steps from before," Olivia said. The acoustics of the room amplified her voice more than she expected.

"Are you crazy?" Mya said. "It was dark."

"It's dark everywhere. You do know the candles aren't nailed down, right?"

She felt eyes on her from the silhouetted face of Christ on the wall.

No offense.

"We need to find weapons," she continued, "and it might give us another way out if we need it. I'm not going back through that front door unless this place catches on fire."

Even then, Olivia thought she might flip a coin.

"Hang on," Angela said. "Let's check the doors in here first. If there's anyone we actually want to find, that's the best place to look."

Olivia didn't argue; at least one of those doors might have a connection to the basement level.

A door opened up top. A flash of black robe swung past the curtain beside the baptismal tank. Something slid on the carpet.

Angela looked hopefully at the others. She led the dash up to the pulpit, their footsteps a stampede through the aisle. "Hello? Father?"

The man in the black robe hoisted something with obvious effort.

The grotesque sight stopped them all.

"Welcome to the temple of Amduscias, angel eyes," he said.

Though they'd yet to have a clear look at him before, Olivia recognized his eyes. They burned with madness and perhaps a limitless faith, if not of the variety they would have suspected from the initial glance of his wardrobe.

"Oh God, it's Brianne," Angela or Mya said.

Olivia barely registered it, too captivated by what he held, and how it could even exist.

He held the body upright like some large brass instrument, carrying it by the wrist and ankle of its respective limbs. The trunk looked to have been turned inside out, with a strange network of tubes fashioned from the internal organs, and various pouches secured by what might have been lengths of tendons. A fan of pieces jutted out like the valves of a pipe organ, perhaps fortified by bone. The eyeballs missing from Steve's head and presumably Brianne's stuck to the valves like the caps on bagpipes. Her head leaned back against his shoulder with one of the tubes routed through a hole in her throat like a woodwind mouthpiece.

Drops of blood plinked from the torn body into the baptismal tank. Red clouds burst like depth charges as crimson overtook the holy water.

Angela, Mya, and Olivia backed up, not taking their eyes from him. He couldn't immediately get to them from up there, but this felt like a scenario to avoid sudden movement and not provoke a mad dog.

"Why are you doing this?" Mya shouted, surely meaning all of it—the murders and whatever he'd done to seal them in this netherworld.

"For him," he answered, as though it should be apparent. "I am his savant and his killer." In a louder voice, he said, "Amduscias, I offer these souls that I may pass through one of your nine gates."

With that, he fixed his lips to the mouthpiece and blew into it. Breath rushed through the entrails. The sacs of hanging pouches expanded and contracted. A low burst of sound blew through the fan of valves, flat and foghorn-like, something Olivia felt in her bowels, as though he'd sculpted the instrument from the clay of her own anatomy.

"Come on," Angela said. "The stairs."

They turned back toward the narthex, the known escape commodity. The doors at the front of the sanctuary might take them deeper into the church, but both could be accessible to him.

A loud cracking sound seemed to rip open the sky. Olivia's first thought was of some winged nightmare swooping in to grab them, which added to her terror when something crashed into the roof of the sanctuary. Broken beams and plaster exploded through a new cavern in the ceiling. Vibrations shook the soles of her shoes as the cross from the steeple punched through the sanctuary, shattering the pew directly beneath it to hammer the ground. It landed upside down, as if the steeple cracked in the middle and tipped over.

The starless sky peered through the puncture in the roof like a black eye, open to anything that wanted access. The noises from slithering appendages outside were louder now, imminent. With a greater accumulation of debris blocking them on the right and the presence of that opening overhead, the three women bore left.

The Christ carving dropped from the cross to the ground. The strangeness of this didn't occur to Olivia at first, not until it became clear the figure wouldn't topple over to the ground. Then she wondered how it could have neatly separated from something that should have been one piece, while that cross continued to hang. Its footsteps thunked on the carpet as it stalked over to the doorway, the movement fluid despite seemingly inert limbs. Arms hung at its sides, no longer confined to cruciform. It stood over six feet tall, waiting in their path, its massive shadow thrown across the doors. The candles lit its face better now, a disturbingly placid expression cross-hatched by shadows from the crown of thorns.

Two rows from it, Angela veered right into the nearest row. Mya's shoes skidded in the carpet as she put on the brakes to follow. Lagging behind, Olivia entered an aisle a few rows away. The pews were too tight to run full bore, forcing her to sidestep.

Mya screamed. The Christ figure had hold of her wrist. Angela tugged at her other arm, trying to wrench her away. She lost. Mya's feet pedaled in the air as the thing lifted her up, its other hand clamped over her throat. Her head jerked as she whipped forward, followed by the crunch of bone as her forehead impacted the crown of thorns.

Olivia took her eyes away to clamber over a pew, stepping on the bench in front of her, then hoisting her leg over the next backrest.

A howl from outside tightened her skin with gooseflesh, the ingress almost directly above her as she propelled herself toward the back. Angela looked at her helplessly, a stricken expression as the horror with Mya played out at the end of the aisle.

She flailed bonelessly in the figure's hands, the thorns punching through her skull, her face, her eyes. Olivia saw what remained as she and Angela stepped over the last row to freedom. Mya's terror and grief were erased, eclipsed by a red moon with several punctured craters. Blood spattered the carpet from the crown, washing the thing's face. It turned toward them as they burst through the doors into the narthex.

IX.

The shrieks and howls beyond the front doors sounded more desperate now, in greater numbers. She and Angela would never get through them. They went for the flight of stairs to the basement level, not stopping for one of the candleholders. Angela employed her flashlight app again, assuring them of solid footing in their descent, though Olivia felt like if the light disappeared, they would simply fall into nothingness.

The sanctuary doors crashed open above they as they rounded a landing at the halfway point. A fireplace glow beckoned through the doorway at the bottom. They reached it as heavy footfalls struck the steps up top, and something hammered the front of the building.

They raced through the basement doorway and the corridor beyond. They may have passed Steve's missing legs, bolted to the wall in another inverted cross shape. The hallway offered only sporadic candlelight, with long stretches of darkness between each sconce. Did the architecture match up with the rest of the building? It seemed like too many steps down and too deep compared to the sanctuary overhead.

Olivia didn't think they would have found the lights, the pews, the Christ carving, any of it had they entered the church this afternoon. Unlike the antique shop, it had changed, become what the man proclaimed—the temple of Amduscias.

Solid bulky steps clambered after them. Olivia looked back as they rounded a corner. The Christ figure passed through a clearing of light to become a solid black shape.

Another corridor awaited, and another, seemingly with no tether to the reality of the architectural structure, until Angela gasped and stopped so suddenly that Olivia nearly knocked her down.

The conjuror stood naked before a grotesque opening in the wall up ahead, the shape of a stone mouth opening its maw to utter black. A chiseled snout and stone eyes completed the demonic effect.

The man's chest glistened, wet with blood and the symbol he'd carved into his own flesh.

Rivulets streamed down his thighs, over his groin. He held a ceremonial dagger.

"Do you hear it?" he asked them. "The music and the grandeur of Hell?"

Olivia thought it was the pounding of blood in her head, or the living blasphemy pursuing them, but she did hear it. A layered, formless dirge as conducted by a symphony of instruments like the one he played in the sanctuary. Bodies reconfig-ured to express approximations of brass, woodwind, and strings with bone, lungs, tendons—a crescendo of moans, howls, and screams, provoked to a spectrum of octaves at the behest of who knew what tortures.

"I go with nothing to the infinite nothingness, the most des-olate of places," he said reverently. He set down his knife and stepped into the abyss, and the stone jaws of the Hellmouth sealed shut behind him with the rumbling of shifting granite. It muted the symphony completely, swallowing it whole.

In the rush of deafening silence, Olivia had a moment to hope his disappearance meant the end to whatever black arts he'd performed. The steady beat of percussion from their other pursuer said otherwise.

Olivia sprinted over to grab the ceremonial dagger. The or-nate handle bore the Amduscias symbol.

"Come on!" Angela said.

Doors branched left and right as they advanced. Angela slowed to aim her light in hopes of finding whichever stairs brought the conjurer from above. At first, empty rooms, but then something humanoid and shockingly pale stirred and shrieked in the light, and after that they just worried about running as fast as they could.

This lasted until another corner, possibly the same distance they'd run previously before encountering the man. Multiple sconces provided the most complete illumination since their descent. The hall terminated in another Hellmouth, its jaws open but this time with the passage concealed by a drum-tight blanket of bloody skin. Angela brought a hand to her mouth as they approached. It took Olivia a little longer to recognize this boneless, muscle-less incarnation of Noel stretched over the opening. His face dangled loosely somewhere in the middle of it, as if skin was something merely draped over the musculoskeletal system like a blanket.

"Stairs!" Angela pointed to a doorway to the right, but a maelstrom almost the equal of the prior symphony bellowed from it. Whatever lurched and crawled outside had obviously made it inside and would be waiting for them, if it didn't come down to find them first.

The Christ carving appeared at the end of the hall, still blood-drenched in the curtain of light before the interceding shadows swallowed it again.

Olivia jabbed the curtain of Noel's skin with the dagger, expecting to perforate it and tear open a new exit for them. The flesh would not tear. She thrust the blade frantically, where it pushed inward like a rubber surface, but did not yield.

The manifestation of Amduscias attained its color as it stepped into the same pool of light with them. Mya's blood streamed through the whirls and angles of the oak face, its expression still unchanging.

Angela grabbed Olivia's wrist and gestured to the stairs. "We have to try!"

She didn't see the dagger slip beneath her chin as she pointed, maybe didn't even feel it at first when Olivia dragged the blade across her throat. She only turned back when a crimson torrent burst from the incision, so dark red it almost appeared black in the soft light. A high-pitched sound whistled from the split windpipe. Her mouth attempted to form words, but only issued a wet choking sound as she fell to her knees.

Behind her, a long tear appeared in the barricade of skin over the Hellmouth. Olivia heard no unpleasant dirge from this one. Another rent and another appeared as she worked on Angela with the dagger. When she fashioned a formidable flap, she dug her fingers in and ripped it aside. The passage of Noel's body tore wide open. Angela fell on her face as if prostrating herself.

The Christ figure waited motionless, as if it had reverted to its original purpose.

"For you," Olivia said, pointing to Angela with the dagger. She slipped her shirt up her shoulders and arms, letting it drop to the ground. Beside her, the reach of the candlelight revealed little of the quiet passage.

What would she find inside?

She hoped for the ultimate menagerie of ruins. Scarred landscapes so embedded with decay, it would be impossible to tell which came first and which fell last. The detritus of eons, repurposed as efficiently as the conjuror's sacrifices. What she'd seen before was a mere thumbnail of the worlds within her, but this would be an excavation and autopsy of a soul so alien and unknowable to her before. Perhaps within, she would find the transcendence hinted at but perpetually withheld in the dying corners of the existence she'd always known.

The most desolate of places.

"I go with nothing to nothing," she said, removing the last of her clothes.

Kneeling in reverence before the manifestation, she studied the emblem of Amduscias on the handle of the dagger.

Then she began to carve the first circle in her skin.

Last Time at Thanksgiving

We impose meaning upon chaos, or at least the indifference of reality. We find design in the purely random. The signs appear to us when we need them, easily dismissed when they portend nothing in the end. The cogs move around us and we call it seconds, minutes, hours. Yet we experience eons of loss and longing in the worlds within, while just our fleeting moments of joy are so precisely measurable.

Only the eons reset.

—*Transitory Bodies*, **Dr. Braedon Obrist**

I.

"You want me to tell you the creepiest Thanksgiving story I ever heard?" Kendall said.

I didn't—not at all—but he launched into it anyway before I got the chance to object.

"Someone I went to school with, his cousin knew a guy who came home for Thanksgiving with his girlfriend, right? Well, the guy's sister brought her boyfriend too. It's a fine Christian home, so everyone gets their own room. Middle of the night, guy's like, *I'm gonna get my dick wet*, you know?"

"Kendall—"

"So, he tiptoes into the room beside his. Girl whispers something about how kinky it is, doing it in the parents' home. And he goes off in her like a stick of dynamite then limps back to his room exhausted. Best nut of his life. Gets in his bed, and not two minutes later, the door opens and his girl slides into bed with him, talking about *Hey, I thought you were going to wake me up with a bang in the night?*"

"Oh, my God."

"Creepy, right? I told you! Okay, now, flash forward nine months later—"

"Kendall!"

"Seriously, this is the best part."

Across the table from me, my mom's mouth curled with extreme dissatisfaction. I knew that look well. "Maybe this isn't the right time for this sort of talk with you and your friend."

My grandfather seemed lost to all of this as he had since we moved him to Amser River Assisted Living, mechanical chewing with a steely expression seemingly his only proper function.

On the other end of the spectrum, my sister had forgotten how to chew, staring at my roommate like something in a jar of formaldehyde at the freak show. She seemed both younger than a high school sophomore and far older in her practiced disdain.

Kendall shrugged. "Okay, yeah. I'll tell you all about it later, man."

"Much later," my dad recommended. His face looked roughly the same color as the cranberry sauce on his plate.

I almost didn't make it home for Thanksgiving, and now I wondered if that would have been such a bad thing.

II.

My girlfriend was supposed to pick me up and bring me home, but the dynamic of our relationship changed earlier in November, from being a *thing that existed* to suddenly not.

Ashley and I dated since our sophomore year, which meant almost three years together going into college. The plan was always to stay together, and it didn't seem to matter so much that we would be hundreds of miles apart at our respective schools. We figured FaceTime, Skype, and texting would be a good enough simulation for reality and then within a few months we'd see other on Thanksgiving break. Winter and spring breaks would last us until summer.

Less than a month away, she said "the long distance thing" wasn't working for her—that we were only delaying the inevitable. I wondered if I would have seen her growing unhappiness for what it was if I examined screenshots of her from every conversation we had since August, like time lapse photography of a wilting flower. I doubted it, though. The situation had changed, but I hadn't.

I thought the same must be true of her.

We didn't have a concept of the difference in time and meaning beyond high school, though. It passes so incrementally then, where weeks feel like months, months like ages. Once I moved out, that ceased to be, despite the continued drudgery of scheduled learning. Time passed like dog years.

Even November flew by, despite the pain that went with it. The very air seemed to be pressing me down in those weeks, but it was always time for another quiz, another exam, another essay, as if to balance out the personal shitty milestones—another call sent to voicemail, another text unanswered, another Facebook message seen and not replied to, before she unfriended me altogether.

If I'd had my car, I might have driven to her dorm that first night, pleaded my case, appealed to history, hoping she would find a world of difference between throwing away me in person versus a pixelated image on a phone or laptop. My college prohibited freshmen from having a car, though. The Nissan my mom gave me after buying her new car stayed back home, and my parents drove me to the campus back in August. I'd been marooned.

Kendall was my roommate at the dorm. He came from out west, a year ahead of me. We stayed out of each other's way for the first couple months, but I had a lot more time to talk to him with Ashley ghosting me. He made for a good distraction with all his stories of people he never seemed to know himself.

My mom would mention Ashley on the phone, and I kept playing it off, acting like nothing had changed. It always felt like it would amount to a confession, some great failure on my part. I planned to tell her on the next call, and then the one after that, but at some point I bought into this idea that I could fix it without anyone back home finding out. The week of Thanksgiving, I said Ashley had car problems and wouldn't be able to come get me, but it was too short of notice for my parents to get off from work without it causing a lot of problems.

I *had* to see her. It was the only way we would get back together. Waiting a few more weeks for winter break just wasn't an option. It would be too late; too much could happen by then.

Maybe it already had.

"I'll hitchhike if I have to," I vowed, two days before break.

"Dude, you'll get raped and dismembered before you're even past the county line," Kendall said. "This kid I went to school with told me about some guy who hitchhiked. A couple months later they found him chopped up in a sleeping bag. All these...pieces just poured out on the ground. Whoever killed him sewed his asshole shut, and when they cut it open in the morgue, they found his dick in there. They think it was crammed in with a coat hanger to really get it in deep, you know? Like a Smore on a stick. Is your girl really worth that? Cornholing yourself in a bag of your own rotting body parts?"

"I'm going," I said, though this hypothetical did put things in a rather grim light I hadn't previously considered.

"Look, I'll take you. I was just going to stay here, eat frozen burritos, and watch a lot of Pornhub. I can still do some of that at your house. You've got Wi-Fi, right?"

III.

"This sucks," he said now. "I wanted to stay at the house."

"Sorry," I said, "but maybe next time, don't tell some story about accidental incest at the dinner table. My parents were *pissed*."

"Okay, sorry. Your mom kept talking about Ashley, you know...it was super awkward."

"Yeah, *that* was the awkward part."

"I was just trying to change the subject. It's not like I did that stuff myself. I never said it was cool or anything."

Mom cornered me after dinner to ask me what I was thinking, bringing home someone with such a lack of manners and good sense. I made some excuse for him, something about his dad beating him with an extension cord back home, an inability to read social cues, a low-grade appearance on the dreaded *spectrum*, etcetera. I felt like I had no choice but to volunteer our services for taking my grandfather back to Amser River. Mom would be tired from doing so much of the cooking, and Dad could get a head start on napping during the football games.

My sister would probably be barricaded in her room with her door locked, per mom's instructions.

I planned to go out anyway for Ashley, but I hadn't planned to have company. Kendall could stay in the car or busy himself otherwise, though. Having a little moral support wasn't the worst thing, I just needed to make sure he stayed far away from her with his stories of incestuous hook-ups and self-violated hitchhikers.

Grandpa grunted in the backseat. He'd become largely uncommunicative since we stashed him at Amser River. I'd heard my dad say it was an act, a long game of petty rebellion. If so, he was really good at it. Maybe it was just easier to believe that than accept the grimmer possibility of him simply winding down, of which there were plenty of signs toward the end of him living with us. He moved in after my grandmother died, right before I started high school. It was a weird time that I never adjusted to, and while I felt guilty, it was mostly a relief when we no longer had to make a family effort to keep an eye on him.

The stereo clock read 3:07—obviously way off. It was correct when I left for college, but now somehow wrong by more than the expected hour from the end of daylight savings. My sister obtained her learner's permit last month and must have messed with the settings. It didn't end there. Music sounded weird to me through the speakers in some indefinable way before I twisted off the volume.

The red-orange glow on the horizon drowned in the rising darkness, and now reflector lights flashed from road crew equipment. It bothered me to see a long line of construction barrels on either side of the turnpike, with several trees sheered away and the ground leveled in my absence. A skeleton of steel frames already stood for one new structure. I wondered how complete it would be when I saw it again in on winter break in a few weeks, like some disease progressing while I slept.

Several cars already filled the parking lot of Letha's. People stood in front of the entrance like angry villagers. Were Ashley and her mother already there? With all the forms obscured by coats, gloves, and hats in the forty-degree weather, I felt that some younger version of myself could be there as last Thanksgiving replayed itself, the future somehow passing behind me. It had actually been a mostly miserable time with so many people hemmed in by the aisles and displays in a claustrophobic nightmare I couldn't wait to escape, but still nice to be included in this family ritual where she and her mother hit the store ahead of true "Black Friday." It seemed like a ritualistic cleansing of Thanksgiving.

"After we drop him off, I need to go to over here," I said, gesturing to Letha's. "Ashley will be there."

"You're sure that's the best place?"

"Yes."

It seemed ironic to hear Mr. Incest Anecdote question the validity of a plan. I already knew she wouldn't pick up my call, and her family might run interference if I stopped by her house.

Oh, sorry, you just missed her. We'll tell her to give you a call, but she's just going to be really busy this weekend, so...

I'd get to talk to her for sure at Letha's. And maybe my own participation in the tradition previously would count for something. She'd be thinking of it. I might belong.

With any luck, I could get her to agree to meet me somewhere this weekend to really talk away from everyone else, and maybe not have to actually go into the store before all hell broke loose.

I meditated on this as I drove, thinking of what I would say, hoping I wouldn't find her there with someone else.

"Not much of a talker, are you?" Kendall said over his shoulder after a minute.

Grandpa broke his silence to say, "Taking me back to all those thieves."

"What does he mean?"

I signaled and turned into Amser River Assisted Living. "He says the nurses steal his stuff."

"Stamps," Grandpa said.

"You gave me those to me, Grandpa, remember?" I said, pulling into a parking spot. "No one stole them."

"You have a stamp collection?" Kendall chuckled. "Dude, nobody even gets letters anymore."

I switched off the ignition. Fluorescent lights showed an empty lobby with no one at the reception desk. Most families who checked someone out probably already brought them back earlier in the afternoon, but it still seemed a little weird.

"Come on," I said, opening the door. "Let's find someone inside. They'll bring out a wheelchair for him."

Grandpa could walk, but not that steadily, and he moved about as fast as a tightrope walker. I felt bad about taking him back, but he spent the day at home with us and barely spoke or changed expression. He could at least watch over his stuff here and make sure no one stole it.

Kendall looked doubtfully toward the backseat. "He's not going to wander off into traffic and get splattered or something?"

I shook my head and murmured, "Child-proof locks." Louder, I said, "We'll be right back, Grandpa."

He didn't say anything.

Kendall and I walked to the entrance. The cold cut deeper here than campus, with the Amser River visible from windows on the south side of the facility. I hoped a receptionist or an orderly would walk through, but the lobby might have been a still photograph.

The first set of automatic doors slid open, then the interior. Grade school kids had traced their hands to draw turkeys on orange and brown construction paper, which the staff taped to the glass on one of the windows. Not so uplifting for the old timers who never actually made it out of here.

We heard sounds through push-bar doors to east and west corridors, but nothing close.

"Maybe in the bathroom," I said.

"Or they're tossing your grandpa's room for some killer stamps," Kendall said.

We stood waiting for someone, anyone to show up. I paced the room, feeling the minutes tick away and my window with Ashley closing an inch at a time.

"You hear that?" Kendall said.

Voices somewhere in the depths of the building, a bit shrill and loud, but some of the people here practically yelled to compensate for not being able to hear their own voices clearly.

I checked the square chicken-wired windows of the double doors to East wing. The hallway sloped off almost immediately and didn't show if any staff might be just around the corner, but this was the wing to Grandpa's room, so I pushed the door open. Kendall followed. This way led to the cafeteria, where my family gutted out a few very awkward meals, including Thanksgiving three years ago in an attempt to make the place seem more like home for Grandpa.

After that, we started bringing him home for any major holiday instead.

We didn't see anyone in the hallway. A few resident rooms were open on both sides of the hallway, but always turned out to be dark and empty.

"Everyone must be back here," I said, wishing we'd just guided Grandpa to his room from the beginning. By the time we flagged someone back to the desk to sign him in and get someone else to bring out a wheelchair, it might end up taking longer.

We heard a lot of clattering as we approached, and immediately saw why as we rounded the open entryway to the cafeteria.

Two staff members dressed in maroon scrubs lay in pools of a deeper shade of red.

Gnarled arms rose and fell around them, knives puncturing the motionless backs again and again. They usually didn't give the residents real cutlery, but they'd found it tonight anyway.

A spry old lady yanked a wall-mounted clock down across the room by the cord, shattering its glass encasing, then dragging it back toward the melee. Trays dropped and rattled on the floor, knocked away by someone flailing on a tabletop.

I saw quick flashes of carnage, still photo shots my eyes found with no memory of moving my head. Each one deepened the shock of the moment; made me aware of only them with no existing world around:

An elderly lady draped over a table, a turkey drumstick plunged in her eye with the bone end.

A security guard with a meat cleaver bisecting his face, layers of multiple grooves from warm-up strikes.

A severed head in a hairnet on the partition to the kitchen prep area.

Most horribly, someone who must have been a relative of one of the residents slumped across a table with his stomach removed, innards strung about like tinsel, and an assortment of fruits and vegetables placed in the hollowed cavity like a macabre centerpiece—bananas, apples, grapes, an ear of corn, likely all transferred from a wax display.

I heard Kendall say something, but his words came with the same lack of coherence as the scene before us. The victims mostly comprised the staff, but there were older residents among the dead, too. I couldn't tell how long all of this might have gone on, whatever it was.

These weren't the foaming rage monsters from the zombie films of this century, but the oldest of them moved with a greater sense of purpose than I remembered from any of my past visits.

A squeaking sound drew our attention to the right. An old woman with a rolling walker edged toward us, barely in control but not worried about falling. She smiled with lips of blood.

Across from us, several of the diners looked up from the tables like a herd of predators.

I don't know how many there were in all, but I would estimate well over fifty. The blades continued to land in the human pincushions, their killers still mindlessly stabbing as they assessed us from the floor. I spotted two nurses among the gathered. At first, I thought some the residents traded out their clothes with scrubs for some deranged reason, but I recognized one of them, a lady who must be closing in on retirement age any year now.

Kendall tore the rolling walker away from the woman closing in on us and slung it at the groups of elders creakily rising. The nurses, both noticeably older than the fallen staff, were already up, slinking around the tables ahead of the pack. The one I remembered from before held a meat fork.

We took off back the way we came before the rolling walker lady had a chance to topple over. Suddenly all those dark rooms on both sides of the hall seemed ominous, waiting to spit out more of these crazies. Shoes scuffed behind us, but we were way too fast for the nurses to have any shot at catching up. We hit the push-bar of the East wing doors and spilled into the lobby, almost in synch with the West doors crashing open. A thin man in custodial clothes and the probable receptionist burst out screaming.

The responsive automatic doors opened soon enough that we didn't have to stop for the interior doors, but the exterior doors held us up for the one second they needed to grab us. Every zombie movie assured me we would be infected if they clawed or bit us, but it seemed like neither of these two had a mark on them.

The custodian swung a pipe wrench at Kendall's head. He ducked. A spider web of cracks traced the glass on the sliding door from the impact. I caught the receptionist by the wrists and used her momentum to toss her through the opening mouth of the exterior doors.

I heard the wrench clunk on the floor, turning around in time to see Kendall seize it and swing in a single motion. He cracked the custodian right between the eyes. The skull caved in with a sickening crunch, a squib of blood bursting from the new crater. The custodian dropped to the ground, arms flailing.

The East wing opened once again. The nurses charged through.

The receptionist had regained her feet by now and rushed through the doors again.

Kendall hit her in the gut with the wrench and doubled her over. I shoved her at the nurses and pulled Kendall back into the cold.

We sprinted for the car. I dug my keys from my coat pocket and hit the pre-start button on the fob. The dome light showed my grandfather pounding on the back windows.

"Shit, he's like the ones back there!" Kendall said.

Was it something in the air?

Were we already doomed ourselves?

"We have to get him out," I said.

Kendall raised the wrench.

"No! I'll get him. You just be ready to drive."

I reached for the back door on the passenger side. The receptionist and the nurses emerged from the entrance, coming our way. I pulled open the passenger door and then the back door. Grandpa scrambled free with a lot less hesitance than he would have several minutes ago.

Kendall dropped behind the wheel once Grandpa stumbled away from the backseat. I threw myself in the passenger seat seconds before the women dived at the car. Grandpa's arthritic fingers snatched at my window for an instant, then the car roared in reverse with one of the nurses on the hood.

Kendall swung the wheel around and she flew off, hitting the asphalt and rolling like tumbleweed. The rear passenger door clunked shut. He threw the car in gear and screeched away as the oldest ones from the group stumbled out of the entrance.

I fumbled in my other coat pocket for my cell phone.

"Where do I go?" Kendall said, not giving me much choice as he wrenched the steering wheel left at the exit, back the way we came.

I punched in 911, but only got a message to hold. I put it on speakerphone so I wouldn't have to hold it to my ear. I almost didn't mind the wait, not knowing how I'd be able to rationally explain what happened.

"They were all acting crazy, the staff, the patients," I said. "What could have caused that?"

"Something in the water supply," Kendall said. "Or a sound...maybe some frequency just fried their brains. If they have stamps, they probably listen to the radio, too."

"That doesn't explain Grandpa. He was fine when we brought him here, at first. We were there and we're okay. Pull over. Let me drive."

He eased onto the shoulder of the road, double checking the rearview as if any of those maniacs could run half a mile in twenty seconds. I hurried around the front and climbed in.

"Dude," Kendall said as I put us back on the turnpike. Traffic seemed noticeably light, with only a minimum of stores opening this early for Black Friday sales. "Boner pills!"

"Huh?" I was suddenly a little less glad I hadn't walked into this nightmare alone.

"I bet a bunch of those old people take pills for heart conditions, like Viagra. Maybe they got a bad batch, and it made them rabid or something. This dude my sister knew, his cousin—"

"It was the staff, too."

"Okay, but what if your grandpa was right, and they *were* stealing from him? They could have still taken the pills, and now they're psychos too!"

"Kendall, most of the staff chasing us were women! They aren't taking fucking boner pills and my grandpa isn't on any of that stuff."

"Oh. Right."

The hold message continued on the line. An operator would be available to assist us soon.

"At least you've got a hell of an icebreaker for Ashley," he said.

We'd be passing Letha's in a minute—though I just wanted to get home to some sense of normalcy, to my family. As the tires hummed on the pavement, ramifications slowly revealed themselves to me, the possibility of quarantine biggest among them. It almost made me hang up. Many would report all these roaming nursing home escapees, might already be holding on the line too. I could only hope that Grandpa wasn't already badly injured or killed. We just left him, but I didn't know what else we could have done. In the movies, there's no going back from this point for the infected, and prolonged exposure to them only increased our chances of being killed or changed like they were.

It wasn't right, but it was as safe as I knew how.

"What the hell's wrong with that guy?" Kendall pointed. "Has everyone lost their mind?"

A car in the oncoming lane made a lazy figure-of-eight motion over the line before drifting back, crashing into a couple of
construction barrels and driving off his side of road.

"It's happening out here too," I said.

"No way," Kendall said. "He's just drunk."

He didn't sound convinced. We picked up speed, as if I
thought we could outrun it... whatever *it* was.

"Shit!"

Letha's appeared to our right and all the people gathered
outside the store earlier no longer stood around waiting for the
top of the hour. Some of them grappled down in the parking
lot, but most of them were rushing toward the turnpike like a
cattle stampede. A few ran in other directions, probably just to
escape from the sudden violence.

"Look out!" Kendall said

The fastest of them crested the slight incline of the parking
lot and streaked into the road. I swerved, veering into the empty
oncoming lanes, then back to the right lane when I didn't think
I'd hit anyone.

"What the hell are you doing?" he asked.

There were three entrances to the store and I slammed the
brakes in time for us to make the last one, burning the tires. A
large segment of the runners branched off from the turnpike to
sprint in our direction.

"I have to look for her," I said. "She needs us if she's down
there."

Needs me.

I powered down the window enough where I could yell out
her name, not enough that anyone could reach into the car. She
might not even be here tonight. Things had been changing this
year—maybe this would be another.

Kendall grabbed my shoulder. I knew he must be mortified to go into the thick of this chaos, but it seemed a calculated risk. We could drive around the runners in circles for an hour with no one ever catching up or able to get to us if they somehow did. We could get through them if we had to, as a last resort.

He reached past my shoulder, his fingers cinching on my throat. I realized that he was a year older than me, that everybody who attacked so far was older than me. Several staff members afflicted, but only the oldest of them, with Grandpa himself on the younger end of the residents. He might have turned into what he did before the automatic doors shut behind us. We weren't looking. Each wave became progressively younger and younger. Probably not my sister yet, but I doubted she'd get chance; it would have triggered my parents already.

I stomp the accelerator, the throng in front of the store virtually shapeless, shadows in a thickening fog. I hit the flank at high speed. The bodies bounce up from the hood on impact, rag dolls with flopping limbs. One or two of them fall beneath the car like I'm guiding a set of metal teeth, chewing them up, each tire another bite into their crumpling bodies. Someone else's face slams the hood before they're thrown back, the white visage now a meaningless red smear. It's all meaningless. The pressure on my throat continues, nails digging into skin. It doesn't matter. I lose a little speed jumping the curb but hit the storefront hard. Airbags deploy on both driver and passenger sides as sheets of glass collapse across the roof of the car, raining upon the windshield and the sidewalk. We lumber forward like some great beast, blind, pushing over the things in front of the car—maybe clothing racks, end caps, mannequins, maybe not mannequins.

The pressure on my throat is gone, but it exists everywhere else, an imperative. When we come to a stop, I leave the car, aware of nothing left behind, nothing ahead, only what cuts, only what crushes.

I don't know where this is.

And though now is the time, I don't know when, either.

POSTSCRIPT TO REPULSION

SOME READERS MAY HAVE expected the return of Von and Greg in this collection, the degenerates from the "Damaged Goods" and "Genital Grinder" stories. We may see them again one day. I get asked now and again if they'll ever get their own book, and I have an idea I've been thinking about for several years. I even wrote the first couple paragraphs so I'd have them saved. I'm sure I'll have their book done long before I have enough short stories for a third collection.

Here are some notes about these stories if you still have that morbid curiosity:

"The Corpsefucker Blues": This was the first one I wrote after *Genital Grinder*. Jeff Burk, then-editor at Deadite, asked me to do it for *The Magazine of Bizarro Fiction* after meeting him in person at KillerCon in 2013. (Founded by Wrath James White, KillerCon is an excellent, highly recommended convention, by the way, and responsible for my collaborations with Lucas Mangum and Kristopher Triana.) I had no short stories in the years between 2004 and 2012.

That's not to say I wasn't still writing during all that time, but I rarely write short fiction unless someone is twisting my arm, and even then it's a gauntlet of self-sabotage and deadline pressure. It doesn't come very easily to me. This probably explains the diary excerpts—an aesthetic I relied on a couple of times in *Genital Grinder*. Those excerpts weren't initially meant to serve a twist. (I thought Chase wrote them.) I didn't have an ending in mind, though, and somewhere while writing the group scene—the one where everyone is still alive, I mean—I realized how I could use those excerpts in a more surprising way. I planned to call this one "The Three-Day Weekend," where the emphasis would be more on if Chase would crack under the pressure of not acting on his impulses with a golden necro-pportunity. Jeff, as he so often does, wanted a more visceral and revealing title. Ergo, "The Corpsefucker Blues."

"The Seacretor": Okay, this one seemed to write itself without too much guidance from me, one false start notwithstanding. I quickly identified the problem and put the group right on the island with allusions to tree-fucking at the outset. This was one I'd thought of sometime before Jack Bantry and Kit Power asked if I'd send them a story for an anthology called *Splatterpunk Forever*. Stephen King's "Beachworld" certainly had an influence here—and directly so in the vulgar intro line. This won the Splatterpunk Award for Best Short Story of 2018. The Splatterpunks honor the more uncompromising spectrum of horror, which is largely neglected elsewhere. I'd shared the Best Novella award with Edward Lee the prior year with our *Header 3* collaboration, but that was all Lee's depraved magic, so it was nice to feel rewarded for my own derangement. *Splatterpunk Forever* editors Jack Bantry and Kit Power also won Best Anthology.

"Threesome": This one pretty much had to appear third in the TOC, didn't it? UK *Splatterpunk Zine* editor Jack Bantry asked me to send him something for his next issue. I approached it with an EC Comics sort of simplicity—revenge porn purveyor Blake ends up filming his own snuff movie. Can you have a morality tale where an avenging woman uses a guy's severed head for oral sex? No. But that's okay: I'm not big on moralizing. When Jack sent me his edits, it changed my Word program to the spelling preferences of the UK, which was quite colourful for a while. The zine marked a first for me—story-specific artwork by Robert Elrod, who nicely rendered the head sequence. Jack used "Threesome" again for the anthology *Past Indiscretions,* which collected several stories from *Splatterpunk Zine.*

"Divine Red": One of the early classics of Dave Barnett's Necro Publications was *Inside the Works,* which collected novellas by Edward Lee, Tom Piccirili, and Gerard Houarner. This was the first appearance of Lee's "The Pig," one of THE seminal works of hardcore horror—and not just because the first sentence involves beleaguered porn talent swigging pig jizz from a shot glass. I would be meeting Tom and Gerard soon after *ITW* in Atlanta at World Horror Con 1999. It's weird to think now that I would end up contributing to the nine-way collaborative novel *Sixty-Five Stirrup Iron Road* fourteen years later to raise money for Tom's medical bills as he battled cancer and in 2016 Gerard would be reaching out to me for a story for his Necro anthology *Into Painfreak.* He had created Painfreak in the Nineties, a recurring club in his stories where the rules of life, death, and anatomy often did not apply. He graciously extended the deadline to give me a chance to write something.

This is one of those stories I really struggled with. I had four or five false starts. It was taking too long to set up because I had a 5000-word deadline and it didn't start working until I put Rob right outside the doors first thing. The haunted house tableaux came from some childhood memories of two different attractions, which helped me set up the symmetry of the end with another wedding of sorts. (And far more amputations.) When I thought of that insane image of the circle of amputees, I knew I could finish the story—*had* to finish it. However, I came in 1700 words over the deadline and had to do some amputating of my own. This version is a little longer than 5000 words.

The song playing in Painfreak is "Ion Storm" from Dodheimsgard's *666 International*, which well suited the chaos of Rob's experience. Coincidentally, that album also came out the same year I met Tom, Gerard, and Dave Barnett himself. RIP Tom and Dave, and fellow *65 SIR* contributors Dallas Mayr/Jack Ketchum and JF Gonzalez.

"Down There": I often feel like every story is this insanely difficult equation I have to solve, but then there will be an anomaly like this one. Matt Shaw invited me to write a guest chapter in his book *The Devil's Guests,* about an HH Holmes-inspired serial killer, and later in 2017 he asked me to do something for his anthology *Masters of Horror.* He was assembling quite a roster with some famous and infamous names of UK horror like Brian Lumley, Ramsey Campbell, Adam Nevill, Shaun Hutson, and Guy N Smith, as well as Yanks like me. While I'm sure he enlisted me for something on the order of genitals and power tools, The Slender Man stabbing case in Wisconsin was back in the news and, with that in my thoughts—as well as and Adam Wingard and Simon Barrett's vastly underrated *Blair Witch*—I started writing about a girl's fear of the woods and this mythic horror inside them. I usually have to know the ending to feel like I can finish something, but the pieces just fell into place here where I needed them—the doll, the leaves, the sacrifice. If Matt was chagrined, it didn't stop him from teaming up with me for the novella *One Thousand*

Severed Dicks, wherein we put paid to the potential of power tools and genitals—and many more implements besides.

"Junk": Gross-Out contests are challenging for me now. I struggle to wrap up a story in a readable five-minute length, but an excerpt from a larger work, no matter how vile, usually fails to land as well. "Junk" was this Cronenbergian concept I thought of one day: What if something going "viral" online affected your body like a real virus or disease? My first version would have required novella length had it not stalled after a few thousand words, intended to build toward the revelation of some grand conspiracy.

When World Horror Con went back to Atlanta in 2015, I wanted to have something to read for the Gross-Out, so I came up with an ending and carved "Junk" below 2000 words.

Like *The Ring*, the afflicted could only heal themselves by exposing more people to the virus. One person was not enough for this theoretical course of antibiotics, so our intrepid hero exposed himself to a playground full of children, assuredly infecting them and fully restoring himself to his former unscrupulous glory. That was version two, which played well for a live audience, but I did not think would work on the page.

Version three came about because Joe Spagnola of Blood Bound Books asked me if I'd contribute a story to *DOA 3*. I'd met Joe and Marc Ciccarone of BBB at KillerCon 2013. I thought if I could simplify "Junk" from its novella origins, I'd have what they were looking for. Randy Chandler and Cheryl Mullenax picked up "Junk" for *Year's Best Hardcore Horror, Vol. 3*. Funny that the third version of this story ended up in *DOA 3* and *YBHH V3*. The former gave me the opportunity to share the pages with one of my favorites, Bentley Little, in addition to some other great talents I've appeared and/or worked with elsewhere. The latter anthology put me with Scott Smith, author of *A Simple Plan, The Ruins,* and sadly no other books to date. Sharing a credit with him seemed about as rare as Halley's Comet: Sure, it'd be nice to have been published alongside these guys with something on the level of "In the Hills, the Cities" or "Gramma" rather than a story where a serial webcam flasher tries to cure his deteriorating junk with an electric carving knife, but I suppose it wouldn't be me without a little genital grinding in here somewhere.

"Angelbait": The vast majority of what I write does not disgust me. In that circumstance, maybe I'm like one of those people whose pain receptors don't work who end up grievously injuring themselves without realizing it. I'm skeptical that some of my most graphic scenes will actually affect anyone, so I make them as grueling as I can to hopefully satisfy the hardcore horror contingent for whom they are written. "Angelbait" is different, though. I went looking for information on the torture and martyrdom of saints a few years back, and found all these stomach-churning anecdotes about pus, scabs, lepers, and maggots. Knowing that people were revered for these acts of debasement seemed rather astonishing. I went back to it when Regina Garza Mitchell announced the anthology that became known as *The Big Book of Blasphemy,* which she co-edited with Dave Barnett. I've been friends with Gina since the World Horror Con days, back when those of us not named Brian Keene only had minor credits and compiled stories for the WHC-released chapbooks *A Darker Dawning* and *A Darker Dawning 2.* The detail that emerged and stuck with me when I reread those atrocities—I'm speaking of the things these saints did voluntarily as well as the involuntary misfortunes they suffered—was the appearance of that angel. I remembered something from an occult encyclopedia about how an angel's voice would have a *Scanners*-like effect on a human. (Disclaimer: the encyclopedia probably did not articulate it in quite that fashion.) I find the idea of any eternal life unsettling, the specter of which looms over this. Maybe I had too steady a diet of *Hellraiser* growing up. "Angelbait" won the Splatterpunk Award for Best Short Story in 2019.

"Orifically Compromised": Every story here was requested by an editor, except for this one. Why would someone like me who struggles with short stories take a chance on a themed submission that might not even go anywhere?

David Cronenberg, obviously.

When the topic of best horror directors comes up, the most popular name is often John Carpenter. Understandably so, given his films shot by Dean Cundey in particular. But for me, Cronenberg's run of genre work from the Seventies through the Nineties—*Shivers, Rabid, The Brood, Scanners, Videodrome, The Dead Zone, The Fly, Dead Ringers, Naked Lunch, Crash,* and *eXistenZ*—is unequaled. So, when Sam Richard and Brendan Vidito announced *New Flesh: A Literary Tribute to David Cronenberg,* I had to try. Once again, not one of the easier stories. More false starts until I stopped frontloading the story with the oSheath. It helped to already have a mysterious conglomerate in the background with InterphaZ, though, as previously seen in "Junk."

Nonexistent trademarks proved a lot more difficult than I expected, where names I tried to invent turned out to be in use somewhere.

I'm not sure quite where the story was going before I had this thought midway through that the whole thing could be an assassination plot. I loved that idea because of the way *eXistenZ*'s ending echoed Max Renn's tumor gun execution of Barry Convex in *Videodrome*, a rare Cronenberg repetition. (Funnily enough, in *eXistenZ* the "real" game turns out to be called *transCendenZ*.) Perhaps that moment resonates for me because in the theatrical print I saw of *eXistenZ*, you hear the assassins shooting after the screen fades to black. It's not like that on the DVD/BluRay. Cronenberg says something on the commentary about that version, but suggests it was only tested that way and not released. Strange. Like "Divine Red," I did some cutting to bring the story in under 5000 words. Fortunately, Sam and Brendan accepted it. This version is a bit longer.

"Temple of Amduscias": This one almost made me miss the days of the four or five false starts of "Divine Red." Maybe it's only fitting to have the devil's own time writing a story about Hell, though. I've been in contact with Jarod Barbee for several years, back before he and Patrick C Harrison III forged Death's Head Press. Jarod had been trying to get me in a couple of their anthologies since, but I'd find out about the deadline too late in the day to make it happen.

Knowing I'm a metalhead, he asked me far in advance to participate in a King Diamond tribute. I had a strange chronology with metal where I started with Mötley Crüe and Metallica, then aside from some slightly less abrasive bands like Sepultura, Slayer, and Celtic Frost, I veered off wildly into death metal, grind, and black metal before going back in the Aughts to appreciate metal bands I originally bypassed like Iron Maiden and Judas Priest—and Mercyful Fate. Jarod wanted something less gruesome and more atmospheric than most of my work, befitting MF and King Diamond. While that approach went simply with "Down There," this one took on several different shapes, concepts and attempts while combing the lyrics of *Melissa* and

Don't Break the Oath for the seed of the right idea. I eventually found it on the *Mercyful Fate* EP with "Devil Eyes." I became fascinated with the idea of voids in one version of this story, and expanded that concept with Olivia here. The exploits of the killer later formed the investigation backdrop of my novella *The Profile,* written for the *Fucking Scumbags Burn in Hell* series orchestrated by Drew Stepek of Godless and collected in the Blood Bound Books anthology *Call Me Hoop,* edited by Marc Ciccarone and Nikki Noir. I've wanted to use that wooden Christ for a couple of decades and given a liberal interpretation of Amduscias's prowess with trees and wood, this finally seemed like my chance.

"Last Time at Thanksgiving": In 2018 I roomed with Russell Holbrook at KillerCon. When he and Trevor Kennedy announced a Thanksgiving-themed antho, I told Russell I would send him something. Floundering at the time with "Temple of Amduscias," a diversion might have been the best thing. I thought of the backdrop of Black Friday, which of course led to the idea of people acting like maniacs, but this wound up being about something more. As they said in *Inland Empire,* it had something to do with the telling of time. I like the thematic symmetry of this collection ending with a story that feels apocalyptic, like "First Indications" from *Genital Grinder.* I say that as one of approximately twelve people who liked "First Indications" based on internet feedback, but hopefully this one fares better with everyone. Credit for the thematic heft of the title goes to Kelly Robinson, who played test reader for me here.

I wasn't sure after the release of *Genital Grinder* that I could come up with anything else in such an extreme vein, not as assuredly as Edward Lee always seems to do. I'm pleased at how much sickness was still left in the well because I enjoy writing hardcore horror. It's as valid to me to explore a story though its most graphic possibilities as its most subtle. There is still art in that which can offer a deeper meaning beyond all those entrails. I'm grateful to everyone who agrees with that and has supported my work in the past decade.

Preesh a lot once more to Kelly Robinson for the aforementioned title and beta-reading some of these stories, as well as Trips, Truman, and the Pawsitive Crew—you guys are the best. RIP Major Briggs, Rusty, Rosemary, and Esmeralda.

My appreciation to the collaborators I've written with in the past several years, who've shared in every kind of depravity with me you can imagine and hopefully several more you couldn't until you read our books—Edward Lee, Lucas Mangum, Shane McKenzie, Matt Shaw, Bryan Smith, Jason Taverner, and Kristopher Triana.

Special thanks to Wrath James White for KillerCon, which has had such an enormous impact on me, and his work with Brian Keene in founding the Splatterpunk Awards. This has been one of the best additions to the horror fleshscape, particularly in its acknowledgement of the legacies of David Barnett before his unfortunate passing and Edward Lee in the extreme horror field.

My sincere gratitude to the editors and friends who requested and/or accepted these stories—Jack Bantry, Jarod Barbee, Dave Barnett, Jeff Burk, Randy Chandler, Marc Ciccarone, Regina Garza Mitchell, Patrick C Harrison III, Russell Holbrook, Gerard Houarner, Trevor Kennedy, Cheryl Mullenax, Kit Power, Sam Richard, Matt Shaw, Joe Spagnola, and Brendan Vidito.

My profound appreciation to Don Noble for his evocative and supremely grotesque cover art for this book!

Thank you also to the following: Chandler Morrison, Brian Keene, Geoff Cooper, Mike Bracken, James Futch, John Wayne Comunale, Jeremy Wagner, Ann & Kelly Laymon, Carlton Mellick III, Christine Morgan, Phil LoPresti, K Trap Jones, Jonathan Butcher, Don Noble, John Baltisberger, Daniel J. Volpe, Aron Beauregard, Carver Pike, Rowland Bercy, Jr., Gabino Iglesias, Christina Pfeiffer, Marian Echevarria, Lisa Lee Tone, Mike Rankin, Drew Stepek, Jason Cavallero, Bridgett Nelson, Jeff Strand, Lynne Hansen, Stephen Cooper, Mort Stone, Chuck Buda, Mike Lombardo, and Judith Sonnet.

Transcendental Mutilation is dedicated to the memory of some of the too-damned-many lost since my last collection: David Barnett, GAK, JF Gonzalez, James Herbert, Dallas Mayr/Jack Ketchum, Richard Matheson, Tom Piccirili, and Peter Straub.

About the Author

Ryan Harding is the author of *Genital Grinder,* the novella *The Profile* in the *Fucking Scumbags Burn in Hell* series, and co-author of the collaborations *The Night Stockers* (with Kristopher Triana), *Pandemonium* (with Lucas Mangum), *Reincarnage: Maximum Carnage* and *Reincursion* (with Jason Taverner), *Header 3* (with Edward Lee), and the Splatterpunk Award-nominated *1000 Severed Dicks* (with Matt Shaw). He is a 4-time Splatterpunk Award winner (Best Novella: *Header 3,* Best Short Story: "The Seacretor" and "Angelbait", and Best Novel: *The Night Stockers*). His work has been published in Polish, German, and Italian.

Twitter: @NecroAF

Facebook: facebook.com/ryanhardmorbid